Hotheaded Heart

Copyright © 2024 by Anna Alkire
All rights reserved.

No part of this book may be reproduced in any form or by any electronic or mechanical means, including information storage and retrieval systems, without written permission from the author, except for the use of brief quotations in a book review.

This is a work of fiction. Names, characters, places, and incidents either are the product of the author's imagination or are used fictitiously. Any resemblance to actual persons, living or dead, events, or locales is entirely coincidental.

ISBN (paperback) 978-1-962780-08-7
ISBN (ebook) 978-1-962780-07-0

Water's Edge Publishing LLC
waters.edge.publishing@gmail.com

Hotheaded Heart

Waterfall Canyon BOOK 1

Anna Alkire

WATER'S EDGE PUBLISHING

CHAPTER ONE

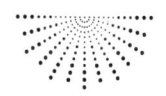

Have you ever coveted a man like he was the most gorgeous pair of peep-toe sandals with a stacked heel you'd ever seen? Or that jacket you try on once that transforms whatever you're wearing into style worthy of a Vogue photoshoot…

I stood by my competition with a smile plastered on my face. My eyelid twitched—everything would change that night. I had a plan. We all waited for the same wide shoulders, wrapped up in a fitted suit jacket, to arrive at the employee party.

"This venue is cute, Raven," Peggy said to me in her flat voice. "Funky. The food smells so good."

Cocking my head, I gave her a slight nod. She'd managed to sound mocking and curious at the same time, as if I'd just love to ramble on about the catering challenges so she could tell me how to do it better. We were so polite to each other that glass could shatter on our brittle smiles.

I handed a name tag to another new arrival walking past us. Peggy was the head office assistant at Good Samaritan River Gorge Hospital, where we both worked, and my number one rival for the most eligible bachelor in town, Travis Dashiell. She stood by the front doors next to me, dressed in a pink skirt and sweater that showed off her curves, waiting for him to arrive.

My foot wobbled a little in my heeled boot. I hadn't slept well the night before—or for a while—mostly because of the hair-raising grunting and wall tapping of my stalker neighbor. He hadn't been having sex with someone, that was his idea of flirting with me. I shared an apartment wall with him, and it was pushing me over the edge.

Also, I'd had an epiphany about Travis: he could take slow burn down to a micro flame. I had to show him there wasn't an iota of rejection in me and lure him closer. My romantic habits were more swashbuckling conquest, like a pirate queen after treasure. That part of myself had to be tied down with knots and stowed in the brig.

Marla, one of the pediatric nurses, smiled gently at Peggy and me. She was such a peacemaker. "It really is nice. Fall themes are my favorite."

"Thank you." I took a sip of my pumpkin-spice White Russian cocktail. "The hospital board decided on quarterly parties. I'm holding them to it."

Peggy sniffed, staring at my drink. "It won't last. Some drunk will mess it up for all of us."

"Excuse me," I said, eyeing the food tables. "I'm going to make sure they remembered to warm up the marionberry and apple pies."

As I walked away, they kept their vigil at the main doors into the Old Cannery Concert Hall. I'd rented the event space to host the gathering. It was an old cannery building turned into an entertainment venue, referred to as The Ruins.

As a public relations specialist at the hospital, I'd been the lead on organizing the Glitter and Gold fall employee party. Of course I'd have a dozen details to check up on.

What Peggy and Marla didn't realize was that there was a second outside door that led straight to the stage area inside—and it was closer to the parking lot. I had the keys to open it.

"Riesling," I said to the bartender.

"You got it."

With the wine glass in hand, I smiled and nodded as I moved through the crowd. Travis Dashiell would be arriving any minute. I knew because I'd snuck a peek at his schedule after hours the night before.

He'd had a family reunion earlier in the afternoon. Knowing him, after scrambling for parking, he'd be a little off-kilter. He'd be rushing in, just about now, to be on time for his performance-awards speech.

Travis, the deep thinking and sensitive introvert—my opposite—had women trailing after him like he was the pied piper of River Gorge, our smallish town. I had to make a move. He was a widower, had been for about four years, and extremely slow to date anyone. We'd been grabbing coffees together a few times a week for the last three months. It was time to make my feelings clear…gently.

The door behind the stage had a sticky lock and creaked when I pushed it open. Daylight was nearly gone as I scanned the parking lot.

My eyes snagged on a man staring down at me from the sidewalk by the train tracks. His teeth bared in a sneering grin. A cold shiver ran down to my clenching stomach. Rob Campbell, my neighbor, rocked his hips.

A semi-truck roared by on the road, breaking our stares. I held up a shaking hand in front of my face and blew out a gasp. *Nooo.* That disgusting shithead would not ruin the night I'd been waiting for. *Come on. Pull it together.*

A car door shut in the parking lot. I stood up straight and sucked in a shuddery breath, refusing to look again up at the road.

"Travis," I called at the figure rushing over in a light gray suit.

He pivoted to me, slowing a little and pulling his jacket straight. One side of his mouth quirked up, that dimple peeking out on his left cheek.

"Wine?" I held out the glass of Riesling—his favorite drink.

He sighed, stepping up on the creaky old wood porch. "Yes." His hooded eyes skimmed over me quickly. He had broad cheekbones and an adorably pointed chin in his clean-shaven face. The dark brown mat of his hair was cropped short, like he only thought long enough about his looks to stay tidy.

Our fingers touched as he took the glass. A little thrill prickled along my skin. There was chemistry there, I knew it. He was a reserved and cautious man and forcing me to be extremely patient.

"It's good to see you," he said while our gazes locked.

I beamed, leaning in a little closer. After being on my best behavior for the last three months, it was past time for one of us to be brave. "You too."

His eyes slid away from mine. "Have you seen Peggy? She has my notes for the speech."

The bottom dropped out of my stomach. I bit my lip hard, my eyes stinging. *Damn.*

I sucked in a breath. What had I expected? The important thing was to show affection and let him know I was there for him. But, of course, I had to screw it up. My face was hot—the internal thermometer inched up to flaming.

I put a hand on my hip and glared at him until he glanced

back at me and blinked owlishly. "I left her locked in a closet to recharge her battery," I said.

"What?" His head drew back.

Shouldn't have said that, especially at a work function. And he never spoke a mean word about anyone. "Ever thought of auctioning yourself off for a fundraiser?" I raised my eyebrows and took a sip of my drink even while my heart hammered in my chest. *Was that clear enough, Travis?*

He huffed out a breath, collapsing against the outside of the building where we stood by the door. "I...wouldn't want that kind of attention—especially if we're talking about work colleagues..."

And there it was, my rejection explained. "For a good cause—"

Something shoved into my back, and cold wet trickled down my side.

"Oh, no—" said a familiar flat voice.

I whipped around, letting my own drink slosh out onto the person that had shoved me. Peggy stared at me. The pumpkin-spice cocktail I had just splashed on the chest of her pink cardigan dripped onto the floor.

"Whoops..." I swallowed fury. There was a wine stain down the side of my tiered lace maxi dress.

"I'll find some napkins," Travis muttered and took off through the doors.

∼

THE BIG OUTSIDE area of the Old Cannery Concert Hall had a stage, dancing area, tables and a bar. The half crumbled concrete walls of a two-story building sheltered the space on three sides. The Ruins—a fitting place for me to hunch over a table and drink fast.

I tossed back the rest of my whiskey sour and stared

morosely at the bluegrass band playing on the stage. I wanted to teleport out of there.

"Hey," said my friend Jada, an ICU nurse. She slid into the other chair at my small table.

"Did you really just have a baby?" I asked, side-hugging her. "What kind of superhuman are you?"

Jada flashed her big smile at me, bright against her smooth coppery complexion. "You know what, I put on a full face of makeup today for the first time in…I don't know. It's amazing. Brian's on baby duty—panicked. He called me three times. I'm, like, you're a firefighter. Figure that shit out."

"Cheers to that. Except, come to the bar with me so I can get another. I'm taking every advantage of our drink tickets."

She followed me over to the outdoor bar, smiling and waving at people who hadn't seen her in months. Jada had started working again that week.

"My word," she said. "I can't believe it's the end of September. This summer has been a blur."

My gin and tonic plopped onto the bar in front of me. We walked away from the crowd, my legs a little wobbly and my jacket covering the stain on my dress.

"I've missed rock climbing with you at the gym," I said.

She blew out a breath. "Yeah. There aren't enough hours in the day."

I glanced to the side and caught Travis's eyes on me. He looked away. We'd done the flirty eye contact thing so many times it seemed meaningless. Trying not to grimace, I took a gulp of my drink, mentally shaking myself. *Stop pouting.*

"Has going back to work been good?" I asked.

"It's a mix. But, yeah—and we need a bigger house. Badly. Sharing a toilet with Brian is not good for our marriage."

Travis had a big house. I forced myself not to find him with my eyes. He lived in one of River Gorge's classic downtown homes—a gorgeous, gabled, five-bedroom with a wraparound porch and a view of the Columbia River and Mount Adams. It was about as far away as you could get from the shitty apartments I'd lived in all my life.

"You all right?" Jada squinted at me. "Tell me what's up—especially if it's juicy."

I swirled my drink around clinking ice cubes. "I have a stalker."

"What?"

"Really pissing me off." I took another gulp and slammed my empty glass down on a table. "My perverted neighbor bullies me every time he catches me outside my door."

And he was probably the one sending me gifts too. For a while, I'd hoped the bouquets were from Travis—but then the creepy notes had begun too.

"Shit. Raven...damn, girl. You got the police helping you?"

I snorted. "They've tried, some of them. It's tough to get proof—like he knows exactly where the line is and stays right on the edge. He sits in front of his door so he can grab his dick and describe his bowel movements. Or tell me we should screw. He shows up where I'm at. Did tonight."

"Oh my God. That isn't enough?"

"Not yet." I twisted the bracelet on my wrist. "I lose it and yell at him." That man brought out a violent side of me I'd hardly known I had. Probably because he scared the crap out of me.

"Do I know him?"

"Rob Campbell. A few years younger than us. Works in insurance. He's like a loner bully type. No friends. Says weird crap all the time."

"Girl, you've got to move."

"Yeah."

Of course, I didn't have the money. There was a giant housing crunch and prices had doubled. Yada-yada, same old doom and gloom dogging my steps.

"Come on, enough about my shitty problems," I said. "Let's get some of that dinner. The vegan cauliflower buffalo wings are actually amazing."

I tried to eat a little to settle the alcohol sloshing around in my stomach, keeping my coat on to hide the stain on my dress. The truth was, my breaking point was barreling at me like an out-of-control train. Campbell the creep didn't know who he was messing with.

CHAPTER TWO

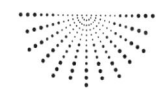

"How's your night, sweetheart?" asked the steel-haired woman driving me home in a taxi.

I sat up out of my slouch. "Work party. They gave us dinner and free drinks."

She nodded. "Grub and company. All you need. And a little booze to grease the wheels with a man." She cackled until she was coughing.

My head thumped back against the car seat. I needed to be as far away as possible from the desperate kid that had lost her stuff every time Mom had been evicted. Or the woman that had to live next to a creep. My eyes burned. *Oh, Mom. I really miss you.*

The driver stopped in front of my dingy gray and tan apartment complex. There were a few broken fixtures, and the parking lot was dim, the asphalt partially covered in a puddle from leaking ground sprinklers.

"Thank you," I said, stepping out of the car.

She flashed me a thumbs-up and sped away for her next fare.

I'd moved back to River Gorge six months ago and had rented out a small crappy apartment to save money. With a lead weight sitting in my chest, I eyed my building. *Could that damn asshole take a night off?*

The only good thing that had come from living at the complex was Cheeto, the orange tabby cat determined to claim me as his human. He usually met me at my front door, or scratched on it soon after I got home, so he could curl up in his spot on my mattress for the night. I'd been a total pushover—after I'd gotten rid of the fleas.

My heels clicked down the walkway toward my apartment, moving faster when I saw the empty lawn chair next to Campbell's door. I kept my phone gripped in my hand with the emergency call button ready. Heart thumping in my chest, I got my key in the lock and cranked the old bolt open.

The beige carpet and drab walls of my apartment greeted me as I flipped on the lights. My bag thumped on the little console table next to the door.

A feline howl stopped me with my jacket half off. The pitiful meowing that followed constricted my chest and had my mouth gaping open. I pulled my jacket back on and yanked open my front door.

"Raven," Rob called in a singsong voice. "Look what ran into my apartment."

On the bark mulch between our building and the road, Rob Campbell was in his underwear. He gripped a squirming Cheeto.

Red ribbon had been wrapped around Cheeto's body and neck and tied into a sloppy bow under his chin. One of his legs was caught. Part of the ribbon was gagging him as he chewed on it.

Fists clenched, I took it all in from my doorway. Cheeto was barely out of his kittenhood, tall and gawky, with soft marmalade and cream fur and white tufts on his large ears. My chest heaved in short jerky pants. Blood pounded in my ears.

Rob had a spray paint bottle pointed at the little cat. He smirked at me, tilting his head to the side. "We've been waiting for you. Except stink-butt shat in my house and needs to learn a lesson."

I whipped up my phone and took a picture. "Put him down," I shouted. "Now."

Rob shook his head, his lips pursed. "Nope. He's a skunky pooper, not a cat." Black paint shot out of the can and hit Cheeto in the back.

I jerked, rage erupting like molten lava. Cheeto made a guttural growl. I ran to the console table and grabbed my pink Comfort Grip Stun Gun out of my purse. When Rob had started harassing me, I'd bought the little shocker. It looked like a mini flashlight. My thumb clicked it on, a red haze clouding my vision.

Cheeto hissed and fought Rob. I stalked out of my door, the stunner held low and behind my jacket.

"Fuck." Rob flinched and Cheeto tumbled out of his hold onto the ground, landing awkwardly. On three legs, he shot off into the bushes.

I kept going, closing the distance between us. Rob stared at me with his mouth open and his eyes wide. He was like someone watching a sports match, leaning in and smiling a little. I pulled up the stun gun and shocked him in the neck.

"You piece of shit," I yelled as he fell to his knees, gagging. "Leave me the fuck alone—do you hear me?"

There was a big brown paper bag the landscaper had left full of leaves and branches. I heaved it up and smashed it down on Rob's garbage-dump face.

"Did you piss yourself?" Smash. "Who's the stink-butt

now?" Smash. The bag broke open and covered him with dirt and mushy leaves. I grabbed one of the branches and thwacked him with it.

"St-stop." Rob covered his face with an arm.

It dawned on me that there were blue and red flashing lights in the parking lot. I stood up straight and looked around. People lingered in their doorways and two police officers were walking toward me.

"Drop the stick," ordered a young cop, his hand on his holster.

Next to him, in uniform, stood Beau Martin, my childhood nemesis and the older brother of my best friend. He frowned at me, his face hard.

∼

"She attacked me," Rob croaked out.

"You were hurting my cat!" My thwacking stick fell from my tingling fingers and hit the ground. *Oh, damn. This is bad.*

Rob flinched as he sat up in the pile of leaves. "Shocked me while I was standing there talking. Didn't touch her."

"Why are you in your underwear, Campbell?" Beau asked Rob, glaring down at him.

"Because he's a goddamned piece-of-shit stalker that follows me around," I ground out, my hands shaking.

"I'm pressing charges," Rob said, one of his eyes blinking convulsively. "For assault."

In the end, I was the one put in the back of a patrol car while a handful of my neighbors filmed it on their cell phones. I hunched over, my face in my handcuffed hands.

Beau crouched down next to the open car door. The other cop was speaking with the apartment manager.

I glanced at Beau's familiar face—there was the strong chin that jutted forward as he stared back at the crime scene.

His features formed more of a rugged and serious man's appearance now, different from the almost pretty teenager I'd known a lifetime ago. How had it been ten years since I'd seen him? We hadn't run into each other in the six months that I'd been back in River Gorge.

"Hey," Beau said. "Somebody found Cheeto and took the ribbon off."

My lips trembled. "That's good."

He leaned in further, his voice low. "I've got your back. Don't say anything until you have a lawyer. Jones over there" —he jerked his head at the other officer—"is on point for this call. He's insisting on an arrest. I'm sorry."

A sob broke out of me. It was settling on me that I'd ruined my entire life. "I really screwed up."

Beau sighed. "Well, it's a pain. Could have a lawyer in your future." He stood up and gently shut the car door next to me.

I was driven to the River Gorge police station in the back of Officer Jones's patrol car. I cried. Beau was in a different car, already off in another part of the city. The radio crackled and spat out cop talk as Jones drove the short distance across town, pretending like I wasn't there.

At the station, I was put in a small windowless room with a single metal chair after they took away my purse and phone. I refused to be interviewed or to answer questions. I was left alone for a long time.

Finally, I was fingerprinted and photographed. Then I had to wait for about three hours more. At last, I was given a release agreement and told to appear at court in three days.

It was two o'clock in the morning by the time I stood in the police station lobby, shakily checking my purse and phone. They'd kept my twenty-nine-dollar hot pink stun gun as evidence. Without it, or any other kind of weapon, my stomach clenched at the thought of being anywhere near Rob.

My "personal recognizance release agreement" meant they trusted me to show up at court—and if I didn't, that would be a whole new crime. Getting a lawyer and paying the boatload of fees and fines coming my way was going to make my money situation go from lousy to dire. I blew out a shaky breath and decided to walk home.

A door opened behind me. "Hey," Beau called. "Give me ten minutes and I'll drop you off."

"No." I scowled at him. "Do me a favor? Go ahead and eff right off."

"Raven—"

"You arrested me," I enunciated slowly. "For standing up to a creep."

He frowned at me. "You're going to walk three miles in those boots?"

I glanced down at my pointed-toe heeled suede boots. Before I could say anything more, he disappeared into the office. I huffed and gathered myself to march home.

I still couldn't believe what I'd done, even after being at the police station all night—that I'd been arrested. A criminal record for the rest of my life...I pinched the bridge of my nose and focused on taking deep breaths.

Growing up, I'd known a few people stuck in the criminal justice loop of doom. It was expensive and trailed you around like a plague—employers didn't want to get near that.

"All right," said Beau, walking out of a side office. "Let's get you home."

He definitely had not been gone ten minutes. I stood up straight fast, then stumbled when black fogged my vision.

"Whoa," said Beau, slipping an arm around my back. "Need some water?"

Swallowing into my dry throat, I shook my head, even

while thirst clawed at me. "No." I stepped away, hitching my bag up higher on my shoulder.

He shook his head, pushing a hand through his wavy blond hair. He still had that young Elvis look to him—small bow-shaped mouth with high cheekbones, and hair that rolled back in an effortless and messy pompadour. The big blue eyes rimmed with thick lashes. Of course, he was notorious for sleeping around all over town.

"Come on," he said. "And I'm buying you something at the drive-through."

I scoffed, trying to muster concrete resistance. I really wanted to be far away from all police officers. My shoulders drooped. I couldn't find the energy to say anything.

Beau was my best friend's brother. If our situations were reversed, I'd have given him a ride too.

He held the door for me. I limped out on my sore feet into the cold night.

"Oh, shit," Beau said, his hand landing on the small of my back.

I halted my wobble down the concrete steps. "What?"

There was a woman glaring at me from a red Corolla parked in front of the station.

Beau lifted his hand in a quick salute at the car before turning away. He hustled us to his pickup. The Corolla revved hard then took off fast down the street. Beau frowned, watching the car speed away as I climbed into the passenger seat of his truck.

He shut the creaky door for me. In another minute, he was cranking on the engine and Queen's "Fat Bottomed Girls" blasted out of the speakers. He turned the volume down.

"Girlfriend mad at you?"

He put an arm along the back of my seat as he pulled out of the parking spot. "She's always mad about something.

Especially me trying to break up with her for the last month."

I rubbed my forehead, trying to ease the headache banging against my skull. "What's so hard about it? Say it straight and be done with it."

"It's always better when they break up with me."

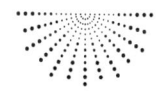

CHAPTER THREE

"Hey," Beau said as we waited in the surprisingly long drive-through line. "How about you stay at Lauren's tonight?"

"At your parents' you mean?"

One side of his mouth crooked up. "Yeah. You're part of the family. You could stay there anytime."

I thunked my head against the passenger seat. "No. Lauren's baby shower is tomorrow. And she has a hard time sleeping right now. I'm not going to go over there and wake everyone up."

"Oh, yeah." Beau rubbed his face. "Forgot about the party."

I turned my head to look at him. "Why aren't you ever over there?" I blurted out, my mouth even more unfiltered than usual.

For most of high school, I'd practically lived at the Martin house. Then I'd actually moved in for my senior year after my mom passed from breast cancer.

He shrugged one shoulder. "Dad and I don't get along."

"Wait—he still wants you to become a lawyer?"

"There's always something wrong with me."

Beau pulled the truck forward to the window, swiped a credit card and took our bags of food. I sucked down my root beer so fast I was hiccuping.

"Thanks for the food," I said after swallowing another mouthful of hot salty french fries. "I love this crap."

"Crap?" Beau pulled into a spot in the fast-food parking lot. "This from the girl that used to stand up and drool whenever a taco commercial played on TV."

I scoffed and eyed him resting in the driver's side corner of his truck with his eyes closed. "Little smarter now."

It had been so many years since I'd spoken to him. In high school, he'd been the guy that always knew where the party was at. Or he'd get a big group together to go hang out by the water. Lauren and I had tagged along every chance we got, which we'd paid for with Beau's constant teasing and pranks. By the time I was sixteen, I'd considered him my mortal enemy—and had retaliated by spiking his shampoo with green hair dye. That prank had gone horribly wrong when his father's hair had turned green too. Beau had kept his hair green until it grew out.

Then he left for college and never really went home again. I'd relished the peace after he left—and missed him a little too.

"What are you going to do about that neighbor?" Beau asked.

I jammed my trash into the paper bag. "Try not to kill him."

"Does he follow you around?"

"Yes."

"You have to document it. Every time."

"Yeah, I know." I scrubbed my hands free of grease with a napkin. "Did you have to arrest me? Thwacking him with a stick was the least of what he deserved."

"That was the other idiot. But it wasn't the stick. It was the stun gun. If you'd called us, you'd have had enough for a harassment charge."

"I know. Damnit." My eyes were burning. I covered my face with a paper napkin. "Take me home."

He turned on the truck and drove me to my apartment while we both sat in silence. I stared out the passenger window and pinched the skin between my thumb and index finger hard, trying to get a hold of myself.

Beau parked by the dumpsters with his hazards on. "I'm going to walk you in," he said.

"Fine."

He followed me as I trudged up the narrow path to my door. Anxious meowing greeted me, and Cheeto darted out of a bush.

I gasped and crouched over. "Hey, buddy." I felt over his back and legs, concerned he'd been hurt when Rob had dropped him. Black paint marred his creamy fur between his shoulder blades. The red ribbon was gone. Cheeto stood up on his hind legs and hugged me, clinging to my shoulders. Sniffling and gasping, I picked him up carefully.

Beau put an arm around my shoulders. I stiffened a little but didn't pull away from his side-hug. Cheeto purred like a stuttering lawn mower.

"Rough night," Beau said. "Let's get you guys inside. Give me those keys and I'll unlock the bolt."

Beau opened the door and turned on every light in the apartment. He was testing the windows when I put Cheeto down on the carpet in the living room. I dumped my bags on the console table, trying to prepare myself to be alone in the apartment once Beau left.

"Going to check the outsides of your windows," Beau said as he brushed by me. "Be right back."

I put food in Cheeto's bowl while Beau was gone. Rob

was being quiet for now, but it wouldn't last. I stared down at the black mark on Cheeto's fur, my skin crawling.

"Okay," Beau said as he came back in, plunking down a step stool by the front door. He stomped over to stand close to me. "You're moving out of here." He pointed at the step stool. "This was under your bedroom window. Call your brother. We're moving you tomorrow."

I jerked back, staring at the step stool in shock. *That asshole watched me through the cracks in my blinds?* My eyelid twitched. I wanted to kick down his door and hit him with a baseball bat.

"No. I'm not going to let that shithead push me around. And I have to work on Monday."

He flung an arm out at my apartment. "You have a love seat, a coffee table, and your mountain bike. It won't take long."

I crossed my arms. It was pathetically sparse—I preferred to spend my money on clothes. And bags. And my chili-red Mini Cooper. "I can't get a new apartment with the snap of my fingers."

Actually, I had been looking for a while. Everything had waiting lists. I hadn't been working long and had student loans, a car payment, and too much credit card debt. My shitty and not really cheap apartment was the key to getting a handle on my finances—or at least not drowning in debt.

He ran a hand through his hair, making it stick up. "We'll figure something out at the baby shower. Lock your door—don't engage with him. Call the station if he does anything."

"I'll be fine."

When he reached out and tucked my hair behind my ear, I just stared at him with my mouth open. I had a touch weakness, as in I craved it way too much.

Heat tingled along my skin. I wanted to put my arms around his chest and beg him to stay with me—but that was fear talking. I was rattled. The man I really wanted was Travis.

"All right," he said. "See you tomorrow."

∼

As soon as Beau left, Rob started screaming at me through the wall.

"You fucking bitch—this isn't over! I'm pissed. Really, really, fucking pissed…You're a whore. Do you hear me? A fu…" And on and on it went.

I made a video recording of Rob shouting and filled out an online police report. After I'd trimmed the paint out of his fur, Cheeto and I curled up on my bed with pillows around us like a barricade. Listening to music with my earbuds in didn't block out the threats.

Lying awake for hours that night, I realized that I probably would rather sleep on someone's couch than share a wall with Rob for another day. Would moving be enough to shake off Rob's fixation with me?

The apartment manager knocked on my door at eight in the morning, waking me up from my three hours of sleep.

"Who is it?" I called through the door while I tied on my bathrobe.

"Shep. Got a minute, Raven?"

I opened my door, covering a yawn. Shep stood oddly bent for someone in his thirties, a tall person's hunch, and always twitched his fingers. He was married to a hard-faced woman who kept to herself and they had an infant that cried a lot. Pulling at his hat, he stood staring toward Rob's apartment.

"Want to come in?" I liked Shep and had gotten to know him a bit during the last six months of living in the complex.

Cheeto darted out past my legs. Technically, I wasn't

supposed to have a pet in my apartment. I glanced at Shep, but he only nodded, his hands in the pockets of his thin coat.

"Sorry—it's early, isn't it?" he asked, glancing around for a clock on my walls. There wasn't one.

"It's eight. Want some coffee?"

"Oh—eh, no thanks. You go ahead."

He followed me into the kitchen, rubbing his chin and staring down at the floor. Shep moved at his own pace, and I'd learned to wait until he had his words sorted.

"Well." He inhaled sharply. "Wish I could do somethin' bout Rob. Evict him, I mean. But the, um, arrest last night set me back there."

"Right." I sighed.

I'd been telling Shep and his wife about my problems since they'd started. Rob was on a one-year lease and so far I hadn't managed to make a charge stick to him—only to myself. My eyes burned. I put my elbows on the counter and let my head drop.

"Lots of folks callin' me to complain."

I nodded, my throat too tight to speak. From the side-eyed glares of my neighbors, I suspected some of them thought we were a messy and loud couple. I'd never, for a moment, considered dating Rob—not even before I knew him.

"I don't like it, Raven." He scratched his stubbly chin. "I ain't evicting ya. But end of the month is comin' and now's as good a time as any for ya to look around. Want you to know I'll do what I can."

"Thanks, Shep."

He nodded, biting on a fingernail. "Rob was mouthing off after you went to the station. Sayin' he'd get a restraining order. You leave today, I think he'll settle—more than a few things he's done wrong."

"Wow." I pressed my clenched fist into my forehead.

"Yep." Shep glared at the wall I shared with Rob. He swallowed, his eyes darting back to me. "One more thing. Newspaper called me—they got hold of the story."

CHAPTER FOUR

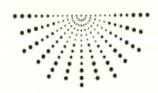

I drove across town, on my fourth cup of coffee that morning, in a kind of disassociating haze. My best friend's baby shower was in a few hours, and I'd promised to help.

Twenty-four hours before, I'd set up a party for the dream job I'd finally landed. One day later, there was a possibility I'd end up in jail. It wasn't real—was it?

John and Allison Martin, Lauren and Beau's parents, owned a custom-built four-bedroom home out on Country Club Road. I backed into my usual spot in the graveled side yard designed for an RV. The Martins kept their cars in the three-car garage and didn't like to have the driveway blocked.

Being the unofficial foster child of the family had been good luck—and also served to remind me of how far I had to go. Their daffodil-yellow two-story, on a private road and surrounded by acreage, always twisted my heart with love, longing, and envy.

I knocked on the wide oak door, then opened it to stick my head in. "Hey. Your party genie has arrived."

Allison Martin came out, a warm smile on her pretty face. She opened her arms for a hug. "I'm so happy you're here. Are you hungry? Thirsty?"

Gladly, and a bit desperately, I walked into her offered hug. "Thanks, I'm okay. Put me to work."

I held on to her hug, blinking my dry eyes, relishing the closest thing I had to maternal love.

She leaned back and stared at me. "You okay?"

Her bright blue eyes seemed to notice everything. She patted my cheek. Allison was a kindergarten teacher and had a well of patience that never ran dry—the opposite of her husband.

I inhaled sharply, nodding my head. "Today is about Lauren." Stepping away, I moved my mouth into a smile.

"Yes, it is. She needs it."

"Everything's so pink. I feel like I should pull out my old Barbies and put a big glittery bow on my head."

Allison rubbed her hands together. "Baby girl is almost here. Would you run up and help Lauren? She needs to eat and, um, do her hair…Maybe this party will get her a little excited again."

"On it." I ran up the stairs two at a time.

Lauren's pregnancy hadn't been planned and it had been with a new boyfriend in the army. They'd married quickly before he'd had to leave for a one-year deployment.

I tapped on her bedroom door. "Hey, prego. It's your chump of a best friend."

"Raven?" She blew her nose.

Oh no. "Who else?"

When I swung the door open, Lauren was sitting on the floor crying, used tissues and crinkled paper surrounding her in a kind of blast zone. Usually, her bedroom was disturbingly tidy.

I crouched down in front of her. "Did something happen with Derek?"

Her husband Derek was deployed in the Middle East; we weren't sure exactly where. Communicating with him was tough for Lauren, and sometimes she didn't hear from him for weeks at a time.

"He doesn't want this." Lauren covered her face with a tissue.

I blew out a breath—at least he wasn't injured. Or dead. "Did he say that?"

"No. But I know anyway."

I kicked some garbage out of the way and sat next to her. Pressing my lips together, I put an arm around her back. "That's his problem. You've got enough to deal with."

She snorted. "Seriously?"

"Yeah. Your little bean is about to sprout. It's time to show off that bump, open presents, and shade your eyes from all the pink."

Lauren sniffed. "I told Mom gender-neutral."

"She's excited."

A tiny smile appeared on Lauren's face. "Yeah, she is."

I patted her arm briskly. "Come on. Pity party is over—hey, you know I don't do mushy stuff. Shower or food first? Everybody and their elderly sister is going to be taking your picture in two hours."

"Fine. I'll shower. But you're doing my hair."

Lauren ate a little dry toast after she'd cleaned up. She waddled over to the stool in front of her white vanity, flinching while being kicked from the inside. I was starting to realize that I might not ever want to be pregnant.

I curled her long blonde hair while she put on makeup. In the vanity, we were opposites, a bit like Betty and Veronica from that old *Archie Comic* about the boy who couldn't decide between the blonde and brunette. Except Lauren was serious and I was…energetic. My Italian father and half Japanese, half white mother had blended to create me—olive skinned with straight dark brown hair.

"Beau's coming," Lauren said, glancing up at me while she brushed powder on her face. "Texted me. He was like, I'm at Target what do you want."

"Golden opportunity for a big-ticket item right there."

She huffed. "I reminded him I have a registry. I think he's single again."

"Oh, yeah?" I didn't meet her eyes. "Who's the latest Beau discard?" I asked like I didn't know.

"Harper. They dated during high school—the redhead who always thought he'd cheated on her."

"Right." She'd been my least favorite person during Beau's senior year.

"Yep. After he left, she got married and divorced. Now she works at the big brewery downtown."

"When do you see Beau? I'm here all the time and he's never around. I've run into Hunter more often—and he lives on the East Coast."

Hunter Martin was the oldest, then Beau, with Lauren the youngest. The age chasm between Hunter and Lauren and me had been like an impassable ocean when we were kids—and he'd been nose to the grindstone with school and sports. He'd seemed like an adult even as a teenager.

"Hunter likes to come home for the holidays. Not Beau." Lauren sat back and rubbed her belly, her face strained. "Mom and I have lunch with him. He's not really speaking to Dad right now."

"Oh." *Wow*. John Martin was harsh at times, but I hadn't realized how far things had gone.

The baby shower filled the house and yard. The Martins

had been in River Gorge for a long time. Lauren was on leave from teaching second grade, and Allison taught kindergarten at the same school. The other teachers and staff that arrived could have populated an office building. There were women from John's law firm as well as cousins, aunts, two grandmothers, and a gaggle of our high school friends. Everyone spilled outside for the baby scavenger hunt and diaper derby, carrying around plates with "bun in the oven" sliders.

I spotted Beau out on the big lawn hitting golf balls with the handful of men that had come, laughing and drinking beers. Lauren's dad stayed inside, watching football and keeping the food table stocked.

The afternoon flew by. Lauren was rosy-cheeked and smiling for most of it, both of us distracted from our problems by catching up with at least thirty different people. Before I knew it, the party was over.

"Hey," Beau said, surprising me out of a daze as I filled up a garbage bag on the back patio.

"Hey." I blinked at him, my shoulders slumping. Exhaustion hit me like a physical blow—or like a rug pulled out from underneath my feet.

"Any trouble last night?"

"A bit. But I don't want to worry Lauren or your mom right now."

He crossed his arms. "Are you staying the night here?"

"Shh," I said, glancing over my shoulder. "I can't leave Cheeto."

"The cat?"

"Yeah. Your dad's allergic—and it's too much."

He ran a hand through his hair. "I have an idea."

"Okay." Why was he so big-eyed and twitchy all of a sudden?

Those blue eyes stared at me for a long moment while he rubbed his cheek. "Did you call your brother?"

"No. But you know he lives in a shack, if that's what you're thinking." It was actually a tiny travel trailer in the backyard of a house he'd bought. He was neck-deep in a huge remodel.

"Your dad?"

I frowned at him. "You know what, don't worry about it." I tied the garbage bag closed with more force than was necessary.

Beau cleared his throat. "I have an empty bedroom." He closed his eyes and took a deep breath.

"What?"

"Three."

"Three what?"

"Bedrooms. I've been subletting rooms in my house. A couple guys live downstairs in the finished basement. Four bedrooms on the main floor—three of them empty."

My mouth hung open. I closed it. He was renting a big house? I tapped my cheek, trying to work through what was happening—the edges of my vision were blurry. "You're offering to rent a room to me?"

He shoved his hands in his pockets and leaned back, raising his eyebrows. "Well, it gets you out of the apartment. You can take stock from there."

"Move in until I find another place?" I twisted my bracelet around on my wrist. "Uh—wow, thank you. I'm tempted but it seems wrong..."

Travis wouldn't like it—or would he care? I stared at the big Adam's apple on Beau's neck that bobbed as he swallowed. What would the maybe girlfriend Harper think? Beau seemed pretty reluctant about it all and I didn't blame him.

Coming closer, he took the garbage bag out of my hand and tossed it away. "It might be awkward—we're a dude house. It isn't pretty. But you've got to move. That asshole is escalating."

I covered my eyes with a hand. *Damnit*. Reality slammed into me. It was really happening—I was moving because a strange guy had fixated on me. He shouted sick threats at me all night through a wall.

Beau patted my shoulder. "I'm sorry this is happening to you."

CHAPTER FIVE

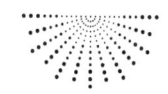

Beau took off right away to run over to his house. Steeling myself, I called my brother, Mason. He was the only one of my father's other children I spoke to. We'd always stuck together—in a grudging kind of way.

The call rang and rang then went to voicemail. I twisted the bracelet on my wrist as I listened to his grumpy recording. "Leave a message. If you have to."

"Hey, it's Raven. I have to move, um, tonight. It sucks and I hate to ask but can you come right away with your truck? Okay—"

He called me back, breaking into my message. I connected the call right away.

"Raven?" he barked tersely with what sounded like a compressor running in the background.

"Yeah," I shouted. "Bad news."

"What—damn. Hold on while I turn this piece of shit off." The phone seemed to fall. Mason cursed.

I squeezed my eyes shut. My brother was like a big unlabeled firework with the fuse burning—you never knew how big the explosion would be. *Did I really need his help...?*

"Damn cheap ass ladder fell over. Bad news? Spill it, Raven. Every fucking bit."

"I have to move—tonight. Beau Martin is letting me stay at his place—"

"No. No fucking way you're staying with that fuckboy. You know he screwed my cousin, Stacy?"

"So what?"

"Jesus, Raven. Wait, are you sleeping with that asshole?"

My head started pounding. "You know what, I don't want to be yelled at. Do you think there's a good reason for my emergency move on a Sunday night?"

He sniffed. "You call for help, I get to ask questions. Why the hell are you moving?"

I took a deep breath. "Stalker. There's a creep in the apartment next to me."

"Did the piece of shit put his hands on you?"

"No. He follows me around and says nasty shit. I beat him up last night and then got arrested."

"He did?"

"No, I did."

Mason grunted. "That's dumb. All right, be there in an hour." He hung up.

My arm dropped to my side. It was so oddly embarrassing to have to broadcast my hideous problem to the people in my life. I didn't want to think about it.

I turned around. Lauren, and both of her parents, were behind me on the back patio. Both women had their hands over their mouths.

"Raven, what's going on?" Lauren asked, like I was about to be sent to timeout.

Head hanging in weariness, I was marched into the kitchen. I sat in a chair, then was ordered to tell them everything—which made me cry. I couldn't seem to pull myself together and I hated that.

Lauren's father gave me the number for a lawyer to call "first thing tomorrow."

"Wait," Lauren said, frowning, one hand pushed into her hair. "You're moving into Beau's? The party house?"

John Martin crossed his arms.

"Temporarily."

Lauren shook her head. "What about here—or at Autumn, Kelsey or Maria's? I mean, Beau's? The guys in his basement are potheads."

Allison rubbed my back and handed me another tissue. "You're always welcome here."

"Thank you," I said, dabbing at my face. "I have a cat now. You guys are allergic. Our friends don't have space. It's all been so messy—and sudden."

"Beau does have spare bedrooms," Allison said. "You'll be a good influence on him."

I leaned my head on her side. "Ha. He won't care what I think."

"Is that cat really worth it?" Lauren asked, rubbing her belly.

"Cheeto. He happened to me."

Shakily, I pushed myself up from the table so I could meet Beau and Mason at my apartment. The other Martins offered to help but I refused, pointing out that they had a party to clean up. Also, my apartment was just too depressing.

~

THE MORE TIRED I GOT, the more the fear set in. I didn't want to pull into my parking space. I sat in my car, on the far side of the complex lot, breathing too fast.

"Okay, okay," I whispered. I shook my head—*what the hell is happening to me?* Clenching the steering wheel, I zipped into an empty spot by the dumpsters.

Shep answered his door when I tapped on it softly. He nodded at me and stepped out, closing the door behind him like his life depended on not making a sound. His infant was a light sleeper.

"It's happening," I whispered. "I'm out tonight."

He nodded, rubbing his chin. "Good, good..."

"Feeling paranoid...have a minute to walk me over there?"

"Oh—sure." He pulled his beanie further down his forehead.

We hopped in my car and drove to my parking spot. My hands were slippery as I turned off the ignition. Rob was sitting in front of his door, staring at me.

"Dang," I said, then had to clear my throat. "That gargoyle gets uglier every time I see him."

"He have somethin' in his hands?" Shep asked.

We stared at the flash of metal.

"His phone, I think." I forced myself to get out of the car and open the hatchback. Unbelievably thoughtful Allison had found some boxes, tape, and garbage bags to help me with the move.

I didn't look at Rob again. Shep dropped off his armload of boxes by my door, then veered off in Rob's direction.

"How're ya, Rob?" I heard Shep ask in the surprisingly firm voice he sometimes used.

"Fucking pissed I was shocked yesterday, Shep. That's how I am."

I didn't stand there to hear more. Gripping the box of garbage bags, I walked to the center of my apartment, quivering a little at the scope of the project—it was already four in the afternoon.

A little adrenaline set in when I thought of my underwear getting tossed around for every soul to see—Beau and Mason would be there any minute. I started stuffing garbage bags as fast as I could move in my bedroom, shuddering at how wrinkled and smashed my pretty lingerie would all be.

"Raven?" Beau called from the front door.

"Yep," I shouted. "Be out in a sec…"

My hands moved faster but my slinky collection of undergarments kept slipping from my fingers and landing on the carpet.

"Hey," Beau said from the door, while I frantically shoved a teddy and garter belt set into the bag. "Good news. I bribed Chuck and AJ into helping out…"

"That's great. I owe you big time for this."

He walked closer. I glanced over my shoulder, hunching forward to hide my naughty bag.

Beau crouched over and picked up a red lace G-string. "Dropped this," he croaked. He bit the knuckle of his other hand.

I snatched it away from him, my ears burning. "Give me a damn minute. And scrub that out of your head."

He punched his chest and stumbled backward. "Never."

"Shit," I muttered after he disappeared through my bedroom door. Heart thumping, I tied the bag closed and set it under my purse in the corner.

"Sister," Mason shouted from the living room. "Put some damn music on. And I want a drink. Then show me the scumbag neighbor so I can kill him."

Carrying my nightstand, I walked out into the living room and worked hard not to look at Beau. "Coke's in the fridge. If you kill my neighbor, I'll be sure to visit you in prison."

"No beer?" Mason stalked over to the fridge and yanked it open. His clothes were covered in paint splatters and what might be wall texture stuff. "Next time, beer and pizza. And where's all your damn food? All you have in here is fake coffee creamer and shorty carrots. Jesus."

"Easy to move," Beau said. "Ready to get this big stuff out of the way?"

Mason grumbled, stomping over to pick up the other side of my tiny sofa. I ran back into my bedroom to shove my bedding into garbage bags so they could get the mattress and bed frame.

Ten minutes later, two guys knocked on the apartment door. "Hey, it's your new housemates," one of them said.

I popped out of my bedroom, lugging sacks of clothing. "Thank you for coming to help. I owe you guys for this."

The bearded redhead waved a hand. "Needed to get off my ass anyway. I'm Chuck. This is AJ."

AJ was a muscular bald guy who nodded his head at me gravely. Both of them seemed like they were somewhere in their thirties.

"Can I set one of you at the kitchen? Boxes are on the counter. This is a last-minute mess—sorry you got dragged in. I really appreciate your help."

Chuck flashed me a thumbs-up and shuffled into the kitchen.

"Want help with those clothes?" AJ asked, his arms crossed as he glanced around.

"Yes, I do. I'm thinking to leave the closet stuff on the hangers, fold it in half and shove it into my hatchback."

"Yep."

AJ followed me to the closet. He wasn't much of a talker so we got right to work and moved fast. I had a lot of clothes.

On the walk to the parking lot, Cheeto was still nowhere to be seen. I unlocked my car and put down the back seats. AJ and I piled the clothing in the trunk while I winced at the exposed fabric trailing close to greasy car parts.

At least Rob the creep wasn't sitting on his front porch anymore. I exhaled and kept my eyes away from his windows. My skin still crawled. I suspected that he was in there staring out like a vicious troll, waiting for his moment to pounce...

"You all right?" Beau asked, suddenly in front of me.

I jumped a little. "Yeah, I guess. It's all happening pretty dang fast."

He wiped his forehead with a sleeve. "Mason and I are going to go unload at my place. Text me when you're done here."

"Yeah, thanks. Have you seen Cheeto?" I swiped loose hair from my ponytail out of my face, watching the bushes where he usually hid.

"No. What are you going to move him in?"

I gaped at Beau. "Shoot—I don't know..."

"I'll come back here with my dog kennel."

"You have a dog? Is he good with cats?"

"Uh, he's interested in them." Beau shrugged. "We'll figure it out. Bubba's a pretty sweet guy."

Big-eyed, I nodded.

Mason walked up and I hugged him, even letting him rub the top of my head. Beau and Mason took off and I went back into my suddenly very empty apartment.

AJ dodged past me with another armload of clothes. I opened my coat closet and felt like an idiot for not remembering my luggage. It really had been a long time since I'd slept. My stomach growled as I finished packing.

There still hadn't been a sign of Cheeto. Chewing on my lip, I tried not to be convinced that Rob had captured him again—what the hell would I do about that? Cheeto did have a few apartments he visited in the complex. Maybe he was happier somewhere else?

Chuck and AJ left while I cleaned. Alone in that almost empty apartment, I missed having my stun gun. The police weren't giving it back anytime soon. Rob cackled on his side of the wall. His television was turned up very loud.

The door swung open and I jumped, screaming a little. It was Beau, holding a take-out bag.

He scanned the room and took a few quick steps over to me. "You all right? Did something happen?"

I crouched over with a hand on my chest. "No—I'm fine."

Beau's face was hard and intent, back in cop mode for the moment. The warm fuzzy spot in my chest—that had been growing for Beau all day—spread a little more. I was really, really glad to be leaving that apartment.

He held up the bag in front of my face. "Brought you a burger."

"Bless you." I snatched the bag out of his hand, so happy to see food I almost kissed him. "I'm so freaking hungry."

I ate on the go, walking the last of my things over to Beau's truck with his help—including all of Cheeto's gear. My key was handed off to Shep. Calling Cheeto's name, I jogged around the complex trying to find him.

Back in front of the locked apartment door, I collapsed on the front step and put my head in my hands. It was almost eight o'clock.

Beau sat down next to me and put an arm around my shoulder. I rested against him without thinking—then stayed there because I couldn't force myself to pull away.

"I don't know what to do," I said.

"Shep said he'd call you if he sees Cheeto." Beau squeezed me a little tighter against him.

"Maybe he wasn't that into me?"

Beau huffed. "He's probably locked in another apartment. If he doesn't end up with you, seems like he'll get fed."

"Yeah...I hope so. His first person left and he's been couch-surfing ever since. I put a collar on him, but it disappeared."

Sighing, Beau pushed to his feet. "Come on. It's almost Monday."

Blinking hard, I took the hand he held out to me and let him pull me to my feet. We stood close together for a moment, the porch light illuminating his blond hair and growth of face bristle. I didn't want to leave my Cheeto—wouldn't have if Beau hadn't put an arm around my shoulders and started moving us toward the cars.

The bushes rustled off to my left and then I heard frantic meowing. I gulped and tears rolled down my face as I crouched and waited. Cheeto appeared, limping toward me with one paw held above the ground. There was a bloody scrape across his ear.

I scooped him up carefully. "That's it, bud. Inside cat from now on."

CHAPTER SIX

From the street, Beau's house appeared to be a squat little bungalow, one story, with an overgrown front yard. *How did so many people fit in there?*

The house was actually built into a slope and as we went down the driveway, the house kept going. From the backyard view, it was a wide two-story.

Beau had me park closer to the front door on the upslope top of the driveway. Cheeto yowled from his tilted crate on my reclined passenger seat.

"Almost there," I said, trying to find the energy to climb out of my car and work for another three hours.

A woman in a camisole and barely there shorts stormed across the sidewalk and onto the driveway, her fists pumping at her sides. She had a ball cap pulled down over her long auburn hair, but she was definitely glaring at me. My eyelid twitched. *Is that who I think it is?*

I stood up out of my car and faced her. Cheeto howled. "Is there something you want?" I asked, putting a hand out to steady myself.

"Saw you at the police station," she said. "You some kind of cheap badge-bunny?"

My hackles went all the way up—there wasn't anything cheap about me. "Are you some kind of stalker, Harper? Grow some manners and back up. I've had a really long day."

"Took your picture, bitch. Leave now, and I won't post it all over the internet."

"What?" The bottom dropped out of my stomach. *What kind of bad luck year was this?* "That's extortion. I will file a police report."

She put her chin up.

I took a step closer and pointed my finger in her face. "You don't know what's going on here."

"Harper?" Beau said from behind me. "What is this?"

"You guys need to talk." I marched around to the passenger side of my car. "Stop confusing her, Beau."

Harper cursed while Beau pulled her down the driveway, shouting and also crying. And that, right there, was why being romantically involved with Beau was a horrible idea—you didn't know that he'd broken up with you until you'd lost your grip on reality.

Cheeto whined inside the kennel box as I carried it up to the front of the gray house. An oak door and concrete step were covered by a small awning protruding out of the low-hanging roof. It seemed like a home built early in the twentieth century that had been added on to many times over the course of its hundred-year life.

I knocked on the locked front door and waited. A bramble of an overgrown rose bush snagged in my clothing.

The door creaked open. "Oh, hey," said Chuck, his eyes barely open. "Come in." He stepped back.

I almost asked him if he was all right, but then the intense reek of reefer on him put two and two together in my head.

Except the smell got worse the further I went into the house—the extremely messy house.

The golden oak floor in the living room was cluttered with piles of torn shipping and product boxes, dog toys, jackets, socks and shoes, and work out equipment. Beau had a big sectional sofa that took up most of the floor space, a coffee table covered with junk, and a giant television perched on a small table. A dog howled from the floor below us.

Chuck pointed at a door in the wall before the hallway. "Stuff's in there. Nice window." He blinked, his head swiveling around. "Where's Beau?"

"Getting yelled at by his girlfriend in the driveway. Why does everything reek like reefer?"

Eyes squinted, Chuck rocked back on his heels. "Trimming my grow in the basement. Almost ready."

"Your grow?"

"Yep."

I opened the door to my bedroom and coughed when a cloud of dust hit me in the face.

It was a long narrow room almost entirely taken up by my full-sized bed—which the guys had already set up. I put Cheeto's cage down on an open spot on the floor.

After cracking the window to let in fresh air, I searched out my sheets and comforter and made the bed. There was a closet in the room, but it was a tiny one.

I worked for the next hour filling my dresser with clothes and setting up my nightstand, moving like a robot and trying not to think. My car was packed to the ceiling with things to unload, but I didn't want to risk interrupting Harper's meltdown.

There was a knock on the door. I glanced up from stuffing empty garbage bags together to see Beau leaning on the doorjamb.

"All right?" he asked, covering a yawn.

"Is she gone? I need to go to my car."

"Oh." He pushed himself up straight. "I'll walk you out there."

We trudged through the front door out to the driveway. Beau immediately grabbed a big armload of clothing out of the trunk.

"There's a closet you can use in the back bedroom," he said.

"You are too good to me. Thank you, I'll take it."

The side of his mouth quirked up. "Meant to tell you to pick whatever room you want. Mason pointed out that the front bedroom put a few walls between us...I thought you'd like the privacy."

I shrugged. "It'll work."

We got everything out of the car by dumping it on the couch. It was a mountain of tangled clothing, but my vision was fuzzing out and I was tripping over my own feet.

"Did you find the bathroom?" Beau asked while we both caught our breath.

"Yeah. Rainbow shower curtain."

"Yep. Decorated by a previous renter. We're gonna have to share it, for now, until I finish the repairs on the other shower up here. Want a quick tour?"

I nodded, too curious to put it off.

The house seemed like a maze of doors and narrow hallways to my foggy brain. The kitchen was all white cabinets and appliances, with a pile of dishes in the sink and a grubby countertop.

"Laundry room through here. Mudroom by the side door." He pointed at a door across the kitchen. "We all mostly come through the mudroom from outside. Stairs to the basement are there too."

I followed Beau downstairs. He told me the basement was a separate apartment. There was a big open room at the bottom, with windows and a sliding glass door that led to the backyard. A tawny pit bull came wiggling over, wagging his tail so hard his back legs slid over the wood flooring.

"This is Bubba," Beau said.

I held still while Bubba sniffed me. He was big and barrel-chested and looked like he could knock down linebackers. He started licking my hand and I yanked it away and wiped off the lingering dog slime on the side of my pants. Cats were so much nicer.

Chuck and AJ were on a couple of recliners in front of two televisions, each of them playing a video game. There was a kitchenette in one corner of the room.

"The guys have their bedrooms and a shower down here," Beau said.

"And pot plants." I leaned sideways and glanced down a hall where a really bright light shone.

Beau shrugged. "Few in the backyard once a year. They're legal."

Chuck's screen lit up with exploding dragon-like monsters. He put down his controller and picked up a giant bong on the side table next to him.

"Your living room stuff is there." Beau pointed to my love seat, put against the wall by the sliding glass door.

"Thank you. For everything." I covered a giant yawn. "I better head up and check on Cheeto."

Beau followed me upstairs. "Sorry about Harper," he said next to my pile of clothing in the living room. "Not sure what I'm gonna do about her."

"Break up with her?" I raised my eyebrows.

He smiled, propped on the couch next to me. I stared at his mouth—his bottom lip was so full and pink, the top a thin bow.

"We went over it again. She's always been a little jealous of you."

CHAPTER SEVEN

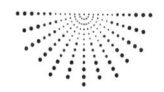

Monday morning, I speed-walked into work wearing a wrinkled light heather-gray pantsuit. I was only a few minutes late—which seemed like a minor miracle after my morning of managing Cheeto and Bubba drama while not being able to find anything I needed.

"Loved the party," called Susan, the finance director.

I smiled. "That's what I like to hear."

Blowing out a breath, I tried to relax my hunched shoulders. Was it possible that my arrest had slipped under the radar? There had been a tiny article in the online local newspaper about it.

My tidy office cubicle seemed like a haven of accomplishment and rationality. The comfortable cage I'd chosen. I collapsed into my chair.

Climbing up the job ladder to my current position had been a high-wire act of pretending to be something I wasn't, like a person that could sit still. Not a problem that morning. Lately, it had started to seem like I could pull it all off. The cursing pirate queen had been locked in her quarters—I only let her out on the weekends.

The morning sped by as I answered emails and drafted content for a social media campaign on vaccines. Right before lunch, an email from my boss, Karen, popped into my inbox. *Come see me right away*, was in the subject line.

I stood up and smoothed down my clothing, knots tightening between my shoulder blades. Karen was a no-nonsense person. With employees she was firm, her steel-gray curls like a war helmet on her round face. I tapped on her door and twisted the knob when she called *Open*.

"Raven," she said gravely, "sit down."

Breathing too fast, I did as I was told.

"Were you arrested on Saturday?"

My ears started ringing. *How the hell did she already know?* "Yes. But I'm fighting it, with a lawyer. My neighbor has been stalking me, and he was hurting my cat. I hope to have this all cleared up soon."

She sat back in her chair. "I'm so sorry. Are you okay?"

"I moved yesterday," I said, not wanting to lie to her. There wasn't anything okay about me in that moment.

She stared at her hands for a moment and hope surged in my chest. *Please, Karen, please...*

"It's unfortunate, but corporate policy doesn't give me a choice. I have to let you go, immediately. When you clear this up, you can reapply."

Nodding, I stood up then had to grip the back of the chair when my vision wavered. "I'll pack my things now."

It took minutes to erase my position as a public relations specialist at River Gorge Hospital. Before it had fully sunk in, I stood on the outside of the building, locked out.

"Raven," Travis called, walking toward me with his briefcase. "I can't do coffee today because Piper has a doctor's appointment...oh. Are you all right? What happened?"

Purse hanging from my fingers, I stumbled to a bench and sank onto it. Travis followed me, his eyebrows drawn together. "I made a mistake. Now everything's ruined." I hunched over, covering my face as I cried.

Travis sat down next to me. "I'm so sorry. What happened?"

"This guy has been harassing me, stalking and saying disgusting things."

"What? For how long?"

"Months—there didn't seem to be anything I could do. When he grabbed my cat, I snapped. Got him with my stun gun."

When I glanced at him, Travis nodded, watching me with what seemed like understanding and sympathy on his serious face.

"I was arrested for assault. Karen just fired me." Shaking my head, I closed my eyes, trying to ignore the lunch crowd walking by.

"Is your cat okay?"

"Yes." I dug around in my purse for the packet of tissues in there.

Travis blew out his breath. "I'm really sorry. And…" He looked down at his hands. "I'll miss having coffee with you."

"Me too," I said, dabbing at my face. Was he ending us? *Reach out to me, Travis…*

He rubbed his cheek. "Do you have a lawyer?"

"Called one. I'm going to fight to have it dismissed."

"Right." He stood up. "I'll let you get to your car. Take care of yourself—you'll get through this."

I nodded, staring down at my bag.

"Raven, I…I'll see you soon."

I stood up. "Goodbye, Travis."

IN MY CAR, I called the lawyer that Lauren's dad had recommended, a criminal defense attorney named David Mesh.

"Any chance he can speak with me today?" I asked the person answering his phone. "I don't mind waiting."

"He's here this afternoon. I think he can see you today."

I drove twenty minutes east on the highway along the Columbia River, the wide stretch of blue water sparkling in the bright sun. Basalt cliffs rose on either side of the gorge canyon around me, the country turning to cheatgrass and sagebrush with every mile I drove away from the rainforest in the west. Mount Hood rose, majestic and high, in the south.

Usually, the scenery was like something out of a fairytale. That afternoon, I was stuck in a nightmare. I'd tried to find a public defender to help me but there was a huge shortage in my area and my income was probably too high to qualify anyway. It would take weeks, or months, to find someone.

After spending time around Lauren's father the prosecutor, I had an idea of what came next. The defense attorney would want me to plead not guilty, go to trial, and fight as long and as hard as possible—and make him a lot of money doing it.

Mr. Mesh's office was an old brick four-story in the old-fashioned downtown of The Dalles, our neighboring city to the east. I filled out client information forms, then paced in the hallway outside of his office lobby. What the hell was I going to do? I couldn't afford lawyer fees...

After I'd worn a few treads into the hallway carpet, at last I walked into Mr. Mesh's office. He was a heavyset man with thin blond hair and a kind smile.

We shook hands. "Hello, Ms. Brown. Have a seat. John

Martin called me this morning and asked me to take your case. I'm happy to do so."

"Thank you. Call me Raven." I twisted the bracelet on my wrist and had to work hard to keep my foot from tapping.

"Okay, thank you, Raven. Would you like a drink—coffee, tea, or water? No? Let me know if you change your mind. We're going to go over everything."

We started with the day of the arrest. Mr. Mesh was very happy with me for keeping my mouth shut at the police station. It took over an hour to talk it all through, including all the evidence I'd gathered of Rob the creep harassing me since I'd moved into that damn apartment.

Mr. Mesh put his pen down and leaned forward in his chair. "I recommend fighting this. Strongly recommend. Your other option is to plead no contest, or guilty, and hope for a misdemeanor fourth degree assault, with probation. However, it will take a year to get through that. And then another year to possibly expunge it from your record. Two years, at a minimum, with a criminal record."

I nodded, rubbing my forehead with three fingers. "All of it takes a long time." And money. Oh no, I wasn't forgetting that.

"First thing we can do is delay. Gives us more time to investigate and prepare."

"Yes. Let's start there." By hook or by crook, I was going to fight.

He nodded. "Good. Now, what are your immediate plans?"

I pinched the bridge of my nose. "Don't know. Find another job."

"Can I make a suggestion?"

"Yes."

"Community service, right away. Show that you're a member of the community that gives back."

I sat up straighter. "Will it help my case?"

"It won't hurt. Keep track of the hours you put in and we'll use it."

"Okay." It sounded like a voluntary penance, and I was totally onboard. "Do you have any suggestions on who to contact?"

"I'll make a call right now."

CHAPTER EIGHT

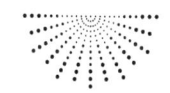

In downtown River Gorge, next to the riverfront, I found the address that my lawyer had given me. The agency office was in a converted industrial building turned into modern office spaces. I straightened my suit jacket and marched inside.

Riverside Hospice was an organization I was familiar with from working at the hospital. I found their suite on the upper floor of the building. It was an open and airy room, with exposed beam ceilings of stained golden wood, and huge banks of windows that faced the river.

A woman over at the one of the worktables waved at me, then held up a finger. I sat down in a cushioned gray armchair to wait.

"This is very…flashy for a hospice fundraiser," said a gorgeously dressed woman with a South Asian accent. I couldn't help overhearing the conversation since it was happening about ten feet away.

"Indra," answered the young woman with black curly hair, "the board already approved. The bachelor auction has a budget."

"Yes, yes. Okay. But I want it to make money, not be a drain on our resources."

Bachelor auction fundraiser? My mouth quirked up—that *was* a flashy idea. And yet, it sounded like an event that would grab headlines in a good way.

I stood up when the woman who had waved at me walked over. She was very tall with dark curly hair.

"Hi, I'm Raven. Mr. David Mesh said he called on my behalf. I'm hoping to volunteer here."

"Welcome. I'm Gail. We can always use more volunteers. Please, tell me about yourself."

We sat down in the chairs, and I gave her my two-minute pitch: Bachelor's in communication and marketing, public relations specialist for the hospital until recently. "My former boss, Karen Owens, emailed a letter of recommendation for me this afternoon. I think it's best to tell you I'm dealing with a court case. A neighbor has been stalking me and I had to defend myself."

That was an extreme simplification, but during our long conversation that afternoon, Mr. Mesh had been very firm about guarding my tongue at all times.

"I'm so sorry to hear that." Gail's mouth pinched together.

"But if you have a place for me here, I'd love to help out."

"I could use some help," called the bubbly young woman sitting nearby—the one planning the bachelor auction.

"Oh." Gail sat up straighter and smiled. "With your PR experience, Raven, I think that's a great fit. This is our intern, Sasha. She's working on a rather, um, large fundraising idea. Suddenly, we're a month out from the date and there's a lot to nail down."

"Right up my alley—and it sounds fun. I'm a local. Already have several women in mind that would enjoy this."

"We need men too," Sasha called.

"Do you have a location?" I asked, getting a little nervous.

There wouldn't be much I could do if she didn't have that. It was still wedding season and tourists flooded our area every day, filling up the empty spaces.

Sasha pushed red glasses up her nose. "Yes. Eagle's Ridge Assisted Living. Their huge ballroom-like dining area."

I nodded, suppressing a frown. Not ideal for an upscale fundraiser but there wasn't time to change.

Gail rubbed her hands together. "Yes, perfect. I still need to do your paperwork, Raven, but if you'd like to start now—informally—perhaps you and Sasha can get started? Perhaps something to reassure the board?"

"You bet," I said. "And I have a firefighter brother, a best friend's police officer brother, and a well-to-do corporate executive friend that I am volunteering, right now, to auction off for charity."

Sasha cheered. Indra and Gail smiled tensely.

∼

After losing my job, apartment, and almost boyfriend Travis, it was like I could sense a piano above me, plunging down to fall on my head, and manic energy kicked in to keep me moving. Could I run fast enough?

Whatever fake and temporary high I was on, I was determined to ride it out as long as possible; I fed the manic beast with extra caffeine and let myself indulge in my weakness for fast food.

I stayed at the agency office until after six, making calls and writing emails, while Sasha and I mapped out the details for the bachelor auction. I spammed every professional I knew with demands they attend or participate. The reality of what I was doing settled in—my reputation would be either made or shattered by this event. I couldn't sit still.

Waiting in another fast-food drive-through lane, I jolted

up and smacked my palm against my forehead. There was a minor detail I hadn't remembered. I took out my phone and texted Beau.

> **ME**
> Hey, are you home?

We'd exchanged numbers at some point during the last seventy-two hours. I'd discovered Beau could be relied on for a quick response.

> **BEAU**
> Leaving now.

> **ME**
> Want tacos?

> Hell, yeah, I want your taco.

> What? Don't start that. Can you meet me in the station parking lot?

> Yes. Be there in ten.

Why was I smiling down at my phone?

Beau was the last person I wanted to be involved with. Not only was he notorious for vowing to never settle down, but I was still holding a grudge against him for about a hundred pranks he'd played on me when we were teenagers. Also, it was about as likely to work out as a lottery ticket.

I did my "dating" in big city Portland to the west, an hour drive away, and far enough removed that Travis Dashiell wouldn't have to know a thing about it. My ability to remain celibate was pretty limited.

When I pulled into the police station parking lot, I spotted Beau right away. He stood next to his truck, grabbing a duffel out of the cab.

I parked close to him and got out of my car. "Hey," I

called, holding up the take-out bag. "Paying forward the bad food habits."

His face transformed when he smiled—from hard and serious to buoyant and playful in a moment.

"I'll take it," he said, closing the door of his truck.

"Realized I don't have a front door key." I handed him the bag. "I can go make a copy right now."

He nodded, pulling his keys out of his jacket pocket. "Yeah, sorry, didn't think about it. Leave my key under the mat by the mudroom door."

"Got it." I took the key. "Lost my job today. Arrest record is a no go for PR departments."

Beau put a hand in his hair. "Shit, Raven, I'm sorry."

I nodded. "Yep—I'm freaking out, on the inside. In Energizer bunny mode at the moment. I'm planning a bachelor auction for Halloween. Counting on you to sell yourself to the highest bidder. Here's the form for you to sign."

He blinked at me. "Can we go back to bunny mode..."

"Please round up other singles in the department too. For a great cause—Riverside Hospice. Sign here." I held a binder in front of him with a pen attached to the flap.

"Um...can I think about it?"

"No. Sign it."

Blowing out a breath, he scrawled his name on the sheet. "I know my rights," he said. "This signature means maybe."

~

BY THE TIME I parked in the driveway at Beau's house, my hands were trembling. I put my head down on the steering wheel.

No job...no job...no job. It hit me hard—how was I going to pay rent, my student loans, and credit card bills? My head honked the car's horn and I sat up with a jerk.

I dragged myself to the front door then stopped, staring down at the red heart box on the door mat. Chocolates. The hair lifted on the back of my neck.

Swallowing, I twisted around to stare behind me at the road. Empty cars were parked along the sidewalk. None of them were Rob's orange Kia Rio.

Stomach tight, I crept forward. My name had been scrawled in thick black ink on the top of the red box. There was a note tucked underneath. I took pictures of everything.

With a tissue covering my hand, I opened the note. *I know where you are.* I dropped it and backed away.

"Damnit." I clenched my fists, trying to find some rage to overwhelm the spiraling need to run, right now, and hide.

Cheeto meowed inside the house, tapping a paw on my bedroom window. I forced myself to move up to the door and unlock it. In Beau's kitchen I found a garbage bag that I used to gather up the chocolate box and note. The heart box opened in the bag and revealed all of the chocolates smashed —and dirty. I closed the front door behind me and locked it up tight.

Bubba howled from the basement, apparently being babysat by the downstairs housemates. After closing all the bedroom doors upstairs, I let Cheeto out of my bedroom. He sprinted out and hid under the sofa. At least his injuries hadn't turned out to be serious.

My heart was an out-of-control racehorse in my chest— the stalker had found me already? Rob had. How could it be anyone else?

I picked up my phone and called my brother.

"Raven?" he answered, sounding grumpy as usual. "What's the emergency now?"

"Hi to you too. Lost my job today and that damn stalker found me already. Left smashed chocolates and a note here."

"Shit."

"Yeah. I'm pissed. Getting scared too."

He cleared his throat. "It's bad. Remember this, if that asswipe lays a hand on you, I will kill him."

I snorted. "Thanks, bro."

"Revenge is my love language."

"I need a favor. Saw an attorney today. He suggested community service to help my case. Now I'm helping organize a big fundraiser. My reputation—career—needs this to work. Can I sign you up to help for one night?"

"Uh—"

"Thank you so much. This means the world to me. I really need it. Make sure you have the Thursday before Halloween free."

"But—"

"I'm counting on you. And find other single firefighters to help too. I need every good-looking man I can find."

"What?"

"This is an extremely good cause—hospice care. The night will be fun. Angels and demons theme, and a bachelor auction. I'm working on really great dates to go with it—dinner at a winery, boat rides, all that. I'm counting on you to get high bids. You aren't bad to look at."

"Raven—"

"It's happening. I'm signing for you. Oops, the cat's clawing something. Gotta go. Love ya."

I hung up on him.

Cheeto had a claw stuck in the rug in front of the fireplace. I picked him up and examined the barb-like nails coming out of his paws. "I think I need to trim these," I muttered, petting him while he purred and rubbed his head on my shoulder.

My ability to sleep had fled. I didn't think I could leave a key outside with that creep possibly watching the house.

While Cheeto explored, I put away clothes and organized

more of my stuff. Did a bit of tidying in general. Messy spaces didn't bother me, really, but I liked a basic tidiness where I was living. Eventually, I showered and wound down enough to lie on my bed with my laptop and Cheeto curled up by my side.

I'd emailed Travis that afternoon about the bachelor auction. In some ways, he was the person I wanted to impress more than anyone—prove that I was more than my criminal record and decapitated career.

Travis was sophisticated in an effortless-not-trying-to-be kind of way. I had to watch myself when I was around him. It made me a better person—or at least sound smarter. A life with Travis would have soft white furniture and thick beautiful carpets. We'd vacation in a different country every year. Our weekends would be a parade of sumptuous meals…

He hadn't emailed me back. I stared at my inbox—putting off, for the moment, filling out yet another online police report. Travis was much more relaxing to think about. I wasn't giving up on him.

CHAPTER NINE

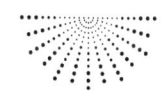

"We have another one," Sasha shouted two days later at the hospice agency office, raising a fist in the air. "Nominated from the real estate office you visited this morning."

"Whoop."

We fist-bumped. I stood up and added him to our whiteboard of candidates.

"And I just sold two more seats to bidders." I added them to our tally.

In an email to single women I knew at the hospital, I'd implied that Travis was participating. Peggy and Marla, my old rivals, had thrown their caps in without a second question.

Sasha fanned her face. "Just looked up the broker guy. Yeah…spicy."

"Need to sell more tickets," I muttered, spinning the dry-erase pen around my fingers. "Do we have more fliers? I'm going to hit up accountants and dentists today—especially the women. We need bidders. And sponsors."

I waved goodbye and rushed out the door, realizing that

if I got to my favorite coffee shop in the next ten minutes, I might corner my quarry.

The last two days of intense party-planning had flown by. I'd also started looking for another job. The problem was, any job had to be flexible enough to accommodate my court appearances. Gig work might be my only option.

Luckily, Mr. Mesh had delayed the first court date for a few weeks with a continuance. We were gathering every kind of photo and recording and other evidence we could find showing how Rob Campbell had been harassing me.

Actually, Campbell was scaring the crap out of me. I hadn't wanted to admit it for a long time, but his unnerving fixation on me had gone from unsettling to terrifying. I needed witness statements from my neighbors in the apartments and anyone else that had seen me dealing with Campbell.

The aroma of roasted coffee and sweet pastry wrapped around me like a comforting blanket as I edged my way into the crowded coffee shop. Travis was there, standing next to a display case. He watched me with a slight smile as I made my way closer.

"Hey," I said. "I was hoping to run into you today. How are you?"

Were his eyes focusing on my mouth or was that my imagination? "Good. Wondering how you are."

"I'm a fighter. My lawyer seems optimistic. Have you seen the emails I sent you this week? About the fundraiser for the hospice charity?"

He rubbed his face, suddenly sheepish. "Yes—and wasn't sure what to say. Was a little confused. Did you know about it last weekend at the hospital party? When you brought up auctioning me off...?"

I shrugged, grinning at him. "No—uncanny, isn't it? Listen, I need your help. Please. I promise it will be fun."

He took a deep breath, his eyes sliding away from mine. "I'm just, um, not sure about the expectations…"

Scoffing, I waved a hand between us. "It's silliness for a good cause. Travis, please. As a favor to me?"

Eyes open very wide, he stared at me. Slowly his chin went up and then down. "I guess—"

"Wonderful," I said, whipping the paperwork out of my bag. "Sign right here. There's a pen on the binder. This is amazing, thank you. I appreciate you so much. Riverside Hospice is a great organization. Go ahead, sign right there. The event is going to be memorable for everyone. At Eagle's Ridge Assisted Living, with some of the residents involved."

At last, Travis scrawled his name on the page. I resisted air-pumping my fist. His worried brown eyes met mine and a rueful smile tugged the corners of his mouth up.

"You're hard to say no to," he said.

"Fire in my belly." I secured the paperwork in my bag. "I need a win."

His name was called for his order, and I waved goodbye to keep running. And because I couldn't afford to buy a coffee anymore.

Selling the bachelor auction all over town turned out to be a decent way to network. I gathered business cards like a bee collects nectar. On a whim, I walked into River Gorge Adventures, a tour company that did fishing and river rafting mostly, and ended up talking to the owner about a position he was hiring for in the office.

Late afternoon, I went back to Beau's house. Cheeto greeted me at the door with a grumpy meow, then darted for outside. I blocked him with my foot. Convincing him to stay inside wasn't going well.

Beau's truck hadn't been parked in the driveway and the house was quiet. Lately, his schedule seemed to be to get home around three in the morning, sleep for six or seven hours, then head out to fish for salmon on the Columbia River before his next shift started.

In the kitchen, he'd actually washed his breakfast dishes. I poured myself a glass of water and fed Cheeto. Beau had left a note for me on the counter.

> Raven, thanks for tidying up around here. We're short-handed at work and the ten-hour days have worn me down. I'm better at keeping things orderly but not at fixing a mess, I guess.
>
> We're doing a barbecue here on Saturday, with music. Can you make it? I'll grill a burger for you better than take-out. Beau

The note was written on the back of a junk-mail envelope. I stared at it, unnerved by my impulse to save the scrap of paper—glue it into a journal or some crap. Instead, I dropped it in the recycling bin and then had to wipe my hand on my skirt to keep from grabbing it back.

It had been a hot day and I wanted to shower before working more on my computer. Inside the bathroom, I stripped down to my underwear and stared at myself in the vanity mirror. Was Beau serious about...flirting? I pressed a damp cotton ball against one eye to remove my makeup, bending forward over the sink.

A shiver ran down my skin when I thought about touching Beau—it was good we didn't see each other much. He was the opposite of what I wanted, in so many ways—a Peter Pan, with his pot-head lost boys. Still, he made my heart race, the devil.

The door opened behind me, and Beau walked in a step.

He froze. Our eyes met in the mirror and his lips parted. He fell sideways against the wall, a hand on his chest. I straightened up from my bent over position—in a thong and matching black lace bra.

"Sorry," Beau croaked. He took a step back.

Heat flashed through me—flushing my face and simmering lower. "Yep."

He put his fist in his mouth and closed the door slowly, his eyes running all over me until the latch clicked closed.

I put a hand over my face. My heart was racing. "Do you need to get ready for work? I can wait."

He cleared his throat. "Yeah—thanks. They need me over there early."

"Okay."

Looking around for my robe, I smacked myself in the forehead with an open palm. I'd left it in my room. I snatched a towel from the shelf and wrapped myself up.

Exhaling when I saw the empty hallway, I stepped lightly onto the creaky wooden floor, determined to wait in my bedroom until Beau left.

"Hey," Beau said from the kitchen as I stepped into the living room, making me jump.

I whipped around, then had to yank the small towel up higher. "Hey. Where's Bubba?"

Beau had Cheeto up on his chest, petting him while the little guy purred. "Dog trainer. He loves it over there."

"Oh."

"What the hell is on the front porch?" Beau put Cheeto down.

"I didn't see it." I'd gone in through the mudroom because Cheeto had a harder time getting through that door.

He crossed his arms. "Withered flowers and a note."

"Huh." I put a hand over my stuttering heart.

He was walking closer.

"Has there been anything else?" He stopped in front of me. I could smell the river on him a little and sweat and coffee.

My nipples hardened. "Let's talk about this later—"

"Jesus." He put a hand over his face. "Why didn't you tell me?"

"I was planning to, at some point…" I tried to stand up straighter then had to pull the towel up again. "I'll photograph and bag it for evidence later—"

"Don't touch it. You need an officer to come out here and document it. And not someone you live with."

"Okay. I'll try. Hasn't worked in the past."

"It will now."

"Ah." I glanced toward my bedroom.

He stared at me, frowning. Sighing, he stepped forward and gripped my shoulders.

I startled again. "Oh…"

"Be careful." He leaned forward, and I gasped as it seemed like our lips would collide, but he turned his head and his mouth stopped next to my ear. "I like your underwear—you in your underwear—a lot. A lot." He groaned. Then let go of me and walked away toward the back hallway.

CHAPTER TEN

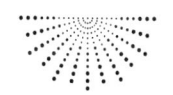

In the morning, I found another note from Beau.

> *I'm worried about you up in that bedroom by yourself. You should come sleep with me where it's safer. Anytime. I would gladly lose sleep.*
>
> *Ordered door cams to put in. Let's get them installed this weekend.*
>
> *I thought about you all night. You know I've always liked you, right? Probably why I teased you so much when we were kids. Are you ready to admit that you've always liked me too? Beau*

Gasping, I crinkled the note up in my fist—then flattened it out and pressed it against my chest. Bent over the kitchen counter, I focused on taking deep breaths, laughing at myself a little while my eyes stung.

Crap. Why am I reacting like this? I stood up straight and set the note down, determined to get my coffee and be rational.

My problem was that it had been too long. I shook my head. Well, and also Beau's wide shoulders and muscled arms. I tapped myself on the forehead.

Before leaving for a long day I was determined to spend entirely out of the house, I wrote Beau a note.

> Don't worry about me and stop flirting! We can't start something. You're getting auctioned off for charity in three weeks and I need your pretty face to bring in lots of donations.
>
> Should I remind you of SOME of the pranks you played on me that I'm still holding a grudge over? You salted my cookies, put vinegar in my apple juice, frozen cereal in my bowl, stuffed my shoes, made packing peanuts fall on my head, and filled my hand sanitizer bottle with clear glue. Those times you stole my towel and clothes while we were swimming so that I had to chase you around, in my bikini, in front of practically the entire high school!
>
> I'm getting mad just thinking about it.
>
> So, no, I'm not going to your barbecue. I'll be over in Portland on a date.

It was Thursday, and I had a long list of things to accomplish—that did not include fantasizing about crawling into Beau's big king-sized bed...I'd had a peek at it when he wasn't home.

By lunch I was dragging—it had been hard to sleep the night before with all the Beau nonsense swirling around my head. I decided to treat myself to a drip coffee and hopefully a run-in with Travis. His handsome serious face would put me to rights, I was sure of it.

I was reaching for the café door when it opened in front of me. Travis and Peggy walked out. She smiled smugly at me.

"Raven," she said in her flat voice.

"Hi," I said, forcing my mouth to move.

Travis just stared at me, his to-go coffee cup held against his chest.

I walked past them and into the shop. *It's nothing. He's getting coffee with her, not walking down the aisle.* Somehow, though, I knew Peggy had completely usurped me as Travis's work wife. She had become the person he did things with. He might tell himself he wouldn't date a coworker but who was he kidding?

Thursdays, a group of women I knew got together for a happy hour at different bars around town for networking. After showing up for the last half a year, a core group of us had become tight friends. I arrived early, starving, and ready to be out of my car.

I ordered a few tapas plates at the bar so I could chat with Pat, the bartender.

"How you been, Raven?" asked Pat, his New Jersey accent strong.

I popped an olive in my mouth. "Lousy. Lost my job because I beat up the prick that's been stalking me."

He collapsed onto his elbows on the bar. "Seriously?"

"Yeah. He thought hurting my cat, in his underwear,

would make me feel some kind of way. I—well, my lawyer tells me I need to shut my mouth. Anyway, a stun gun was involved. The cops showed up and arrested me."

"Fuck." He shook his head. "Cat okay?"

"Yeah. He made it."

"You know what? Women that beat up their stalkers get a free drink in my bar. Good job."

"Thanks." I hunched over, eating another olive.

"You gonna be all right?"

I nodded, cocking my head. "Course."

He pushed a big glass of white wine across the bar to me. "Try that. It's nice."

Mustering a smile for him, I forced myself to sit up straight.

A few minutes later, Kelsey came through the door and saw me. She walked over, staring at the floor and holding her hands together in front of her.

"Hi. Do you want to grab a table?" she asked.

"Yeah. How about that big one by the windows?" I stood up. "Phenomenal wine," I called to Pat.

A little Riesling in my empty stomach and I was almost cheerful. Kelsey seemed even more tense than usual.

"How are you?" I asked her as we settled into seats at our table.

She frowned, folding her beautiful caramel cashmere trench over her chair. Her long light brown hair shimmered. It always had that gorgeous movie star wave.

"Oh, Gerry has been…uptight lately—didn't get his promotion," she mumbled, staring down at her water glass.

Pat appeared and took Kelsey's drink order. He put some lovely bread and olive oil on our table.

Kelsey was an accountant, making a nice paycheck. For some reason, she was determined to marry her asshole boyfriend. He was attempting to be a big deal in the local banking community.

"Does Gerry make you happy?" I asked her as Pat walked away.

She blinked, darting a glance at me. "Yes. Of course he does."

"All right. I just…wonder sometimes if you realize what a catch you are."

Her mouth quirked a little. "Thanks. I…really want a family."

"Yeah. Those are nice." I swirled the wine around in my glass. "I told you about Travis, right? I saw him today, getting coffee with another woman."

"A coworker?"

"Yeah." I sniffed.

We sat quietly. I wanted Kelsey to tell me to give up, that he obviously wasn't interested in me. Or to say be patient, he's a widower with a child that needs time. But Kelsey was too polite, and thoughtful, to give her judgment.

"He's just not…trying," I said.

Kelsey bumped my shoulder with hers. "Hey, you're a catch too."

I huffed, my eyes burning a little. Having a criminal record was on me right now like a constellation of facial warts. "Thanks."

The door to the restaurant opened. Our friend Autumn came in wearing red heels and gloves to match. She sauntered over to our table, smiling and tossing her blonde chin-length hair.

"Thursday at last," she said, pulling off her gloves. "Did Pat really wipe down this table? It seems a little sticky. This week has been so busy for me—rush rush before winter sets in. Oh, hi, Pat. I'll take a vodka soda, thanks."

Autumn was working her way up in a real estate firm,

putting in long hours, and was as tenacious as a bulldog. She was short, curvy, and didn't really accept the word no. A winner in my book.

Other friends showed up after that in quick succession. There was Maria, a party girl and even more of a clothing hound than me. Naomi, a graphic designer and all-around artistic type who changed her hair color on a monthly basis.

There were more that hadn't made it, like Jada, Isabella, and Lauren too—the married with baby or pregnant crowd. I ordered another drink and tried to enjoy being single. The problem was Beau and Travis sat in my thoughts like a couple of tiny devils poking at me with their prongs.

"Listen up, everyone," I said, tapping on the side of my glass with a spoon. "I'm organizing a fundraiser for Riverside Hospice. It's going to be a bachelor auction. Buy your tickets now. I need your support on this, badly. Check your phones. I sent a link."

Naomi, who never really put her phone away, squeaked. "You're selling men?"

I nodded, solemnly. "For a good cause. And with their consent—mostly."

Maria laughed, tossing her dark brown hair. "All right, since you twisted my arm. Are there cute young ones?"

"There's a page with the bachelors," I said.

"Beau Martin's doing this—Lauren's brother?" Autumn asked. "And your brother, Mason."

"Yes and yes." An ache twisted in my chest—watching Beau or Travis go on a date wouldn't be my favorite thing ever...

"I'll come to the dinner," said Kelsey. "Cheer you all on."

"Oh," said Maria, sitting back. "Travis Dashiell? But... Raven, why are you giving him away?"

I put my hands up in a shrug. "Maybe it will push him out of his no-dating stalemate."

She shook her head at me, a funny look on her face.

They all bought tickets. And I talked Pat into sponsoring a tapas date at his restaurant. I tried to ignore how much I wanted to get home to see if Beau had written back.

He'd seen me in my underwear...it seemed like it might shatter our platonic coexistence in his house. I ate a bacon-wrapped date, nodding and smiling as my friends talked about the bachelor auction.

I'd written to Beau that I was going on a date in Portland on Saturday. Hooking up through the apps wasn't something I did super often, but sometimes I got desperate. There was a nightclub owner I'd messaged that afternoon. We were meeting Saturday night.

CHAPTER ELEVEN

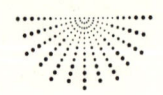

Beau had already left for work by the time I got back to his house. He didn't leave a note for me.

I put on my pajamas and told myself it was a win. Cheeto and I curled up on the living room couch and watched a couple of shows.

Friday morning, I was up early for another day of hustling. Cheeto tapped on my bedroom window with his paw, staring at me and meowing plaintively. Bubba started whining from Beau's bedroom, where he was locked in with the door closed.

"Hush," I whispered at Cheeto, filling up his food and water bowls. "We don't want them out here."

Tiptoeing around, I tried to get out of there as fast as I could so Beau could sleep. After four over-ten-hour-days on shift as a patrol officer, I suspected he finally had a three-day stretch off.

In the kitchen, I froze on my way to the fridge. There was a new note on the counter.

Raven, seeing you in that sexy ass underwear

yesterday was better than forcing you to chase me around when we were teenagers. I used to live for when you'd jump on my back and try to pull my hair...

Now I need you to show up and protect me from my stalker. It's what we do for each other. Let's pretend we're together and make it easy on everyone.

Please, babe? Don't go to P-town. Is it an app hookup? Hmm mm, not good. There's somebody right here, ready for you. Really ready. Beau

Blowing out a long breath, I rubbed my forehead. *Oh my God.* I didn't know what in the hell I was going to do.

Beau, you're too damn much—mow the freaking lawn and stop messing with me! If I start yelling at you, maybe you'll wake the eff up!

Without stopping to eat, I got the hell out of that house.

That day I begged every news outlet in the city to cover the bachelor auction—even managed to get a video interview. I emailed promo information for all social media platforms to anyone even the tiniest bit interested. We still hadn't sold nearly enough tickets.

Lauren rang me while I was stepping out of a beauty salon—where way too many of the women had been married to be worth my time for the fundraiser.

"Hello, Mama," I said, walking to my car through the bright afternoon sun. It was windy, as usual for River Gorge, but still warm.

"Please," Lauren panted, "help me."

"Oh shit—are you in labor?" I started jogging across the parking lot.

"What? No. Going up the stairs." She huffed, struggling to catch her breath.

"Dang it. Are you trying to give me sweat stains?" I unlocked my car and then stood back from the heat blast as I opened the driver's side door.

"Hey, I can barely walk. I'm harboring an alien life form. Please come and get me. I'm freaking out."

I looked at my watch. It was after four. "Okay, sure. What are we doing?"

"Zucchini cakes."

"Like, at a restaurant?" I asked, hopefully.

"Let's cook them. At Beau's. And barbecue drumsticks... Apple cobbler for dessert?"

I groaned. "You're a lot of work."

"Stop." She sniffed. "But it's fine. Forget I asked..."

"Oh my God. Pack your tissues, I'll be there in twenty."

Hanging around Beau all night had not been in my plans. I hung my head between my arms propped on the car. On the other hand, Cheeto seemed to need me. I'd bought a cat harness for him that afternoon so I could bring him out of the house. Maybe I'd try the thing that evening...

Grumbling, I decided to warn Beau that his kitchen was about to be invaded.

ME

> Hey, Lauren wants to cook a big meal in your kitchen tonight. Cool?

I was blasting the air conditioner when he texted back.

BEAU

> As long as you cook enough for me. Should I fire up the grill?

Yes. She wants bbq chicken drumsticks.

> Buy two family packs. Band's practicing. I'll pitch in. I'd run to the store but I'm too busy mowing the lawn, as ordered.

My mouth tried to stretch up. I shook my head and drove to Lauren's.

The Martins' beautiful home was quiet as I went up to the door. My phone rang.

"Hey," said Lauren, panting again. "I'm in the garden. Freakin' massive zucchini back here."

"Be right there." I glanced down ruefully at my pantsuit and heels.

Lauren was down on her knees, digging in the spectacular backyard vegetable patch when I found her. "Let's do a potato salad as well. Oh, you look nice. Onions and tomatoes and then we're done."

"My heels are sinking into this soil. Hand me that box and I'll carry it for you. Where are your folks?"

"Date night. Every Friday—they eat out, anyway, and call it a date."

"That's sweet." I sighed. John and Allison Martin made marriage appear easy. They seemed unshakable.

Lauren cut a pile of big beefy heirloom tomatoes and some herbs. Then we were off to the store. We picked up the chicken and a few other things, Lauren grimly marching—kind of waddling—by my side with her face set.

"Are you okay?" I asked when she insisted on going all the way back to the dairy aisle for sour cream. "Shouldn't you be resting with your feet up?"

"No." She took a big breath. "The walking keeps me sane."

"Oh." I bit my lip.

"This sucks, in case you couldn't tell."

"Sorry, hon." I put my arm around her.

"We're buying ice cream too. I've earned it."

"Yes."

When I parked in Beau's driveway, there was an incredible amount of noise coming from the detached garage. Lauren and I went to investigate.

The old detached garage had its big door closed. On the side facing the yard, a door was open. We peeked inside.

The interior looked…insulated. After a moment, I realized it was soundproofing with egg cartons and old blankets. Beau, AJ, and Chuck were all rocking back and forth in rhythm to their Pink Floyd cover, their ears covered with headphones, and dripping with sweat. Glancing up from his guitar riff, Beau saw us.

His eyes slid down me. One side of his mouth quirked up. My heart sort of flopped over and fainted in my chest. He had his shirt off…everything was hard and toned. His cargo shorts hung off his hips a little. He was so much bigger—filled out—than when we were kids.

Sucking in a breath, I hightailed it back to the car and started unloading the groceries. The man was so much trouble. Did he really want to sleep with someone he was living with? I'd be homeless in a matter of weeks.

"Oh, my goodness, Cheeto is like a creamsicle." Lauren cooed, bending over to pet him in the kitchen—and wobbling precariously as her big belly tilted her too far forward.

"He's mad at me for keeping him inside. I'm going to change—be back in five. Don't hurt yourself lifting things while I'm gone. I've got this."

She scoffed. "You do coffee and cereal."

"You're going to eat those words," I called from my

bedroom, "along with my amazing cooking. Which you'll tell me how to do, every step of the way."

In jeans and T-shirt, I tackled the mountain of food on the countertop. We grated massive zucchini—troll penises, I decided, holding up a couple of tomatoes next to an extra-large one. Lauren rolled her eyes at my vegetable dick jokes.

I scrubbed then boiled potatoes. I chopped a million things and peeled a mountain of apples from the big tree at Lauren's house. She directed me like a maestro even though she had to lie down from a cramp.

"Wait," I said, knife poised over a bunch of fresh parsley, "is that a contraction?"

"No." She waved her hand at me. "Don't say the c-word."

"Um…"

"What's going on with you and Beau?"

"Nothing." I glanced over my shoulder at the garage. They were still playing music so presumably he wasn't about to walk in on us talking about him.

"Uh-huh. Tell me another. Did you sleep together yet?"

"Nope." I dumped chopped parsley on the steaming potatoes. "But he wants to."

"And you don't?"

I couldn't tell if that was a sincere question. Staring down at the cutting board, I refused directly. "A fling with him seems…complicated."

"Because you like him too much."

Oh shit. "Damnit, did you have to say that out loud?"

She was on her feet, limping over to sit at a bar stool on the other side of the counter in front of me. "It's okay. No risk, no reward. No pain, no gain."

"You sound like our old basketball sergeant, Coach Phinney."

"Mayo, mustard, vinegar, and pickle relish for the potato

salad dressing. Oh, and squeeze out the grated zucchini. I want you to be happy."

"I'm stuck on Travis Dashiell. He's playing hard to get and I'm...I don't know, determined to win. It's dumb. But after all of it, I don't want to give up."

Lauren pulled out a pickle. "Leprechaun dick?" She sucked on it.

"You're seriously grossing me out right now."

She ate her warty disgusting pickle. "Travis has a lot going for him but..."

"What?"

"What does he do for fun?"

"Well, he has hobbies. Writing. And woodworking, I think."

"Thrilling." She put her elbows on the counter and rested her head on her hands. "Actually, I'd like that. My idea of a good weekend is reading a book and using up the garden produce."

I pursed my lips. Her point was hitting me hard enough to be a punch in my back...Was Travis a homebody?

"Are you okay?" I asked.

Lauren's eyes were fluttering closed. "Great."

"Do you want to lie down on my bed for a while?"

She sat up and shook her head. "No. No—you need to mix that zucchini cake batter."

"On it. Half a cup of flour, baking powder, two eggs, salt, pepper, zucchini, and grated onion. Wait, it says two medium zucchini. The troll dick was not medium. Should we double it—triple it?"

"Triple it. We're the band bitches. Makin' food for the rock stars."

I groaned. I'd be frying the damn vegetable pancakes all night.

Butter and olive oil sizzled in Beau's big cast-iron pan as I poured in my first saucer-sized dollop of batter. Bubba barked from the basement, and I realized I could hear things easily again. The garage music had stopped for long enough that the guys seemed to be done practicing. Butterflies swarmed my stomach.

"Still haven't heard from Derek," Lauren said, scratching nail polish off a fingernail.

Dang it. I'd hoped he'd finally emailed her back but hadn't wanted to ask in case it made her cry. Derek and Lauren had barely known each other when the pregnancy happened. He was a little younger than Lauren and me, more like twenty-five instead of twenty-seven.

The guy had been cute, cheerful, and easygoing. He was helping Lauren financially with an automatic deduction out of his pay. Since they'd married, she had access to his healthcare through the military. They were planning on moving into military housing in the next year. But there was no denying that he wasn't staying in touch, not like a person in love anyway.

"When does his deployment end?"

"Next month. Hopefully."

"Bubbles are popping on these zuc cakes. Time to turn?"

"Yep."

They were golden-brown on the done side. "Whatever happens, I'm here for you. We'll figure it out. Right?"

She sniffled. "Yeah."

"Baby Athena is going to be amazing."

"I know. I love her so much already."

"Derek might be freaking out a little," I said. "But he's going to come and see his girls—hopefully for Thanksgiving."

The mudroom door opened, and Bubba came barreling in, head swinging back and forth as he took in all of the delights. Cheeto hissed and ran for my bedroom. Beau had found a gate that kept Bubba out of my room.

"Whoa." Beau grabbed Bubba's collar before he could chase after the cat. "Smells good in here. Hey, Laur Laur. Don't leak too much. Baby girl might get thirsty."

"Shut up." She wiped her face.

I jogged over to my bedroom and closed the gate door so Cheeto had some peace. And to keep Bubba away from the cat food.

"Grill's goin'." Bubba ran free. Beau went into the kitchen and rummaged around for a big metal bowl, tongs, and a basting brush.

I had to sidle in next to him to reach the frying pan. He glanced at me, a wicked smirk on his face. I glared at him, then turned resolutely to my zucchini cakes, trying to ignore the heat shooting down my spine.

"Food in here is close," Lauren said. "Should we bring it outside? Do you have paper plates or something?"

"Just bring your plates out. The guys can come in here to load up." Beau poured sauce over the raw chicken in the bowl. "Thanks for cooking. This is going to be good."

We all focused on wrapping up dinner. Lauren felt well enough to do the finishing touches, dressing the sliced tomatoes with olive oil and vinegar, then salt and pepper and sprinkles of herbs. The apple cobbler came out of the oven, and I opened windows to let in cool night air.

Lauren and I ate at the outside table set up by the garage. Beau served us the first done pieces of chicken. The guys seemed to be waiting until we were through to go after the food, drinking their beers and throwing a ball for Bubba.

Every time I glanced up, it seemed like Beau's eyes were on me. My heart thumped in my chest—it was dawning on me how much trouble I was in. I'd either be moving out or sleeping in his bed.

CHAPTER TWELVE

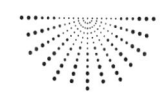

"Come stay the night at my house," Lauren said with her head on my shoulder. "Please?"

Cheeto sat on my lap, wearing his harness and very tense. He stared around the backyard with his ears up. The experiment of bringing Cheeto outside with his leash on had not gone great, but we'd made it to the table—after I'd picked him up.

The guys were on a beer run, which also served as a Bubba walk. Part of me really wanted to hang around and see what happened with Beau. I bit my lip, disgusted with myself.

"Yeah," I said. "Let's go."

I settled Cheeto in the house for the night, brushed him, and checked over his food bowls and litter box. He seemed sleepy. I crossed my fingers, nervous about leaving him on his own.

Lauren's parents were home when we got there, sitting together in the family room watching stand-up comedy on the big television.

"Raven's staying," Lauren called out. "Spare bedroom's ready, right, Mom?"

"All set. Help yourself to some wine, Raven honey, if you feel like it."

"Thank you."

Lauren had taken over the formal dining room as her puzzle work area. She booted up a big tablet on the table.

"Let's put on a really raunchy reality dating show," she said. "And I'll let you help me with this puzzle."

"'You don't stop gardening when you get old,'" I read from the art deco style puzzle image. "'You get old when you stop gardening.' Thrilling. How could I resist?"

"I know. It's challenging because everything's green."

"Um, what's with the intense puzzle fixation?"

She threw a piece at me. "Find that or I might panic. Not losing pieces is my ultimate goal in life right now."

"Relax, I've got it."

"I'm in the last weeks of my pregnancy. What else do you need to know?"

"Oh." After thinking about it for two seconds, I felt really dumb. "Yeah. Totally makes sense."

The show got going and we were both sucked in to the ridiculous premise—hot people stuck on a beach and they couldn't have sex. I distractedly sorted puzzle pieces by shades of color. Lauren would pick one up, stare at it for a while, then fit it together with another piece. Who knew she had a hidden puzzle superpower?

My phone buzzed with text messages.

BEAU

where are you?

please come back here.

I put my head in my hands. He was moving too damn fast.

> **ME**
> I'm staying with Lauren tonight. But I don't know what to do about you. You're seriously ready to jump into something? Would be a little complicated don't you think? I mean we live under the same roof. And sister's best friend.

I wiped puzzle pieces off my arm when Lauren glared at me. Probably questioning Beau at all would make him back a million miles off.

> **BEAU**
> Yeah, I'm ready. We're attracted to each other. Why not enjoy it? I'm not a worrier. If things get hairy, we'll figure it out.

I rolled my eyes. Of course, just that simple.

> **ME**
> I don't do flings in town. You'd ruin my reputation as a good girl.
>
> Okay, honestly? I think we've known each other too long.

> **BEAU**
> Come hang out with me tomorrow. Let's go do something.

> Don't you have a party to get ready for?

> It's ready. It's Chuck's show. He's picking up a keg.
>
> Cheeto misses you.

> Is he crying?

> He's purring on my lap. Where you should be.

> I still can't believe you're doing this.

I like you.

> Really? Why? Because you saw me in my underwear?

That did burn away the doubts.

You're you. Raven. Beautiful. A little mean. I like it. That smile…

> Stop

You like it when I touch you.

> You're so full of yourself.

I'm serious. I like you. Do you like me?

> I don't know. I'm thinking about it.

HOPE

> But I'm going on that date tomorrow. I already said I would.

> You're moving too fast for me.

Fine. Please don't sleep with him.

> Not your call.

RAVEN

> Your sister is falling asleep with her face on the table.

How would you feel if I slept with someone?

> Is that a threat?

No. But now I'm pissed.

> Put Lauren to bed. I'll talk to you tomorrow.

∽

SATURDAY MORNING, I didn't see Beau. His truck was gone from the driveway and Bubba wasn't barking in the house. All signs pointed to fishing.

My lawyer had sent me a whammy of emails to respond to. Bouncing my leg, I worked on the statements he needed and reached out again to my old neighbors in the apartment.

The walls of Beau's living room seemed to be closing in on me. I stood up and paced around. The people living closest to Rob in the complex weren't responding—I suspected they were afraid of him. Without those neighbors speaking up for me about the constant harassment, I wouldn't have much of a case.

Cheeto meowed and pawed at the door. We did another outing with the harness—Cheeto clung to the ground and cried, flopped on his belly, refusing to take a step with the contraption on him. I gave up and put him back in the house.

I was determined to distract myself on my date. There were too many worries, like spiders eating me up from the inside, and I was tired of it. I pulled out my favorite fit and flare cotton dress in rich bright green. Sleeveless, it had a square neck, a matching belt, and a skirt that hit above the knee. With my black faux-leather motorcycle jacket and ankle-strap black sandals with a chunky heel, I was a little edgy but still dressed fine.

Beau walked in as I was slinging my Louboutin knockoff handbag over my shoulder.

"Damn," he said, leaning back against the kitchen island and sticking his hand in his hair.

"Gotta go," I muttered. "Cheeto's in my bedroom. All set for food and water. Have a good party—"

"Wait." He stalked across the room to where I stood, my pulse picking up with every step he took forward.

I inhaled—he was so...rugged. His face was tanned and a little rosy from too much time in the sun. He was unbearable. I had to find another place to live. Rummaging in my bag, I took a step away from him. He still stood way too close.

"Don't do this. Raven, look at me." His blue eyes were more intense and serious than I'd ever seen them.

Was he hurt? I didn't believe it.

"This"—I pointed from him to me—"is too complicated for me."

He shook his head, the muscles in his neck tense. "It's not."

"You're impulsive."

"I'm impulsive? Who's the one meeting up with a stranger? Oh, walk away. I'm fucking pissed. Don't be surprised if someone else is in my bed tomorrow. I'm done."

My heart wrenched as he stomped away from me, cargo shorts hanging off his hips and his thin T-shirt showing a hard muscled back. I smoothed down the skirt of my dress. My face wrinkled up. Then I left.

During that hour-long drive to Portland, I had to force myself not to slouch so I wouldn't wrinkle my dress. It was like there had been a taut string connecting me to Beau and it had snapped. I wanted to curl up in a ball and mourn the loss.

Dominic, I reminded myself. He was so handsome I was half expecting some kind of catfishing—not the dark-haired gorgeous man in his profile picture. Older, in his late thirties, Dominic owned a restaurant and a nightclub.

When I saw him, waiting for me at the bar we'd agreed to meet at, my breath caught. There was not catfishing happening—he was, if anything, even more gorgeous in person. Tall, broad shouldered, in a fitted chestnut blazer and white shirt, and dark jeans that hugged powerful legs, I was entirely won over by his style.

"Raven?" he asked, sultry gaze assessing me, one side of his mouth curving up slightly.

"Yes." I smiled, putting my hand in his. "Very nice to meet you, Dominic."

"Likewise." He gestured at the barstool next to him. "Please, order a drink if you'd care for one."

"I would. A gimlet," I said to the bartender.

"How are you?" Dominic asked.

His eyes were so distracting—warm brown flecked with amber and ringed in dark lashes. There was something distant and removed about him. Beau flashed into my mind —that mischievous and warm smile of his. I tried to swat him out of my thoughts.

"Happy to be out on a date, with you, on a Saturday night. There isn't anything I like better than getting dressed up for a nice dinner out."

Was that really true though? I wanted it to be...

"How are you?" I asked as the bartender slid my cocktail across the bar to me.

He was a very still man. Contained. "I'm well. You're even more beautiful in person than online."

"You know what? I was thinking the same thing about you."

We stared at each other, each of us sipping our drinks. He had a tumbler of golden-brown liquor. There was a gentle chemistry between us—it was saying *yes, this person checks the boxes*. Green light. Except, it was like the Beau string was still pulling on me...

"Can I take you to dinner at my restaurant?" He leaned forward and his scent was pine and rum and very yum.

"I'd love to."

"It's a block away. Do you mind walking?"

"No, sounds nice. How long have you been in the restaurant business?"

He swirled his drink. "One year."

"Oh?"

"I've been in Portland for about eighteen months. I moved here from New York."

"Intriguing," I said. "What did you do in New York?"

"Investment banker," he said. "Like my father."

"Wow. Are you out of banking now?"

"Mostly, yes. I needed a change. So, here I am. Sidus, the restaurant, is the chef's creation. I am merely the financing."

"And the nightclub? Do you love electronic dance music?"

His mouth quirked—the man didn't seem to smile. "It's fun. But again, I'm involved on the back end."

We left to walk to the restaurant. Dominic insisted on paying for the drinks—and considering the kind of wealth he seemed to have, I was happy to accept.

He held the door for me, his hand on the small of my back. Warmth tingled through me. It was nice and yet…his gaze was so far away, as if he was already thinking about tomorrow.

"You're in PR," he said as we walked. "What are you working on?"

"A bachelor auction fundraiser," I said, grinning at him.

He blinked at me, putting an arm around my back when a group of people passed us on the crowded sidewalk. "For which charity?"

"A hospice organization. It wasn't my idea—but I'm starting to love it. It will be a mix of working professionals and older adults living in a retirement community. Close to Halloween. With an angels and devils theme. Live music. It's going to be a blast."

His eyebrows pinched together. "That's...unique."

I laughed. "I know."

"How will it work?"

"Silent auction. In a big ballroom with live music and plenty to drink. Each bachelor will have a romantic date given to them as part of their package. Dinner at a winery. Boat tour. I'm trying for a helicopter ride, but the company has stopped answering my emails..."

"You're tenacious?"

"Yes. Horribly."

He gave me what might be a sultry look. "Intriguing."

The restaurant was small and intimate, with artwork all over the walls and a big bouquet of orange marigolds in a ceramic pitcher on the bar. The server rushed over to seat us when we walked in, obviously recognizing Dominic.

My date's demeanor changed—he seemed harder. Was he keeping the employees on their toes?

"A vegan restaurant," I said. "With kombucha? Did I say that right?"

"Yes. It's fermented tea with fruit or botanical flavors."

"Ah." I stared at the menu, reminding myself that I wasn't eight. I didn't hate beets or mushrooms anymore. Much.

"Would you like to do the flight and try everything? The chef is talented. Once you see it plated, you'll know what you like."

"Hey, I didn't tell you I was a horrible eater and addicted to fast food. How did you know?"

"My guess was that, like most people, you'd hesitate to choose a restaurant like this. It's changed the way I eat." He signaled to the server.

Our meal began with some very nice bread, to my relief. Dominic and I settled into small talk about Portland and the Pacific Northwest. I was brave and tried all of the food, including the beets. The mushroom ravioli surprised me by being delicious, even though it had a dressing on it that tasted like ground-up salad.

"I think this meal added a few years on to my life," I said as we finished.

Dominic was an extremely polite eater—reminded me of Travis. "I'm glad."

His attention, and the nice meal, were flattering. I kept thinking of what he'd written to me before we'd met. *Strictly casual. No strings attached.* Apparently, with him, that included a very nice date. And one night together.

My heart thudded in my chest, the Beau string yanking on me. Dominic was paying the bill—the wealthy owner still paid? He'd mentioned a musician at his club playing that evening.

"Excuse me," I said and stood up.

Dominic nodded at me and picked up his wine glass.

In the bathroom, I stared at myself in the mirror. I needed to reapply my lipstick. Dominic was the perfect fling for me —what else could I want?

I pulled my phone out and stared at the notifications. Five missed text messages from Beau.

BEAU

Hey

How's the date?

I'm still mad but can't stop thinking about you

Please don't sleep with him

Do you like him?

I pressed my forehead against the cell phone screen. WTF?

Here's the thing about Beau: He'd always been too much.

Too wild, too rage-inducing, too good-looking. There had been more than once, when we were teenagers, that I'd thought I could kill him—mostly for stealing my clothes.

If I was being totally, brutally honest with myself, yes, I'd always been attracted to him—in an involuntary, it's-so-wrong kind of way. He was what I wanted physically but a far cry from the kind of partner I imagined myself with.

Travis Dashiell was who I should be with. If I started sleeping with Beau, the chance to be with Travis might disappear forever.

ME
Hey

It's fine. He took me to a vegan place. I was good and didn't throw up.

Would you relax? Think of me as the bachelorette. When I am with you, I'm with you...

Just kidding. Talk to you soon.

BEAU
I miss you.

Come home.

I shook my head, stuffing my phone back in my purse. As I walked out of the bathroom, I had no idea what I was going to do. Then I looked out at the restaurant and froze.

My stalker was looking in through the big window by the door. I stepped back and flattened myself against a wall. My chest rose and fell in quick pants. *It's just pathetic Rob—you can take him.* Except everything in my gut was telling me not to let him near me.

Leaning forward slowly, I peeked around the shelf in front of me. He was gone. Had I imagined him? *No.* He'd had on that tan jacket he always wore and sunglasses tucked into the collar of his white shirt.

One hand on my chest, I walked to the table where Dominic waited, relaxed in his chair and reading something on his phone.

He glanced up and saw me. "Ready?" Rising to his feet, he stared at me more intently. "Is everything all right? Are you upset?"

Other people in the restaurant were staring at us. I sat down in my seat and then so did he. "No. I saw someone that really scared me." I took a gulp of my ice water, my hand shaky.

"What is it? Or who?"

Blowing out a breath, I closed my eyes for a moment and shook my head. "I hate having to talk about this. At the last apartment I lived in, my neighbor became, like, fixated on me. He followed me around. Bought me things. Then he hurt my cat—everything got worse. A moment ago, he was looking in the restaurant window."

Dominic startled, then sat up straighter. "He's here?"

"Yes. Out there—how did he find me? I live an hour away. God, I'm so sick of this shit. Will you walk me to my car?"

"Of course. But shouldn't you report this?"

Chewing on my lip, I thought about it. "Not enough there. Believe me, I've looked into it."

"Is he violent?"

"He's a bully."

Dominic took my hand on the table. I gripped his back.

"I'm sorry," I said. "It was such a nice evening."

He nodded, his eyebrows drawn together.

We left and walked quickly back to my car. I kept my hand wrapped around my cell phone. Dominic was alert and tense at my side. I didn't see Rob on the crowded sidewalk, but my car had a note stuffed under the windshield wiper.

Whore was scrawled across a piece of printer paper in thick black ink. I photographed it, then scooped it up into a plastic bag from my trunk.

"Can I email you for a statement about what you saw tonight?" I asked.

"Of course." Dominic pulled me in for a hug. "I'm sorry you're dealing with this."

"Thank you," I said, a little warmth streaking back into me. He smelled nice. The lining of his jacket was silky red and smooth, as I found out when one of my arms ended up on the inside around his waist.

He kissed my cheek. "Message me."

My mouth quirked up in a smile. Dominic was turning out to be warmer than I'd thought. "I will."

CHAPTER THIRTEEN

Beau's house was crowded with people when I drove past the jammed driveway. I had to park a block away on another street.

The front door was wide open as I edged my way up the crowded front porch. Normally, I liked parties. That night, after spotting Rob following me, I was clenched up with a no-doubt sour face.

"House is closed," I called out to the people on the porch.

"What about the bathroom?" asked a small brunette that appeared to be about eighteen.

"One bathroom pass, if you're a woman, and I like you. Wait at the back door."

"What—"

I closed the door and locked it. Then I kicked everyone out of the living room and kitchen. I taped a piece of paper to the mudroom room with *WE'RE CLOSED* written on it and locked that door too.

It was ten o'clock and I wasn't in the mood—and not afraid to be that bitch. Cheeto frantically meowed at me when I opened the door, his little head bobbing around as he peeked past my legs.

Eventually, we cuddled on my bed together. With a sigh, I took out my phone.

> ME
>
> I'm back. Kicked everyone out of the upstairs and locked the doors.
>
> The creep followed me to Portland. Left a note on my car. How the hell did he do that?
>
> It freaked me out. I saw him too. Looking through the restaurant window.
>
> Is he tracking my car somehow? WTF

There wasn't any response. It dawned on me that the music I was hearing was live—Beau's band was playing.

"I guess I'll go out there," I said to Cheeto.

His ear twitched. He seemed pretty conked out.

The heels came off and I found a pair of flats I could stand to wear with that dress. I poured myself a glass of wine and trudged out to the backyard.

People swayed back and forth in front of the detached garage. With the sliding door up, Beau, AJ, and Chuck were easy to see at the bottom of the driveway.

Beau had on an awful black shirt, half covered in red and orange flames, and drawstring shorts, his feet in flip-flops. It didn't matter. I couldn't take my eyes off him.

He swayed, his head moving to the beat. Then he leaned forward, with his eyes closed, and started singing the old Pink Floyd lyrics, about wishing someone was there, in his deep voice.

My heart quivered. The man was sweaty and a little grubby and yet seeing him sing was like seeing him for the first time, remaking him in my mind. My chest was tight. He was so beautiful—despite his fashion choices.

Beau could really perform, and the band was good. Some of the neighbors were out in lawn chairs, the couple next door holding hands and swaying. I stayed in the shadow next to the house, a little giddy with my unchecked staring at Beau.

He scanned the crowd in brief glances, seeming lost in the music. They played another song, moving seamlessly into it without a pause. The finish left my pulse thrumming and my ears tingling.

"That's it," Beau said. "Thanks for coming out."

"Encore," a few people shouted.

But Beau was already switching off his equipment and putting his electric guitar in a stand. I huffed—it was so odd seeing him follow the rules. Or maybe not follow exactly, but at least respect. He'd probably negotiated with the neighbors to be able to throw a party with live music. And also kept on the right side of the city noise ordinance…barely.

The crowd started to thin out a bit. I spoke to a couple of people I'd known in high school. Chuck and AJ led a big group of people into their basement. I waited while Beau closed up the garage, weirdly glad he hadn't noticed me yet.

Harper appeared, striding down the driveway toward Beau. She wore a tight sheath dress with a bottom hem that barely covered her ass. I was a little impressed that she pulled off the look as well as she did, pairing it with tennis shoes and a jean jacket.

"Beau," she called, an extra sway in her hips as she ambled down to him.

He glanced up from the padlock, a wide-eyed startled rabbit expression on his face.

Sighing, I walked across the yard and up onto the driveway.

Beau had a hand over his face. "Hey, Harper."

I walked in front of Harper, forcing her to take a step back. Beau's head jerked up and his mouth dropped open. It was a slightly gratifying response.

"Party's over, Harper," I said, glaring at her. "Most of the people that were here are headed to Whiskey Tango downtown."

Beau put his arm around me—and I let him, for Harper's sake, of course.

Her nostrils flared. "You bit—"

"Night," said Beau. "Take care, now."

"Are you kidding me? I deserve more fucking respect than this."

I opened my mouth, but Beau grabbed my arm and tugged me away. Resisting the urge to scowl over my shoulder at Harper, I swallowed my words and let him hold my hand as we walked to the house.

Harper sobbed behind us. Beau flinched, his shoulders hunching as he unlocked the mudroom door.

"Damnit, Beau. I love you."

I pushed Beau into the house and closed and locked the door behind us. Running footsteps went up the driveway. I peeked out the window and Harper was gone.

"Phew," I said. "Maybe that one will stick."

Beau pulled me against his chest. His arms wrapped tightly around me, and he buried his face in my hair. "You're here."

"Yeah."

"I stopped checking my phone. Was too pissed." His hands slid up and down my back.

His body against mine was furnace-hot and a little musky. I wanted to nuzzle my face in his neck. My chest tingled as we both breathed. A snake of desire wound down my spine in a sinuous coil.

I cleared my throat. "I'm...still thinking."

He groaned, squeezing me tighter against him. "You look so good."

Swallowing, I tried to ignore the rush of warmth moving through me. "I like watching you sing."

Leaning back, he gazed down into my face. "You were there. I didn't see you."

"Stealth spying on you."

His fingers slid into the knot of hair on the back of my head. "You scare me a little."

"Really?" Touching him was messing with me—I tried to keep my hands still on his muscled back, the texture of his cotton shirt enticingly rough under my fingers.

"I really like you." He pressed his lips against mine.

It was like electricity shot through me and made all of my hair stand on end. I inhaled sharply and my knees turned to mush. He rubbed his lips over mine, then molded our mouths together. The shock of it zapped all the way down my spine.

He lifted me up onto the kitchen counter. My skirt slid up my thighs and my legs wrapped around his back. Beau was not a shy or slow kisser—he was demanding. It was too good. In another moment, our clothes would be off.

I turned my head away. "Hey. Can we talk a little bit?"

He groaned, hugging me to him and putting his face in my neck. "Raven."

"Yeah, that's me." I put my fingers in his hair, ran them through one time, then forced myself to put my hands behind my back.

Frowning, he took a step away from me. He turned and went to the fridge.

I hopped down from the counter clumsily. Uncomfortably aroused, I crossed my arms. And squeezed my thighs together. *Damnit.*

"Did you see my text messages?" I asked.

"No." He opened a beer with a bottle opener attached to his keychain. "Left my phone in my room. After I asked you to come home."

My cheek twitched. What were we doing? I'd been on a date with another guy a few hours ago. Beau's ex-girlfriend was out there crying somewhere.

"Rob followed me to Portland."

Beau's head jerked up. "You saw him?"

"Yeah. Looked in the restaurant window. And he left a note on my car."

"Jesus." He pushed a hand through his hair. "He's tracking your car. Fuck, should have thought of that."

Cheeto meowed from the bedroom. I walked out of the kitchen and opened the door for him. He shot out and dove under the living room couch.

"Something scared my cat," I said, turning on the bedroom light.

Everything seemed normal. The blinds were bent open in the spot where Cheeto liked to push his head through to see outside. I pushed the blinds up to double-check that the latch was locked.

"Ahh!" I screamed.

There was a note taped to the outside of the window with *sweet dreams* written in black ink, facing in for me to see.

Beau rushed over. "That piece of shit left a note? Damnit."

I covered my mouth with a shaky hand.

"You can't sleep in here." Beau grabbed my hand and pulled me out of the room. He hugged me by the couch. "Go get on your pajamas in the bathroom. You can have my bed and I'll sleep on the couch."

"What—no. What about Bubba?"

"He's at a sleepover. It's okay, relax. I know you don't want to sleep with me."

I squeezed him tighter. "If we sleep together, I don't want it to be on a night I was on a date with another guy."

He gave me a quick kiss on the mouth. "I'm going to go search outside. Where did you park?"

"About a block east. Are you sure? What if he's armed or something?"

Beau gave me a look, his mouth twitching. "You beat him up with yard debris. I can handle it."

"With a Taser?" I asked hopefully.

He nodded and took off. "Call the station. And lock the door behind me."

CHAPTER FOURTEEN

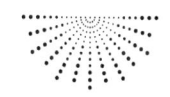

I moved my blankets to the couch and got ready for bed in plushy velvet cream sweats that were my cutest loungewear.

Beau popped back in and grabbed my keys so he could move my car. Then he disappeared outside for a long time.

Cheeto and I curled up on the couch with the big television tuned to Saturday Night Live. I yawned. The party in the basement was a little loud. Maybe Beau had gone down there?

The mudroom door opened. Cheeto and I both tensed, raising our heads.

"It's me," Beau called. The door shut and I heard the bolt twist. "Found the tracker." He held up a plastic bag as he walked over. There was a black box inside with wires sticking out.

"Okay. That makes me feel better." And I'd be emailing my lawyer about it first thing in the morning.

"Is there an officer coming out?"

I shook my head. "Doubt it. I called and they sounded busy. I did an online report."

"We're sleeping on the couch?" He frowned at me.

"I am. You've got a nice bed to go to."

He flopped down on the cushions next to my head. It was a big sectional couch with room for two people to stretch out on.

"Let's both go there," he said, scratching Cheeto's head. "All we'll do is cuddle."

"Uh-huh. I'm fine here for tonight. Little spooked for my room but I'll get over it."

He wrapped my loose long hair around his hand. "Nope. We stay together."

"Aren't you awake until three or four in the morning?" I really liked how much he touched me—it wasn't good.

"Nah. I'm tired. Have been losing sleep to go fishing."

"Catch any?"

"Oh yeah." He grinned at me. "Stocked freezer in the basement."

"Nice."

We both watched a raunchy comedy skit on the television and laughed. Beau slipped off his shoes and lay down with his head next to mine.

It was amazing—like we were in a settled relationship. I swallowed, too much longing welling up in my tight chest. If I wasn't careful, I was going to embarrass myself by crying. I hated being alone.

A commercial came on. "Can I ask you about Harper a bit?" I asked.

Beau sighed softly. "Sure. I guess it wouldn't kill me to open up a little."

"If your heart starts failing, speak up and I'll give you a minute to recover."

He reached over and took my hand. "Fine. But now you have to hold my hand."

I ran my thumb over his wrist. "What happened? I remember she really liked you in high school."

"She'd made up her mind that we were it for each other when we were kids. I...didn't feel like that. I was too much of a dumb selfish teenager to do what I should have."

"You guys did break up. Your senior year."

"There was a pregnancy scare," he said, starkly.

"Oh." I glanced at his face. His hand covered his eyes.

"Condom failure. I felt like such a piece of shit. And scared. Her mom found out, somehow, and we both talked her into taking the morning-after pill."

I blinked, not really understanding where all the drama came from. People that had a lot of sex sometimes had that happen.

"Right," I said. "I mean—that's practical. I've taken the damn thing before."

He squeezed my hand a little. "Her mental health can be shaky. Don't repeat that, please. She struggled with school. When I broke it to her that I was leaving for college, and didn't want to do long-distance, she...dropped out."

I had a vague memory of her showing up at the Martins' house and crying on the front lawn. Beau's father had been really angry with him all the time.

"So I went all the way down to Arizona for school. Then I worked for a while in Phoenix. Came back up to Oregon and tried Eugene for a bit. Did more school. Moved back here about two years ago when River Gorge hired me."

Of course, I'd heard about him a little from Lauren. I hadn't seen any of the Martins much during my time away.

"So you got back together?"

"No. I kept my distance—until a couple months ago. She was always showing up and persistent. I drank too much one night, and things happened. I'd been upfront about not getting into anything. But she still had strong feelings for me.

So, I said it wasn't right. She refused to accept it. I screwed up...I really want her to be okay."

I pulled his hand next to my face and laid my cheek on it. "Thank you for telling me."

He propped himself up so he could see me. "Not angry with me? Convinced I'm an asshole scumbag?"

"No." I let go of his hand so he could move freely. "I think I understand Harper a little better, though. That's good. It'll slow me down the next time she shows up and I want to punch her."

He grinned and leaned over to kiss me upside down. After almost having his tongue in my nose, I pulled away. I shook my head at his goofy grin. Cheeto jumped up onto the top of the couch backrest.

"My turn," Beau said, scooting down so his head was against my side. "Soft." He rubbed his cheek against my sweatshirt.

"You're a little odd, aren't you?"

"Yep. Enough about me. Tell me about you. I know a little, from Lauren. Like that you were living with someone for a few years."

"Yes." Frederic. "I thought he was it. His family practically adopted me. Took me a while to figure out that he was a cheater. And a liar...Even about stupid stuff."

"Damn."

"Yeah, it was tough." I'd been shattered. Had decided I would force myself to make a better choice. No more smooth-talking playboys—like Beau.

He'd actually reminded me of Beau a little, back in college, blond and lively. Except Frederic had played competitive golf and been a fraternity guy. Beau had always seemed like a country boy to me.

He rolled onto his elbow. "You've been single ever since?"

"No. That ended four years ago. There was another year-long relationship. He moved for a job. I didn't think there was enough there."

"You're picky."

"Very. Aren't you?"

He collapsed onto his back. "Yes. Slow to commit and quick to leave."

Wow. There it was, confirmed out of his own mouth. "That's some self-awareness, at least."

His eyes met mine. "It's different with us, Raven. I know you. And I really like you."

My mouth dropped open. He swooped in for another kiss, hard and fast.

"Get some sleep," Beau said. "I'm going to shower. Then the other half of this couch is mine."

∾

IN THE MORNING, Beau was asleep on the other side of the big couch, one of his arms hanging off the side. A paperback novel and little night-light had fallen on the floor next to him.

I stared up at the ceiling, blinking away the sleep haze at the edges of my vision. A lot had happened the day before—and I was still getting over moving out of my apartment. But now I lived with Beau and we'd kissed.

Cheeto tapped my chest with his paw and meowed.

"Shh." As quietly as I could, I got up and fed him.

I took him out in the backyard on his harness. He flattened his ears and hung his head but did explore the big grassy space a little.

With coffee and toast, I tackled updating my lawyer on everything new that had happened. I messaged Dominic about a statement describing the note on my car.

My back hunched as I looked over everything I had on

Rob so far. The problem was that there wasn't a direct link to him—I couldn't prove he'd left any of the creepy stuff. I was paying for private fingerprint tests on the chocolate box note he'd left and would send in the new pieces of paper as well. But Rob Campbell, I'd found out, didn't have a criminal record and so probably didn't have fingerprints in the databases.

Pots and dishes clattered in the kitchen. I rose from Beau's office desk and stretched.

I found Beau whisking eggs in front of the big television. He'd turned on a Sunday morning football talk show.

"Morning." I started folding up blankets, keeping a little distance between us. We'd both had a bit to drink the night before—it had been an aberration. Time to get back to normal. "Shouldn't you get more sleep?"

"Morning, beautiful. I'm fine." His whisk was moving fast, and he shifted from foot to foot. "Let's go do something. Windsurfing or mountain biking? Windsurfing. Little heat this afternoon. Might be our last chance."

"You have boards?"

"Two in the shed."

I bit on my knuckle, trying to hide my smile as I stared at him. As teenagers, we'd always been the ones dragging everyone outside on the weekends. Rock climbing had become my hobby and light mountain biking, but I would say yes to just about any outdoor adventure.

"First, we eat." He quickstepped back into the kitchen.

With swimming in the cold Columbia River in my near future, I dashed around packing, searching for my sporty swimsuit, and tightly braided my hair.

Beau made breakfast burritos for us, then wandered off to the back shed with his food in his hand. I cleaned up the kitchen. We took off in Beau's truck just as the sun rose high enough to start baking the asphalt.

We drove ten miles west to Viento State Park to launch from the sandy beach there. Driving through the canyon, along the mighty river that had cut its way through a mountain range to get to the Pacific Ocean, always put little wings on my heart.

Ice age floods and ancient volcanoes had created the river canyon, pushing up granite and basalt cliffs and creating the largest concentration of waterfalls in the world. Many of us referred to the area as Waterfall Canyon. It was a part of my heart—and it was looking like I'd have to move away again.

"Did you miss the gorge?" I asked. "When you were away."

Beau nodded, darting a quick smile at me. "Oh yeah."

"Me too."

I kept sneaking glances at him. How did he already seem like a best friend? I needed to lose my temper or have a bitchy day—I was very capable of that—and pop the weird bubble floating around us.

I squeezed myself into an old shorty wetsuit Beau had found in his shed. Out on the river, I yelped the first time the wind jolted me forward and fell in the cold water.

Beau shouted instructions at me—that I couldn't really hear. Rather than relearning how to windsurf, I spent too much brain space admiring Beau's tall body, muscled and lithe, in his wet suit.

My arm muscles were twitching by the time I got out to lie in the sun and watch Beau. He caught a wave and a gust of wind launched him up into the air. He managed to stick the landing on his board. I cheered from the shore.

He came out and collapsed on the sand next to me. "My balls are frozen."

I smiled down at him. "That water is cold."

In the next moment, he'd rolled on top of me, ignoring my squeaks and gasps. "Need you to warm me up. Before I injure something down there."

He kissed me, our legs entwined on the sand, his chilly lips still managing to send heat shooting into me. My hips pushed up against his. Every time he kissed me, it was harder to stop. Luckily, we were in a public park.

Bracing on his elbows, he pulled back and grinned down at me. "You're all turned on and fluttery."

I squinted at him. "You give yourself too much credit."

He was right—even with a damp and clammy wetsuit on, I was seriously fluttery.

"Relax. We both need this."

Relax? So, it definitely was casual for him. There was a feeling like falling in my belly. "What—like to blow off steam?"

"Sure." He shook his head at me. "That makes you unhappy?"

"Yeah, I think it does."

He rolled off me and sat up. "You'll like being in my bed. I'm going to get you there and then we'll figure out the rest of it."

I stood up and picked up my board. "Not really worried about the consequences, are you?"

He pushed damp hair back off his face. "I'm an optimist. Come on, let's go get Bubba, then I'll make you a burger for lunch."

CHAPTER FIFTEEN

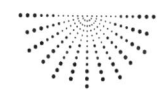

The afternoon turned into a backyard barbecue party. Chuck set up a card table in the shade and harassed us all until we'd do a poker tournament with him.

Beau grilled burgers and the guys threw on their own grub, sausages for AJ and his girlfriend, and an eggplant for Chuck—with teriyaki sauce on it.

AJ's girlfriend, a petite and sharp-eyed woman named Samantha, was nearly done with veterinary school. She looked over Cheeto for me and showed me how to cut his nails.

I drank wine and lost two dollars to Chuck and watched Beau watching me. In so many ways, he was right about what he'd said at the river park. I needed to blow off steam, badly. Everything about him turned me on.

He would be a handful in bed, demanding and unafraid. It unhinged my mind and made my underwear too tight.

I was washing the lunch dishes in the kitchen when he found me alone in the house. He caged me against the counter with his body, his front pressed along my back.

"Want you so much," he muttered into my neck, pulling my hips back.

"Oh," was all I could say, my breathing shaky. Everything between my legs throbbed into aching readiness, crying out for action. *Right now*. It was impossible to think.

His hands slid up and cupped my breasts. We both gasped. I forgot everyone and everything while he kissed my neck. It was more than a kiss—way more. My eyes closed and my head tilted back. The need reached a fever pitch.

The doorbell rang. "No," Beau moaned, pumping a little against my backside.

I cleared my throat. "Um…"

Knock, knock.

Beau's hands slid off me. He stalked into the living room and glanced out the window.

"Lauren," he said, grumpily. "I'm taking a shower."

Dazedly, I splashed cold water on my face at the sink. *Crap*. That had seemed unstoppable. Why the hell had I lost it like that? I bit my lip, too wound up. That had been…wow.

I opened the door, flushed and uncomfortable. "Hey, come in," I said, forcing a big smile on my face.

"Hi. Mom and I did a bunch of baking." Lauren struggled to get through the door with a big box in her hands.

Waking up, I took the box out of her hands and brought it to the kitchen counter. "Whoa—this is amazing. What's in here?"

"Zucchini bread, blueberry scones, carrot muffins, and apple cake. Garden produce. Summer squash, green beans, corn, jalapeños, and a tomato—mostly. Can't remember what else now. Yeah, yeah, I'm sitting down. Dang, it's hot. When's the fall finally going to get here? It's October."

I stared at her. "Aren't you supposed to take it easy?"

She flapped a hand at me. "I decided I'm ready. To not be pregnant anymore."

"Right, okay. Thirsty? There's orange juice."

"Water. With ice. Please say you have ice…"

"Yep. Coming right up. This box is blowing my mind—look at those pretty peppers."

"What are you doing? Want to turn on the football game?"

"Yeah," I said, my voice high-pitched. I coughed.

"Oh, good. Mom needs a break. From me." She sniffed, her face crumpling into a quivering frown. "Sorry. I'm sick of myself."

"Stop." I hugged her. "You're doing great."

"Not working has been hard." Lauren's doctor had been worried about some swelling in her legs, so she'd quit teaching a week or two earlier than she'd wanted to.

"Totally understand that one. Let's get you to the couch where you can put your feet up."

And so I was saved from myself by Lauren's timely arrival. Beau stayed in the shower for a long time and I… envied him.

Lauren had her ice water, reclined on the couch with her swollen legs up on pillows. Then she started crying during one of the commercials—it was about insurance.

"Yeah," I said. "That was some powerful marketing. Was it the old couple dancing that did it?"

"I think it was the music."

I handed her a box of tissues. "Yep."

"There's a big favor that I want. But, first, do you love me?"

"You're all right. What do you want?"

"My feet—could you…do you think you might, um, like, massage them a little…"

Groaning, I collapsed on the couch. "Ugh. You don't even have pretty nail polish. Those things were in the garden an hour ago."

"Forget it. You're right—I'm too disgusting to touch." She blew her nose.

"Stop...you're soaking them first. Girl, why not get a pedicure?"

She blinked, fanning her face with one hand. "Too many chemicals. I'm organic everything."

I rolled my eyes—when she couldn't see me. Since I did my own pedicures, I dug out my kit, imagining a halo over my head and hoping Beau would appear soon and handle the massage. Feet made me squeamish and a little sick to my stomach. I tried not to look at them.

Beau's feet had trimmed up toenails and an acceptable shape and I pretended they weren't there. He passed me in the hallway, a towel around his waist. I sagged sideways against the office doorjamb, watching the long muscles of his back as he walked to his bedroom door. Despite him having feet, I liked everything about his body. He smirked at me over his shoulder, then disappeared inside his room.

A knock pounded on the front door. I sat a basin of warm water on the floor in front of Lauren and dropped a towel on the couch. She had her eyes closed with a pillow over her ears.

Mason frowned at me when I opened the front door. "What are you wearing?" he demanded, shifting the six-pack of beer under his arm.

"Oh, shut the freak up. What are *you* wearing? A homeless person would have used that T-shirt as a rag."

He shrugged. "Painting today. What'd you do, go swimming or something?"

"Come in, a-hole. Windsurfing." I had on my bikini top and a cropped tank top and a pleated A-line miniskirt with a shirred waist. One of the many differences between Mason and me was fashion. As in, he thought it was a foreign word.

"Look," he said, "that dickwad used to be my best friend. I know him. Stay the fuck away."

"Mason, eat some zucchini bread and shut up."

He halted when he spotted Lauren on the couch. "She's preggers?"

Lauren opened her eyes and sat up. "Yes, I am." She plopped her feet in the soaking tub. "Hey, Mason. Still farting on all the girls and burping the alphabet?"

Mason sighed. "You know what? It's been too long. You look so cute I might have to rip one on you."

"Oh my God," I said, pushing Mason to the kitchen. "I thought you were housebroken."

Bubba came barreling out of the back bedroom, barking viciously. Mason crouched down and opened his arms, cooing at the snarling dog. Bubba backed up, eyeing him suspiciously.

"Don't forget about my foot rub," Lauren called.

"Foot rub?" Mason asked in Pluto's voice, Mickey Mouse's cartoon dog. He dropped his beer on the kitchen counter and scampered into the living room.

I watched, halted with my mouth open, as he plopped himself down on the sofa next to Lauren. He grabbed her wet feet and swung them in his lap, sloshing water all over his dirty carpenter pants.

"Towel," Lauren squeaked, pulling the skirt of her dress down as she scooted back against a pile of cushions.

"Mmm mm," Mason said. "Love me some feet. Gimme lotion—I'm gonna lube these babies up so good—"

"Ahh," I shouted incoherently.

Lauren covered her face with her hands. "I'm so desperate. I'd put up with anything for a foot rub."

Mason stilled, his eyes locked on Lauren's stomach. "Moving." His hand shot out and rested on her bump. Then he leaned over and pressed his ear against her belly.

"Would you take it easy?" I stared up at the ceiling, shaking my head.

Mason sat up and squirted lotion all over both feet. Lauren's face was red, and her eyes were closed.

"Dad's having a birthday party." Mason frowned at me while his hands massaged hard enough to make Lauren twitch. "At the bar."

I took a deep breath. Mason and I had the same father and different mothers. I had other siblings as well, but they all hated me. "So, you're going?"

He grunted. "Figure I better be there to get him back to his trailer."

Twisting the hair tie around on my wrist, I paced back and forth. "He never calls me. I'm lucky if he returns a text message."

Mason pursed his lips. "I know."

"I'll think about it."

He cleared his throat. "About that bachelor auction—"

"You're single, aren't you?" I asked.

"You know I am. Sworn off relationships until the ball bust passes. Like in my next life. Deidre just signed the damn divorce papers."

"I'll be sure to include 'not emotionally available' in your auction profile. Nope—you're doing it. And it's going to be fun."

"Raven—"

"There are already women signed up because you're listed," I flat-out lied.

He sat up straighter. "Oh, shit."

When he didn't hide underneath torn and stained clothing and ratty ball caps, my brother had the whole Italian stallion thing going for him. He worked out, obsessively, and was a big strapping dude. The unfortunate personality wasn't apparent at first glance.

"Yeah. It's happening." I pointed at him. "And you don't have to do a damn thing except show up—in nice clothes. Maybe like a polo with your fire station logo and chinos. Barbered. And you better smell like a freakin' Irish spring."

Beau walked in and gave me a sultry smile. "I like it when you start yelling."

"I wasn't."

"Uh-huh." He slung his arm around my waist.

Lauren and Mason gaped at us. "What the hell…" Mason began.

"What are we going to do about dinner?" I put my hand on my hip and stepped away from Beau. Misdirection is a powerful weapon.

"I'm grilling the salmon that's in the fridge. Caught yesterday. Right now, I'm installing those security cameras."

"I'll help," said Mason, frowning at Beau.

CHAPTER SIXTEEN

The guys slammed out of the house to install a door cam.

"You're finally—you and Beau..." Lauren gaped at me.

"No." I wrinkled up my nose. "Maybe. I don't know."

Lauren's eyes were getting watery again. "I love it so much—but are you ready? I'm afraid one of you will screw it up..."

I threw my hands in the air and stomped over to sit close to her. "I'm still stuck on Travis. He's a serious family man. Please don't cry."

"It isn't going to work." She covered her face with her hands.

Not sure if she meant me and Travis or me and Beau, I frowned. Then I put an arm around her shoulders.

"I'm crazy attracted to Beau. Like, I'm hanging on to caution with my fingernails here. But he...doesn't want to settle down. Bad strategy for me. You know what I want—and it's not being in a rental with a bunch of stoners and pot drying in the basement."

Lauren's eyes opened wide. "That's the smell?"

"Yeah. I'm worried about my clothes."

"This is Beau's house. He could change things anytime—and will, I think."

I twisted my hair up into a bun on the top of my head. It was Beau's rental house and he'd turned it into a laidback kind of party central. The gatherings were fun and yet the opposite of what I needed for myself.

"Okay," I said. "Your turn. What was that with Mason?"

"Huh?"

"Please. Stop giving me that innocent face. I thought you guys hated each other."

Lauren sucked in her upper lip and stared off into the distance. "Yeah. It was nothing—just a little…teasing. Made me feel like more than a pregnancy for a second."

"Wow, nice deflection."

She rolled her eyes. "Let's do rice and beans with the fish. Go raid the pantry."

It turned into another party night at Beau's, with Mason on his way to earning a noise complaint from the neighbors all on his own. AJ set up a badminton net. Chuck brought out a whiteboard for his badminton tournament and insisted we all throw in a dollar.

"Mason," I said after my brother lost a match against AJ and threw a cursing tantrum, "come help me with dessert."

A few friends of Chuck's had shown up, including a couple of giggly women. It was like Mason had gone into strutting rooster mode.

"Fine." Mason started to slam the racket against the ground, pulled up at the last second, and then tossed it up above his head, so it flipped around. He caught it with one hand. Handle first, he handed it off to the laughing woman next to him.

Beau stared at me from where he sat next to Lauren. We'd been a little shy with each other, not talking much, but I was always aware of where he was.

Mason stumbled a little next to me. "Fucking ground," he muttered. "Need to level out this lawn."

"You can crash here," I said.

"Yeah, yeah." He held the mudroom door open for me. "I'll sleep in that garage. Got my cot with me."

Mason drove a junky old truck with a canopy on the back and kept it loaded with camping gear for his frequent forays away from the camper at his construction site. He met up with a group of buddies in the woods, got drunk by a campfire, and usually ended up blowing things up—like aerosol cans and glow sticks. One year, they made a thirty-foot blaze out of old Christmas trees. He was a firefighter who loved fire and explosions. It seemed wrong.

"Fucking Beau, Raven?" Mason filled up someone's used cup at the faucet and chugged from it.

My hackles rose. "Are you talking about the guy that insisted on protecting me from a stalker?"

Mason burped. "He'll disappear. As soon as things get tough—and they will."

I crossed my arms. "Your cousin is an alcoholic with a speed addiction. She hides it well but, no, I'm not surprised he took off. What was that, eight years ago? A party hookup that lasted while he was home from college."

"I'm still right."

"You guys used to be best friends. What happened?"

Mason scratched his face, collapsing against a wall. "We both suck at phone calls. Whatever. Get your heart broken."

I picked up the plate with Lauren's apple cake. "Maybe I'll turn the tables on him."

His face wrinkled up. "Gimme Lauren cake so I feel better."

"You're all about Laur—"

"Shh." He pressed the side of his finger against my nose. "No, no. Not with the ringie poo."

Actually, Lauren wasn't wearing her ring because her fingers were swollen. She did have it on a chain around her neck. I took the cake out and found Lauren with her head on Beau's shoulder.

"Better lie down for a minute," Lauren said, slurring her words a little. She hadn't had a drop of alcohol; it was pure exhaustion.

"Come on, sis." Beau pulled her up to her feet.

"Let's watch a movie," Lauren said to me, blinking.

"Sure." I gathered up plates and made sure the garage was unlocked for Mason.

In the kitchen, I loaded up the dishwasher and started it running. When I turned around, Beau was there, leaning against the counter. That wicked smile pulled at his mouth.

"Hey," he said.

"Hey." I didn't know what to do with myself—mostly I wanted to walk into his arms. Instead, I kept my hip against the counter.

The Star Wars theme played in the living room. Most of the lights were off. Lauren was on the couch under a blanket.

Beau pushed his hand through his hair. "Evening shift again this week. It's pissing me off I won't see you until Friday."

"Oh." I stared down at a speck on the counter, unable to keep the smile off my face.

Beau came across the kitchen and put his arms around me. "Those dimples. Damn, Raven. Why are you smiling— because I'll miss you?"

I inhaled, really distracted by his hands moving up and down my back. "You talk about what you're feeling. Surprises me. And I like it."

We stared at each other, his arms tight around me. He smelled like cut grass and beer and soap overlaid with Beau sweat—it was heady. My heart flip-flopped in my chest.

"We fit," he said. "I can feel it."

He kissed me. His mouth was unhurried and sweet while his hands glided over my skin. My arms snaked up around his neck.

"Come to bed with me," he said in my ear.

I shook my head. "You mean later?"

"Whenever. Please."

He pulled me up off my feet and kissed me again, urgently.

Lauren coughed in the living room. People laughed in the backyard. Bubba barked from Beau's bedroom.

I pulled away from him, hot and bothered—and frustrated. I didn't want our first time together to be noted audibly by a group of people.

"Not tonight," I said, stepping sideways.

He put his fists against his forehead. "I don't know what you're thinking."

I straightened out my skirt. "Wondering...if you're thinking ahead."

"To what—the bachelor auction?" He threw up his hands. "Come on. There's more to life than that."

He grabbed a beer out of the fridge and stalked away toward his bedroom. After a moment, Bubba came charging out, whining and his tail lashing from side to side, ecstatic to be let out of the bedroom. He ran to me, ran to Lauren, then Beau and Bubba disappeared out of the mudroom door.

I hadn't been thinking about the bachelor auction, although I should have. Beau wanted to start screwing and it would be hot and fun. But we were already living together, and I was practically a part of his family. Mason was right, it would be ugly when Beau disappeared—which happened pretty easily when he didn't get exactly what he wanted.

∼

Lauren and I slept on the couch. She woke up very early, uncomfortable and cramping, and paced around the house.

"Go for a drive?" I asked groggily.

"I'm buying us breakfast," she said, rubbing her belly.

Lauren showered after I did. Her clothes went through a speed wash while I sat at the breakfast table with my first cup of coffee. I opened my laptop and tried to refocus my brain away from Beau. The bachelor auction was two and a half weeks away. A jolt of adrenaline hit me as I scanned over my list of things still to finalize.

My criminal case was on hold, which was exactly what my lawyer wanted. Dominic had sent in a statement about what he had seen on Saturday. I forwarded it on to my lawyer. There was still so much missing—including statements from my apartment neighbors.

I fired off more messages when I could find some of those neighbors on socials, unashamedly begging for statements. What I needed to do was find a way to see them in person...

The day turned into massive party prep for the auction and cold calls to everyone I could think of to sponsor balloons, flowers, decorating, printing, and photography. The band I'd hired made noises about possibly pulling out. I went to the singer's day job, at a music store, to level with him—and show him pictures of the hospice patients he'd be letting down. He backed away with his hands up.

"That was fun," Lauren said. I'd returned her to her house, and she sat with her feet up in a recliner. "I never knew you were such a hard-ass."

I sniffed, opening my laptop. "I'd already made graphics

and posted on social media. Hell hath no fury like a PR manager forced into retractions..."

My email had a big surprise waiting for me. The Adventure Tours place had offered me a part-time job. It would be as an office assistant and the media manager. I sat up, chewing on my lip.

"Looks like I have a job offer," I said, slowly nodding my head.

"Oh?"

"That tour place downtown. The pay is low but it's still in my field."

"They do fishing stuff, right?"

"And more."

Lauren fanned herself with a magazine. "Weren't you thinking about starting a tour business? Rock climbing, women empowering women...to get in the woods?"

I leaned back against my chair. "Yeah, if I can ever raise the capital."

"Maybe you could start smaller. With hiking. And, like, touristy stuff."

It would be a good use of the free time I suddenly had. I spun around in the office chair I'd borrowed from Mr. Martin's office. Ridiculously, Beau flashed into my mind. When would I see him with so much going on?

My foot slammed down on the ground, and I stopped spinning. How had I even gone there in my head? Beau and I weren't a thing—we were a possible experiment.

"You're right. I'll take this job and use it as research."

I went to the Adventure Tours office that afternoon, in downtown River Gorge, to negotiate and file the paperwork. The office was a desk surrounded by piles of river rafts, kayaks, windsurfing boards, mountain bikes, fishing poles and more.

Mike, the owner, a middle-aged man with streaks of gray

in his hair, met me there. He had a hard time getting off his cell phone and seemed pulled in about ten different directions.

"One minute," he said to me, scratching his beard while he paced with his phone to his ear.

I walked around the office until I found their calendar. It was solidly booked with tours, especially on the weekends.

"Yep," Mike said, stuffing his phone in his pocket. "My life is chaos. Wife just had another baby."

"Congratulations."

"Thank you." He rubbed his face.

I pulled out my cell phone so he could see it. "I'd like to record you talking about the job, if you don't mind. There's a lot going on here and I don't want to miss anything."

He nodded, straightening up his hunched-over back. "Great idea."

By the end of an hour, I was on my way to running the office, even though I could have used a lot more of Mike's time. He had to spend most of our training setting up access for me and finding things. Clearly, the organization of digital assets was toppling into utter chaos. Mike and I hammered out initial priorities and a schedule. I would start the next day.

Unable to stop myself, I drove back to Beau's house. *Cheeto needs me*, I kept telling myself. It was true. My teenager cat was getting very restless from being cooped up indoors.

Beau's truck was there in the driveway. It was like I'd poured champagne straight into my belly as I headed for the mudroom door. Bubba barked greetings at me, then whined and licked my hands, barely letting me slide by his quivering body.

The house smelled like bacon and fried eggs. Beau had left a plate out on the counter with a pile of bacon. Underneath it was an old envelope with my name scrawled on it in his jagged handwriting. And to counter my heart melting into a puddle all over the floor, there was also a pile of dishes he'd left for me in the kitchen.

"Hey, babe," Beau called.

"Hey." I smiled—because I couldn't help it.

"Come in here. I have a surprise."

The ghost of Beau pranks from the past made my steps slow. Would he spray a confetti cannon at me? Maybe he was hiding behind a door waiting to jump out and scare me? Of course, there was the classic throw a rubber snake or giant plastic spider...

When I stepped into the narrow dining room, where I could see the living room, I stopped. My hand pressed on my chest as I stared.

"What do you think?" Beau pushed his hair off his forehead.

"Oh my God. It's so amazing."

He grinned at me and tossed a screwdriver into a toolbox. "Just finished. Cheeto approves."

In the corner of the living room, partially in front of the big picture window, was a three-tiered cat tower. Cheeto was perched on the very top, about four feet up, his tail swishing back and forth as he stared down at Bubba. The middle tier was a cubed den type of thing, and all of the posts were wrapped in sisal rope for scratching.

"Wow." I drifted closer. It had a sturdy wooden base with a light birch kind of veneer, and all of the platforms matched. Instead of carpeting, there were attractive fluffy white pads. Cheeto grabbed a dangling ball from the lower platform, pulled it up, and chewed on it, rolling around on his back.

"Careful, buddy," Beau said, pushing Cheeto further toward the center.

"What—how?"

Beau wrapped an arm around my back. "Cheeto's a little

unhappy when you're not here. Now he has somewhere to get away from Bubba without being locked in the room."

I turned and wrapped my arms around him. "Thank you. I thought you were about to prank me. I'm so surprised..."

Standing up on my tiptoes, I kissed him. He lifted me onto the back of the couch and perched my butt on it. I wrapped my legs around his waist—it was like we picked right back up where we'd left off the day before.

His hands slid up my sides and our mouths were locked together, his tongue sending shivers down my spine. An alarm went off somewhere nearby.

Beau pulled away and pressed his forehead against mine. "Gotta go."

"Right." I rubbed his back a little, trying to feel relieved.

"I'm sorry I was impatient. Last night."

Smiling, I touched his nose with mine. "Okay."

His hands cupped the sides of my face. "This is big. You and me."

I smiled, my heart going all mushy. He kept saying things like that—and hearing them was a little addictive. Had anyone ever been this affectionate with me?

The alarm sounded again, and he stepped back. "Damn. Station needs me early this week. We're short-handed and Billy's out sick."

"You're doing twelve-hour days?" I asked, following him out of the living room.

"Four in a row. Can you watch Bubba tonight? I like the added security for you."

"Sure. Text me if you need anything."

He pulled me in for a quick, hard kiss. "You. That's what I need."

I pushed him toward the office where he kept his go bag. "Took a job today. Part-time at the tour place downtown."

"Oh?" He glanced at me. "What's your shift like?"

"Weekday mornings, for now. It's flexible. I...don't think I'll really see you until Friday." I didn't want to try to start sleeping together, somehow, during the hours we were both home.

Eyebrows pinched together, he marched toward the front door. "Damn Mondays."

CHAPTER SEVENTEEN

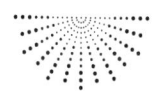

Monday night, the house was too quiet. Chuck and AJ didn't seem to be home. I paced around, wondering if Rob the creep was out there watching the house, and glad Bubba was with me.

My bedroom's big window, which you could step through from the front porch if the pane was opened, loomed right next to my headboard like a cave with a monster inside. After sitting on my bed for ten minutes, trying to work on my laptop, I gave up and moved out to the couch.

The animals and I settled in the living room for the night. Bubba whined and tried to get close to Cheeto. My cat had a breakthrough when, instead of running away, he swiped at Bubba's nose with his claws extended. Bubba immediately backed off. We all fell asleep on the couch together.

I woke up when the mudroom door opened, and Bubba snuffled and made excited growly noises.

"Hush," Beau said. The door closed lightly, and they were both outside.

Putting a pillow over my head didn't accomplish anything. I glanced at my phone, and it said four twenty-five.

Giving up on more sleep, I sat up and turned on the table lamp and switched on the television for the morning news. Beau and Bubba came back in as I was leaving the bathroom.

"Morning," I called while yawning behind my hand.

The kitchen lights switched on and I blinked blearily. Beau dropped his bag on the floor in front of the laundry room. He closed the distance between us and wrapped his arms around me.

"Damn long night," he said, pressing his face in my hair.

"You okay? Want to talk about it?"

He sniffed and squeezed me in tighter. "Nah. Try to leave it on the job. Hate being reminded that people aren't good. A lot of them. Anyway, I did what I could. Showed up."

"My hero," I said, kissing his shoulder. "Hopefully this time it wasn't a woman stunning her stalker that got arrested."

He groaned. "Jones is getting nonstop shit for that at the station."

I harrumphed. Officer Jones and I would never have peace between us. "Not sorry."

"He's a bonehead."

"Want some tea? I have herbal nighttime stuff."

He yawned. "No. Just going to shower and hit the sack. We're still on the couch?"

I leaned back to stare up at him. He smiled down at me.

"I'm up for the day," I said. "Go sleep in your bed. You need it."

Pouting out his bottom lip, he hung his head. "I need cuddles."

I went to the coffee maker. "We're waiting on cuddles. I'm...still in shock that I'm here. A lot happened in the last week."

He followed me into the kitchen and propped himself

against the counter with his arms crossed. "Are you talking to that guy you met in Portland?"

"No. I did message him about a statement to send my lawyer—he saw Rob Campbell's note on my car."

Actually, Dominic had hardly crossed my mind. Even though he was the wealthy and handsome man, with impeccable clothing, that I'd decided to find for myself. *What the hell?*

The timing hadn't been right for me to get involved with him—entirely Beau's fault. What I needed to do was tell Beau about Travis Dashiell. However, it was far too early in the morning for that.

His haggard face cracked my heart a little. I leaned in and kissed him briefly. "It won't kill us to take this a little slow. You know, talk."

Sighing, he rested his cheek on the top of my head. "It might."

"Go shower. Before you fall asleep on your feet."

"Come home for lunch. I'll make something."

I pushed him to the bathroom. It wasn't that I didn't want to spend time with him—I'd woken up three hours early so I could—it was his assumption of assent. One of the oldest selling tactics in the books, an assumptive close gave me that backed-into-a-corner edginess. I could be contrary down to my manicured toes.

Beau made me squirm by walking into a room. I constantly craved his hands on my body. Was it smoking my judgment? I liked who he was—now that he wasn't a prankster anymore. Cheeto jumped up onto his new cat tower and opened the blinds with a paw. Everything inside me was melting and yet…a lot still held me back.

My first day on the job at Outdoor Adventures flew by. I met a couple of the guides, extremely fit outdoorsy types, one of whom was vaguely familiar because he'd been the state swimming champ and so had his picture on our high school wall. Mostly I answered emails and called potential clients who'd left their phone number—managing to close a few tours, with deposits paid.

Mike, the owner, came in just before lunch and asked me to stay longer to set up more executive access. I smiled and nodded, trying to ignore the punched-in-the-gut disappointment of missing lunch with Beau.

"Need a moment to cancel some lunch plans, Mike," I said. "Be right back."

"Ah—okay." He hunched over the computer.

I stepped out into the wind, realizing I should have brought a jacket. First I texted Sasha, the bubbly intern over at the hospice office to let her know about my schedule change. Then I called Beau.

"Hey," he answered, sounding like I'd woken him up.

"Hey. I can't make lunch today. New boss asked me to stay for training. Did you sleep well?"

He grunted. "Crashed hard. Glad you woke me up though. Hate sleeping past noon."

"I hate missing your cooking. Especially when I'll be doing your dishes anyway."

He laughed. "Oh, burn. I'll leave you something in the fridge. Did you do a BLT yesterday? Those tomatoes from Lauren are awesome."

"I did. Thought I'd take Bubba out to your parents' tonight. Lauren is sending me text messages with pictures of puzzle pieces. I think it's a cry for help."

"Yep. I'll tell Bubba to be good for you. But he likes bribes."

"I know where his treats are."

"I'll miss you," Beau said. "See you in the morning?"

There was a goofy smile on my face. "Yeah. See you."

The afternoon flew by. I had a balloon and flower shop

willing to donate their time for the bachelor auction, if the materials were paid for. I met with them, along with Sasha, and nailed down the details.

With everything going on, it was after five by the time I got back to Beau's house. He was long gone. Wandering around the empty upstairs of the house, I tidied up this and that, and even started a load of Beau's laundry for him—handling his clothing made him seem a little closer.

Bubba and I went out to Lauren and her parents' house for the evening. I brought a bottle of wine for Allison and John and fresh raspberries for Lauren. Bubba panted and drooled all over my backseat but was, in general, manageable.

"You're here," Lauren said from the rocking chair on the front porch as I walked up with Bubba on a leash.

"Brought you berries," I said, holding up the package.

"Yay." She smiled wanly, appearing even more exhausted than she had two days ago. Her face was pale, the skin seeming stretched over her high cheekbones.

"Do you want to walk a bit?" I asked.

She nodded. "Backyard. Bubba can run around. The fence is in good shape."

After I ran inside to say hello to her parents and drop off my goodies, we ambled around the house and through the back gate. Bubba's tail wagged a mile a minute.

"Baby's close," Lauren said, holding on to my arm as we slowly walked across the path through the cut grass. "She's lower."

My eyes opened wide. "Like, today close?"

Lauren shrugged. "Not sure. My back is killing me. I hope it's soon."

I patted her hand. "I'm excited," I said, my voice squeaky. Actually, I was terrified for her, but that wasn't the right thing to say—obviously.

"Still haven't heard from Derek." She stopped, hunching over and pressing on her side.

"Contraction?" I rubbed her back. "Should we get you off your feet?"

"No. It's fine. Tell me about you."

So I rambled on about the bachelor auction, my new job, and my stalled-out criminal trial. I didn't know what to say about Derek. It wasn't good that he was so quiet—and it was breaking my heart for Lauren. Maybe he was in a difficult part of the Middle East?

"Okay," said Lauren. "But what about Beau? Are you guys, you know, together together now?"

Bubba ran up to me with a stick in his mouth. He was already covered in dirt and mud and tried to put his front paws on my shirt. I ignored his pleading watery eyes and cocked head, anxious for rowdy play. In some ways Bubba reminded me of everything rough and messy about life with Beau—not the beast I'd pictured myself with.

"I'm trying to take it slow. He's in full boyfriend mode and I...really like him but...wonder if he's thinking past the easy sex. For some reason, I can't stand the idea of a meaningless fling with Beau."

Inhaling, I shook my head. *Wow.* Despite his bad fashion choices, dish washing procrastination, and party house lifestyle, apparently, I was falling for him. Hard.

"Me too. Athena needs a cousin."

I snorted. "Don't hold your breath for Beau. What about your older brother? When's that guy going to get married?"

"I don't know. He's pretty anti-relationship. Should we try to set him up? Who do you think..."

"Autumn, Kelsey, or Maria...I don't know if any of them really seem like an officer's wife, willing to relocate all over the world. Kelsey. Because she needs to get away from Gerry."

"But Autumn's so, like, take charge and organized."

"And all about her career. Can't really see her sacrificing making money for a husband."

"Naomi," we both said at the same time.

"A graphic designer that works from home." Lauren nodded. "How did we forget about Naomi?"

I pursed my lips. "She has blue streaks in her hair right now. Not sure Hunter would like that. He's so serious…"

Lauren swatted a bug away from her face. "You're right. I give up. I'm putting all my money on you and Beau, for the win."

My stomach clenched. The small-town pressure was piling on already—it was why I rarely dated close to home. I'd been so sure Travis was the one. But he'd let me go like a fish that was too small to keep.

CHAPTER EIGHTEEN

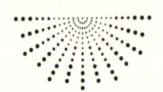

There was a package on the front step when I returned to Beau's Tuesday night. Cheeto meowed anxiously inside as Bubba and I walked from the car to the front door.

I was shaky, goosebumps breaking out on my arms. My legs were stiff as I stared around at the overgrown yard. Bubba sniffed the ground but was otherwise quiet. It should have reassured me since he could tell when a car pulled into the driveway from across the house. I didn't see anyone in the cars parked along the street—but the back of my neck was prickling.

There was a box on the front porch. I leaned closer and saw it was Summer's Eve Vaginal Douche, extra cleansing. Underneath was a piece of paper. I shifted the box over with my foot. The writing said *YOU'RE A WHORE*.

Trembling, I took Bubba inside, locked the door behind me, then checked all the doors and windows. I called Beau and left a voicemail and sent a text message about the package as well. Pacing back and forth, I waited.

My phone finally rang. "Hey," Beau said. "Hang tight.

Officer Smith will be by sometime tonight to gather the evidence."

"Not you?" I really wanted to see him.

"Can't, babe. Wouldn't be good for your future case against Campbell. I checked the door cam footage, and he stayed hidden under a hoodie and wore a mask. Still, it's enough to get a case going for you."

I blew out a breath. "Okay. Thanks."

"Gotta go. Hang in there, honey."

"Bye."

Collapsing on the couch, I pressed the phone against my forehead. How had Rob known about the cameras? Beau and Mason had hidden them. Why was that creep always one step ahead of me?

It took me a long time to fall asleep that night. I waited for an officer to knock, but they never did. When Beau opened the side door around four in the morning, I slept through it.

My third cell phone alarm woke me up, with barely enough time to be ready for work. "Dang," I muttered groggily, sitting up.

Beau was asleep on the other side of the big sectional couch, his arm hanging off the side. Bubba opened one eye and winked at me.

I stared at Beau, his long body wearing boxers only half covered by a worn quilt. There was pressure in my chest—I was getting too used to thinking about him as a part of my life.

If only I could talk to Mom about it. I closed my eyes and pinched the bridge of my nose. Thinking about her hurt too much.

As quietly as I could, I dressed and slipped out of the house. The douche package was still on the front porch, covered in dew from the foggy morning. I sighed. Maybe a detective would have time that day, but I wasn't counting on it.

While waiting in a fast-food breakfast line, I called my lawyer and left a voicemail. I turned the bracelet my mother had given me around and around on my wrist. There wasn't enough direct evidence against Rob and time was running out.

One of the neighbors that hadn't responded was Mrs. Garcia. An older woman, she kept to herself, except with the other Spanish speakers in the apartment complex. My own Spanish was horrible. I texted Lauren.

> ME
> Have some time this afternoon?

She responded right away.

> LAUREN
> All I do is try to kill time. What's up?

> How's your Spanish these days?

> Rusty. Functional.

That probably meant she was completely fluent. She'd been really good in high school and had studied the language in college.

> ME
> Help me corner a suspicious older lady and convince her to give a statement about the creep that lives below her?

> LAUREN
> Sure. Then I want FroYo.

> She has like three jobs. There will be sleuthing.

Going to the apartment building would be another step. I chewed on my lip, stomach clenching at the thought. It was time to be brave—I had to stop letting that creep scare me. And I could go while he was working.

After another full morning hunched over the computer at Outdoor Adventures, I managed to get out of there on time. Bubba met me at the mudroom door, anxiously whining. I let him out and waited while he ran laps around the backyard and peed in three places.

Beau was in the bathroom when I went inside. I took the chicken salad he'd made the day before out of the fridge and toasted bread. Staring out the windows at the gray overcast day, I couldn't get my shoulders to relax.

"Morning," Beau called. "Mine anyway."

"Hi." I couldn't seem to stop myself from smiling as he walked toward me, his hair sticking up and crease lines on his face from sleeping.

"Don't worry, I brushed my teeth." He rushed in and swept me up in a hug. My feet dangled above the floor. "Finally, we're both awake. Let's go cuddle."

I leaned back enough to stare into his sparkling eyes. "You think I'm an easy booty call, don't you?"

He grunted. "That's me."

His mouth pressed against mine and I forgot all about my questions. He tasted like toothpaste, and before I'd had another thought, my legs were wrapped around his waist and his tongue was in my mouth.

Smoke cut into my heady escape from reality—my toast was burning. The fire alarm went off.

"Damn," Beau muttered, putting me on the floor, then

darting away as Bubba began howling. The high-pitched beeping stopped.

I opened the kitchen and dining room windows. "Sorry. Forgot about my bread."

Beau grunted, hugging Bubba. "Woke me up."

After checking on Cheeto, I settled at the table with my sandwich—on cold bread. Beau joined me with a giant bowl of granola and milk up to the rim. Some sloshed out onto the table.

"So," he said, "what are we doing this weekend?"

I collapsed against my chair, staring at his cheerful face as he took his first big bite of cereal. Perhaps what we both needed was a hard talk.

"Might be rainy," I said. "I think we should talk. Right now."

His spoon stopped, dripping milk, on its way to his mouth. "Now?"

I shrugged. "Why not?"

"Because I'm sober."

"It'll be interesting." Well, that was true. But my belly was quivering. "Where are you at, career-wise? Do you see yourself in River Gorge long term?"

He slouched a little and took another bite of food. "Yes." He swallowed. "I want to stay here, get promoted to detective in a few years. Might have to look elsewhere if they don't take me seriously."

"How so?" I nibbled on a piece of my bread.

"Some of the guys that knew me as a kid can't get past it." He pushed a hand through his hair.

I nodded. It was a small town, if a growing one, and most people had long memories. My history felt like a dark cloud —the poor kid with the proud mom that couldn't hang on to housing.

"What about you?" Beau asked.

"I don't know if I can stay in River Gorge now. Career-wise." I twisted my small plate on the table. "Maybe. I'd thought so. But living in the same town as Rob might be too much for me."

"Hey." Beau covered my hand with his on the table. "It'd be worse if he followed you somewhere new."

"Where I didn't know anyone, you mean? Yeah, that's a good point." Changing my identity was an option. Actually, I really hated that idea.

I wanted to turn the tables on Rob the creep somehow—make him scared of me. Maybe it would be worth a misdemeanor to thwack him with a stick again...

"I'm getting serious about starting a business," I said. "Tours, to start. Hiking and climbing mostly. If I don't land another job I like, freelance marketing as well."

Beau nodded. "You could do it. You're like that battery bunny that never stops. The Ravenizer."

I raised an eyebrow at him. "That sounds like a weapon."

He grinned at me. "A sexy one. That shoots black laser beams."

Cheeto jumped on my lap and sniffed at my plate. "Do you ever think about buying property?" I asked.

Beau waved his spoon in a circle above his bowl. "Well, I have this place. Wouldn't mind a fishing cabin. Got into this right before the big price increase. It suits me. Guys downstairs are easy to live with."

I hadn't realized Beau owned the house. "Smart of you to buy young."

He shrugged. "Like the freedom to do what I want. Have a dog. And a band. Store a bunch of stuff. Fishing boat, someday."

There was a knock on the door, and it turned out to be an officer from the station. She asked a lot of questions and reviewed the door cam footage. Beau transformed into his working persona, serious and hard-faced. He also put his arm around my waist—surprising Officer Ortega and me.

By the time we were done, Beau was rushing off to prepare for another twelve-hour shift, shouting gratitude at me for doing his laundry. I took Cheeto out on his leash, staring around at Beau's property like I'd never seen it before.

CHAPTER NINETEEN

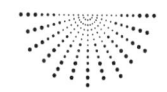

I sat with Lauren on a dinky bench in front of the discount grocery store where my old apartment neighbor, Mrs. Garcia, was finishing her shift. The schedule I'd spied next to the employee break room had showed she finished at three, in a few minutes.

Lauren rocked slightly, a hand on her belly. "I'm not sure sex is worth it, anymore."

A passing teenager stared at us, his skateboard tucked under his arm. I rubbed Lauren's back a little.

"The weirdest thing is," she went on, "Mom says I won't remember."

"What? Like a trauma block?"

"Yes. Especially the birth…"

I hugged her against my side. "We'll get through this. Easy births happen—your mom's was, right?"

She nodded, reaching out to hold my hand and gripping it hard.

I wasn't much of a friend-hand-holder, but I would do just about anything to help Lauren in those moments. Her situation was crushing my heart—and had me thinking about what Beau would be like as a daddy-to-be. He'd do the foot massages and the cuddles. It made me a little melancholy. I didn't think he was ready to settle down.

"Señora Garcia," I called, jumping up off the bench. "Un momento, por favor."

She paused, a plastic grocery bag hitched over her shoulder. Frowning, she stared at me, her body still pointed away toward the parking lot.

I pulled Lauren up off the bench. She began speaking in Spanish, in a soft friendly way—everything sounder kinder in Spanish—gesticulating with her hands.

Mrs. Garcia gave short, clipped answers, shaking her head.

Lauren gestured at me, words I didn't follow flowing, then held out a greeting card envelope with contact information inside. Reluctantly, Mrs. Garcia shoved it in her plastic bag, saying a few terse words.

Flinching, Lauren pressed on her belly as Mrs. Garcia walked away. "Let's go," Lauren gasped. "I want my FroYo."

Moving slowly, I got Lauren in the car. I started driving to our next stop. Lauren's breathing became easier, and she sagged, lying on her side in the reclined passenger seat.

"Okay?" I asked.

"Eh. It passed."

"What did Mrs. Garcia say?"

"She doesn't want trouble." Lauren sighed. "I think she's scared—of Rob but also of any kind of attention."

I nodded. "What else?"

"She said Rob is quiet these days. There's an older man living in your old apartment. Everything's okay now. Why should she stir up trouble? I told her he's threatening and following you. She said she'll think about it."

I gulped—that hadn't gone the way I'd hoped. My foot tapped on the floorboard of my car.

"Can I sleep over?" Lauren asked. "I did well on that couch the other night."

"You bet."

"Best to give my parents a chance to talk about me when they aren't afraid I'll overhear," she said, staring out the passenger window as we drove.

"Maybe. Or watch Thursday night football and eat a frozen pizza. They'll miss your cooking."

She huffed.

There wasn't a package on the doorstep. My shoulders dropped. Cheeto greeted us at the door, trying to push past my legs and dart outside.

Lauren and I relaxed with the animals, leftovers, hot tea, and a show to binge-watch. I carefully did not mention Derek. We both fell asleep on the couch with the television on.

I woke up for a bit when Beau opened the mudroom door. He had been warned with text messages about the slumber party and quietly went to his room. Flipping onto my side, I almost followed him. Lauren snorted in her sleep. With a sigh, I came to my senses.

Lauren waved me off in the morning. "Beau can bring me home. I want to hang out with Cheeto."

"Okay. Drinks tonight with the gal gang. Do you want to show off your bump and do a virgin cocktail?"

She shook her head. "No. Too noisy. Say hi for me. I'm going to redecorate my character's house in Animal Crossing. Cottagecore all the way."

"The video game? Don't forget to buy cute clothes from the hedgehogs."

I left, struggling to shake my worry for Lauren. She was an introvert and fairly self-contained, but it seemed like she was slipping into depression. Then again, she was processing a lot. I tended to try and keep emotions at arm's length, but they were unavoidable at times.

The bar for the meetup was within walking distance of Beau's house. I left my car in the driveway and hiked downtown, inspired by Chuck and AJ. They bicycled everywhere and spent their evenings drinking away from the house. I was ready for a few drinks that night.

Kelsey and I were the first ones there again. She was very pretty in a fuzzy cream sweater and slacks, sparkling drop earrings, and polished shoes—impeccably dressed and put together for her day job in accounting. Except her face was even more strained than usual.

"How are you?" I asked as we took our jackets off at a table.

She inhaled sharply. "I'm…a little on edge. Sorry. How are you?"

The server stopped by—Maria's cousin—and I ordered a jalapeño pomegranate mojito and deep-fried oysters. He winked at me, scribbling on his notepad, then bustled back to the kitchen. I couldn't help grinning, even though he was practically a teenager and made me feel old.

I raised my eyebrows at Kelsey and bit my bottom lip. "I might jump in bed with someone. Tonight."

Her head jerked forward. "Really?"

I nodded, taking a sip of my water. "Lauren's brother, Beau. I don't know. Still trying to talk myself out of it. He isn't my type, and he isn't serious about it…"

She fingered one of her dangling earrings. "Not talking to Travis anymore?"

"No." I slouched. "Maybe another time…I don't know."

She fiddled with her napkin on the table. "Gerry is… becoming more difficult to live with."

"I'm so sorry."

She smiled sadly. "Thank you."

"Let me know if you need any kind of help. You know what?"

"What?"

"Don't miss that bachelor auction. It's going to be fun. You have almost two weeks—be ready and be single."

Her eyes opened up very big. "I don't know…"

"Get it done, girl. You'll be one step closer to happy."

She covered her cheek with a hand. "I'll…maybe."

Our drinks arrived. I raised my glass. "Here's to those who wish us well. As for the rest, they can go to hell."

We clinked glasses. Kelsey sipped her wine, a smile tugging at her mouth. "I love toasts."

I grinned, holding up my glass again. "Here's to steak when you're hungry. Whiskey when you're dry. A lover when you need one and heaven when you die."

Kelsey leaned forward. "In Italy they say, 'While we live, let's live.'"

"Hear! Hear!"

Our glasses chimed again. The spicy tequila in my cocktail burned down my throat. Maybe I could put my plan for a normal life on hold for a few weeks—let a fling with Beau flame out. A little heat pooled in my belly.

Maria and Autumn arrived, frisky and ready to party. There was live music, and Maria danced with a man that bought our table a round of drinks. I ate my oysters and laughed—mostly at Maria when she tried to hide behind her hair from an earnest ex-boyfriend.

When Kelsey rose to leave, I followed her, waving goodbye to Autumn and Maria at the bar. I couldn't really afford the Thursday night outings anymore and had already spent too much. Glumly, I shoved my bill receipt in my pocket.

"Do you mind dropping me off up the hill?" I asked Kelsey.

"Not at all." She beeped her white Toyota Corolla hatchback open.

Her car was very clean and still had that new scent on the inside. "Thanks," I said, buckling my seat belt. "I've been a little nervous outside at night lately."

"Did something happen?"

I slouched, reluctant to end the evening talking about the creep. And yet, maybe Kelsey and I needed to open up with each other more.

"An old neighbor is stalking me. It's...completely annoying."

She gasped. "Oh my God, I'm so sorry."

"Thanks."

"Beau's a police officer, right?"

"Yeah. Turn right here. This is his house, actually."

She parked in the driveway. "Raven—I'm still processing...a stalker? Are you okay? Can I do anything?"

"If I disappear, be sure to ask around."

She gaped at me. "What?"

I grinned, shaking my head. "Sorry. Dark humor. What you can do is spread the word about the bachelor auction. That would really help me."

"I'll do that."

Kelsey waited while I ran inside. Bubba and Cheeto greeted me at the door in an otherwise quiet house. I turned on all the lights and checked the doors and windows.

I walked down the hallway and propped myself against the doorjamb of Beau's bedroom. He'd left his door open, as usual. There was laundry scattered around the room, bags cluttering the surfaces of the dressers, dog beds and toys, and an acoustic guitar on a stand tucked into a corner. An old surfboard was mounted on the wall above his large bed.

There was a tug of war happening inside my chest. I had always had strong feelings about Beau—half hating him when we were teenagers and half eagerly anticipating whatever he would do next. Allison and John had been very firm that sexually messing around would not be tolerated between Beau and me. And my brother had been like a guard dog capable of vicious retaliation.

Mostly, I liked to pretend that I was completely in control of my emotions. The longing for Beau, the soft gooeyness inside my heart, was flooding me with warmth. I bit my lip, my skin tingling. Resisting wasn't in me anymore.

I texted him, light-headed.

> ME
>
> I'm tired of sleeping on the couch. Your bed looks pretty good. Come find me when you get home. xx

CHAPTER TWENTY

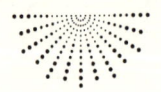

I took a long shower with a new razor and my favorite perfumed bodywash. My breathing was shallow, my breasts aching as I pressed my face into the stream of hot water.

A message flashed on my phone while I lay in Beau's bed, trying to wind down enough to sleep.

BEAU
Don't go anywhere.

The alarm I'd set woke me up at four—my face scrunched up and then a ripple of adrenaline opened my eyes. I sat up and turned on the lamp on the nightstand. Bubba popped up out of his dog bed and trotted through the cracked bedroom door, tail wagging. Cheeto stretched.

Grumbling at my own absurdity, I brushed my teeth and splashed my face. With a robe on, I shuffled out to the kitchen, yawning.

I'd gulped down half a glass of water when headlights flashed in the driveway and Bubba began whining. Moments later, the mudroom door opened, and Beau's head appeared.

HOTHEADED HEART

"Hey," he said, grinning at me.

"Hi," I croaked.

"Be right back—God, you look good."

My mouth quirked up—he was still in his uniform. A river of heat shot down my spine.

His head disappeared and the door snapped shut. I blinked, staring at where he had been.

Cheeto meowed at my feet. I gave him food in my room and fresh water. While I was washing my hands, Beau came in and fed Bubba.

He caught me in the hall, pulling me against him and burying his face in my hair. "Raven." His hands ran up and down the back of my robe. "I couldn't concentrate all night. Are we doing this? Please say we're doing this…"

"I don't know—isn't this a little old married couple? Should we fight or something first?"

"All I need is to see you. What are you wearing under this robe? I'm really, really turned on, you have no idea…"

He bunched up the back of my robe. My breath caught. Everything tightened and throbbed between my legs. When I looked up, his mouth captured mine and everything went into the fast lane.

I slid my arms around his neck. He bent over and lifted me up and my legs wrapped around his hips. He braced me against the wall, his hands squeezing my butt, our mouths open and ravishing each other's.

He moved us down the hallway, still kissing, bumping into doorways with his back, until he stumbled into his bedroom and kicked the door shut behind us. We landed on the bed with him on top. Groaning, he kissed down my neck, his hands working at the knot of my robe.

"This is so good," he mumbled against my skin, pushing my robe open. "You're so beautiful—and sexy. Fuck, Raven. Look at you."

His hands massaged my breasts through the lace teddy, cupping and kneading. My head tilted back, and I lifted my hips. "Am I in trouble, officer?"

He huffed, his thumb pressing cleverly between my thighs. "You like the uniform?"

"Yes," I squeaked.

His head moved lower, and he kissed my belly. "You want to be naughty and I'm...Raven, I'm so happy."

My fingers combed through his soft waves. He talked so much, his words like sunshine filling up my chest. I shivered as he pulled up the bottom of my lingerie. My body was awake and humming, my mind still half asleep.

"Oh," I moaned as his hands stroked between my legs until I was shuddering. I slid over the waterfall's edge, breaking into ripples of pleasure.

He stood up and I heard him unzipping. Clothing rustled as he undressed. "Don't fall asleep on me yet. Babe. I'm so ready. It's been torture every time I can't touch you."

A condom package ripped. I opened my eyes to see him, muscled and lean, staring down at me with hooded eyes. I smiled at him as he crawled between my legs. He thrust into me, his eyelids fluttering closed.

"Yes." He pumped hard, braced up on his arms, the muscles of his back flexing under my hands.

The sliding throbbing pressure coiled deliciously inside me. I looked up and Beau was staring at me, his eyes narrowed. We moved together and I came with deep hard clenches.

Beau groaned, pumping harder, his head thrown back. Our hips locked together. He collapsed on top of me, pressing his forehead against mine.

He wrapped me up in his arms and held me tight. "This is so good," he mumbled against my hair, nuzzling and kissing.

"You're not sleepy, are you?"

"I'm too excited." His hands were gliding over me, down my back and over my butt. "I love your ass." He squeezed.

I bit his shoulder, gently, meaning to tell him to let me sleep. He twitched against me—and it was like a jolt of heat shot between us.

"Oh, babe," he growled. "You want to be a little naughty. I won't forget."

"Maybe." I touched his neck with my tongue and grabbed his shaft with my hand, pumping and stroking. I slid down and put my mouth on him.

He writhed, pulling my hair. "Yes...yes..."

His dick was long and thick, already rigid and pulsing. His long arm stretched across the bed, and he groped around for the packet of condoms on the nightstand. I lifted away when he ripped one open and crawled up next to him on the bed.

"Caboose style," he said, grinning at me while he rubbed between my legs.

He sat against the headboard of his bed and pulled me onto his lap, with my back against his front. I slid onto him, shuddering at the deep penetration. My neck arched while his hands gripped my breasts and he nudged up. The top of his cock struck an intense G-spot inside me.

"So beautiful," he groaned. One of his hands slid down between my legs and his fingers rubbed my swollen clit.

I groaned, in a totally abandoned place, shivering from the scrape of his face against my ear, his hand on my chest and his fingers below while the big drum pounded inside me, louder and higher.

"Yes," Beau said. "Bend over. Now, babe."

We rolled forward together, and I eased down onto my arms. Beau pulled my hips up higher and thrust hard. I screamed a little, pressing my face down onto the bed, riding the wave until I was clenching, cresting before crashing down into a rippling surge. He pumped faster, groaning, then shouted. Shuddering, he planted kisses along my shoulders.

Huffing, he rolled onto his back. "Oh, man. This is giving me chills. Raven. Talk to me, babe. You're feeling this, right?"

His hand grabbed mine on the bed, weaving our fingers together. I turned to stare into his twinkling blue eyes, a smile pulling at my mouth until I couldn't resist it.

"Yeah, I felt it. I'm all melted inside."

He grinned. Then yawned. "I need like five hours. Come snuggle with me?"

I yawned too but sat up. "No. You need to sleep. Having a naked woman around is too distracting."

He pulled me down for a kiss. "A naked you."

"Rest," I said, cupping one side of his face. "And use the bathroom first."

CHAPTER TWENTY-ONE

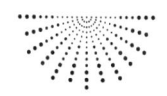

Beau tried to get me to shower with him, chasing me down the hall and then wrapping his arms around me so I spooned against him while he kissed my neck.

I told him to go get some sleep so we could do something while it was still daylight. He squeezed my butt, groaned, then trudged off to take a quick shower.

The clock said it was barely five in the morning. I started coffee and ate a bowl of Beau's granola—the stuff was growing on me. A text appeared from Lauren.

LAUREN

I think I'm in labor

This freaking hurts

Can you come over here?

Tripping over my feet, I raced around seeing to Cheeto and Bubba, showered, wrote a note for Beau, and packed up a bag for myself. Beau needed to sleep so I didn't disturb him —and I assumed it would be a long day of waiting.

I met Allison in the driveway of her house, loading bags into her car. "How is she?" I asked.

"Doing fine—although she doesn't think so." Allison hugged me. "She'll be glad you're here."

Inside, Lauren was pacing around her puzzle table, her face pale and tight. I hugged her, patting her back while she cried a little.

"I hate Derek," she said. "I think I'm done. With him."

Nodding, I guided her to a couch. "Is this what you want to wear to the hospital?"

She stared at me blankly for a moment, her bathrobe gaping open showing her T-shirt and underwear underneath. Then she hunched over, keening, and blowing out through her mouth. She gripped my hand and squeezed hard.

Allison kept us all pointed in the right direction. She had me time the contractions and finally, in the middle of the afternoon, we drove Lauren to the hospital. My heart was ripping open, watching my best friend get through what had to be the toughest day of her life. I couldn't do anything but be there.

Beau arrived at the hospital waiting room with take-out dinners in the evening. Allison stayed with Lauren in the birthing room—pushing was finally about to start. I tiptoed out of the room while Lauren had her eyes closed. I didn't mean to be gone long.

There was a long hallway to get to the visitor waiting room in the maternity ward. It was fairly calm that evening with staff staring down at their work tablets or checking whiteboards on the wall.

Beau was standing with his back to me, his shoulders tense, as I approached. His father John was standing too, with his arms crossed.

"I'm asking," John said in a hard tone, "when you're going

to start living like a responsible adult. Do you think your chief takes you seriously?"

"The answer is never," Beau spat out.

"Ah, what a surprise," John said sarcastically, glaring at his son.

My steps slowed. It was so odd to hear Beau speak like that—a side of him that only seemed to come out around his father.

"I'm not planning to tie myself down to anything or anyone. Life is too short."

I cleared my throat. The bottom dropped out of my stomach, and it was like my chest was trying to fall through. Beau whirled around, staring at me with his eyebrows pinched together.

"Hey," I said, twisting my bracelet around on my wrist. "Lauren's getting close. I better grab my food and head back there."

Beau crouched down and picked up a big plastic bag full of take-out containers. "Tacos," he said, seeming to examine my face. "Mom's are in there too."

"Thanks." I took the bag, looking away from his red face.

"No complications?" John asked.

"Allison says it's going well. Lauren is tired but getting through it." I pushed hair off my face. "Okay, I'm going to head back."

"Raven," Beau said, then swallowed, seeming unsure what he wanted to say next. "Let us know."

Something inside of me had folded up, diminished down into a tidy lump I could shove in a dark compartment. *Get a grip—so what?* I hadn't been taking our fling seriously either.

"Yep." I glanced up briefly at his frowning blue eyes. Then I turned and walked away.

At ten twenty-five that Saturday night, Lauren delivered a healthy baby girl. Baby Athena weighed a smidge over seven pounds.

I cried, and so did Allison. Lauren was exhausted but smiling, staring down at her red little wrinkly infant snuggled up against her chest.

"Will you take a picture on my phone?" Lauren asked me. "I want to send it to Derek."

"I'm so proud of you," I said, dabbing at my eyes.

"And look at this little girl." Allison bent over the hospital bed. "That swirl of hair on her head is red."

Lauren grinned while I took a photo. A big bouquet of flowers came in, delivered in her father's arms. I stepped out into the hallway to make room.

On impulse, I sent the photo of Lauren to Mason, letting him know the baby had arrived. He sent back a heart emoji and demanded updates.

"Hey," Beau said, walking down the hallway with his hands in his pockets.

I showed him the photo of Lauren on my phone. "Are you going in there?"

"The nurse said two people is the max."

We stood there awkwardly, not touching. I tucked my phone away in my purse. "Cheeto and Bubba okay?" I asked.

"Yeah. I've been running back. Think you're about ready to head home?"

My eyes jerked up to his face. He stared at me, his full lips pinched together. I wanted to go back in time to that morning—it seemed like we'd never be there again.

"No. You go ahead. I'll be staying with Lauren for most of the weekend, I think."

He rubbed his face. "Raven, fighting with Dad brings out the worst in me. That argument wasn't about us—"

"Ah," I said, cutting him off. "No. It was just about your life plan."

His head jerked back. "Seriously?"

I shrugged, taking a step back. "Hearing it…changed the way I was feeling."

"Damnit, Raven—"

The door opened and Allison and John walked out, holding hands. I held the door for them and forced a smile onto my face. Beau raked a hand through his hair and slid past me into the hospital room. I followed him in.

"You're an uncle," Lauren said.

Beau's face relaxed into a smile. He bent over, touching one tiny hand the size of his finger. "You all right, sis?"

Lauren's head flopped against the stack of pillows behind her in the inclined hospital bed. "I think so."

"How long are they keeping you here?"

"Overnight, I think. Should be released in the morning."

"You're tired. Is there anything you want?"

Lauren gave him a wobbly smile. "Babysitting—someday. Thanks, bro, for being here."

Beau wrapped them both up in a hug. We helped Lauren put Athena in her hospital bassinet, rolled next to the bed. Lauren collapsed on the bed and shut her eyes.

I dimmed the lights and followed Beau out, closing the door gently behind me.

"Walk out to my truck with me?" Beau asked.

"Yeah, okay."

We trudged through the hallway in silence. I veered to the stairwell and quickstepped down to the parking-garage level, Beau keeping pace beside me. There was a kind of static in my head—I didn't know what I wanted to do.

"I missed you today," Beau said as we walked across the concrete garage. "I miss you right now."

"Thank you for taking care of Cheeto," I said—because I

was grateful but also because I didn't know what I wanted to say to him. "I'm not sure when I'll be back."

Beau blew out his breath, and we stopped in front of his truck. It was dark and chilly outside. I wrapped my arms around my chest.

"Raven, please." He locked his hands together behind his head. "I go on autopilot when Dad starts picking at me—it's an old stupid argument. He's conservative and religious and I'm not. It pisses me off that I'm some kind of crusade for him."

I chewed on my lip. "Okay. But this is why I've been hesitating—we are a part of each other's lives. And I'm not like you."

He nodded, his eyes searching my face. The corner of his mouth twitched up. "You've always been hard on me."

"You've gotten exactly what you deserved."

"Hey." He came a little closer. "I really like you."

I backed up against the side of his truck. "Uh-huh."

"Can't wait to see you every day. Think about you all the time."

I rolled my eyes as he put an arm on either side of me. My heart beat too fast in my chest and my fingers tingled from wanting to slide them up his sides.

"We're living together," Beau said, smiling down at me. "And I love it. I don't want you to go anywhere."

I kissed him—I couldn't help myself. The man could probably talk himself out of any corner. Besides, I wasn't deciding anything, except that he was irresistible.

We pulled away to breathe and he picked me up in a bear hug against his chest. I managed to restrain myself from wrapping my legs around his waist.

"Ugh," Beau grunted. "Damn, that scared me. Don't do that again."

Shaking my head, I laughed and buried my face against his shoulder. "You're always in trouble with me."

He groaned, grabbing my hips. "Stop talking dirty. Dang it, woman."

I pressed my mouth against his one more time then slid down his chest onto my feet. "Are you on the same schedule next week?"

He tucked my hair behind my ear. "No. I'm on day shift. Nine to seven."

"Nice."

"You really have to stay here and sleep in a chair?"

Another night wrapped up in Beau pulled at me like a fast-moving river. When I was with him, I forgot about the criminal trial, my stalker, imploding career, dire financial straits…I sighed.

"Lauren asked me to stay. She doesn't want to be alone right now."

He nodded. "Okay. But Cheeto and I want to see you tomorrow."

I put a hand on my hip. "I'll be nagging you to do yard work."

He grinned. "I'm going fishing in the morning. Forcing myself to wake up early. Not sure I'll have time…"

I pointed a finger at him, but before I could say anything, he grabbed me and kissed me—and I did wrap my legs around his hips that time. A few minutes later, someone honked at us and we pulled apart.

Beau grabbed my hand. "I'm walking you back to the hospital. At least your shithead stalker won't be able to get into the maternity ward."

CHAPTER TWENTY-TWO

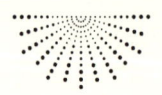

Leaving the hospital late Sunday morning, after Lauren had been discharged, I questioned my ability to drive. I blinked in the bright sunlight as I sat in my car, trying to resist going to my favorite coffee shop—and failing.

A few minutes later, I stumbled through the doors and shuffled over into the line, hoping no one would see me in my wrinkled clothing.

"Raven," Travis Dashiell said, appearing at my side. "It's really good to see you."

"Hi." I plastered on a big smile and kept my arms flat against my sides—why hadn't I remembered to pack deodorant?

Travis was immaculately dressed, as usual, in a Havana blazer, navy polo cardigan and trousers. "I've been wanting to check in with you."

I nodded and wondered why he hadn't. "I'm...excited about the fundraiser coming up. How are you?"

Damn—I'd lost all my ease with him. Actually, I hadn't really thought about him in a while.

He frowned, wrinkling his nose at me. "Not looking forward to that."

"It's going to be fun. And we're counting on you."

The old lopsided smile appeared on his face. "I won't let you down. But it's a favor to you. Can you join us for a bit? I'm with my daughter and mother at that table over there."

I glanced over and saw his cute eight-year-old, Piper, with beribboned pigtails, setting up a checkers board. His mother was also there. Below her bob of pretty white curls, she glared in our direction. Victoria had never spoken to me. She turned away and said something to Piper.

My throat was difficult to clear. "Oh, I—"

"We've missed seeing you in church," Travis said.

"It's been a chaotic time for me."

His name was called at the counter, and he left to pick up his order. Tall and slender, he strode across the room, at ease and confident. His freshly cropped hair was attractive, and also emphasized his slightly floppy left ear. I blinked my dry eyes and forced myself not to stare at him. There was still a piece of my heart tied up with Travis and yet…he didn't seem like the same man.

I kept myself still and my posture straight, aware on some level that he was glancing at me. There had been so many times I'd thought something was happening with him and then it wasn't. We'd had a work relationship that had seemed like more—and the answer to my interior battle not to be a risk taker. The good man I'd been searching for. I'd clung to him for a long time.

From an early age, I'd wanted a pretty home, with what I'd thought of as a lucky family—all together around a big dinner table every night. My childhood had not been that. I'd had a mother who loved me, but she'd been adventurous and fearless. My rebellion was that I wanted no rebellion.

And yet, there was a pirate queen inside me that was restless—like I couldn't escape my DNA no matter how hard I tried. Flipping the bird to a corporate desk job and going rogue entrepreneur was my constant psychological sword fight with myself, the pirate queen flourishing her cutlass and daring me to try. But I knew the risk wasn't worth the reward.

Travis was reserved and cautious—the opposite of Beau. My shoulders tightened. Beau had kept up a steady stream of text messages saying he missed me and wanting to make plans. There was so much affection I was practically floating in it. And yet, I didn't trust Beau to know what he wanted. Travis, on the other hand, was like a scientist contemplating you, and himself, under a microscope.

After I put in my drink order, I made my way over to the Dashiell table. Travis smiled and gestured at an empty chair he'd pulled up to the table between Piper and his mother.

"Hi," I said to the table. "Is it okay if I sit here?" I asked Piper and Victoria.

Victoria gave a quick nod, not glancing away from her phone.

Piper looked solemnly up at me. "Hi, Raven. Daddy said you was coming over."

I sat down. "Yeah, thanks. It's nice to sit down while I wait. I've been at the hospital all night."

"Really?" Piper cocked her head at me.

Travis settled back and crossed his legs. "I thought you seemed a bit tired. Are you all right?"

My grin faltered at being called tired—but who was I kidding? "My best friend had a baby last night. A girl. I stayed in the hospital to keep her company and help look after baby Athena."

"Oh," Travis said, his eyes crinkling. "Congratulations to Lauren."

"Is the baby pretty?" Piper asked.

I nodded. "She's a little red and wrinkly right now. But so tiny. With a swirl of strawberry blonde hair."

"Did you say *Athena*?" Victoria asked, frowning.

"Yes."

Travis cleared his throat. "Really happy for her. Is she home now?"

"Should be. I'm headed there next. How was church this morning? Did you do any singing, Piper?"

"Yes. I practiced. We're doing Christmas songs."

"That's so fun. There's my drink order—see you all soon."

"I'll help you carry them to your car," Travis said, standing up.

He followed me up to the counter. I only had two drinks, a peppermint mocha for myself and Lauren's favorite blueberry smoothie. Travis picked up the smoothie and we walked out of the coffee shop.

His hand touched the small of my back as I beeped my car open. I startled a little and he pulled away.

"Raven," he said, standing close to me. "I've…I'm glad I ran into you."

I opened my car door and set the drinks inside. "Me too."

He gazed down at me, and I thought he was staring at my mouth. "The auction is coming up fast. Next Thursday."

Blowing out my breath, I nodded. "Ten more days. Wow."

"I…" He took a deep breath. "Will be looking forward to seeing you there."

A flush heated my cheeks. That was more than he'd ever said before—and still practically nothing. Travis at his most direct flirting. I couldn't quite make eye contact with him.

"Don't forget to answer Sasha's email question. Angel or devil?" I managed a weak grin at him and fled.

When I pulled into Beau's driveway that evening, there was a bundle of shriveled dead roses on the front porch. The note said *Till death do us part.*

I took pictures, then left the note and flowers untouched and called the police station. Beau and Bubba were gone, not home yet from a fishing trip on the river. Cheeto meowed at me anxiously as I hustled inside and locked the door behind me.

My heart raced in my chest—it seemed like I could feel Rob's eyes on me as I'd found his package. Time was running out. Soon I'd be in front of a judge and forced to demand a jury trial for my criminal case. The whole thing would drag on and on and be more money than I could pay.

Unless...I could draw Rob out. If I caught him, my case might be dismissed before I even went before a judge. I collapsed on the couch and let Cheeto jump on my belly. The problem was, how? I was out of ideas.

The mudroom door opened, and Bubba galloped inside, dashing over to try and dive into my lap. Cheeto flew up onto his cat tower.

"Down, Bubba," I said, pushing him off me and standing up.

Beau was in the backyard, putting away his fishing rods and other gear. I yawned and shuffled into my bedroom to take care of Cheeto's needs. For a moment, I stared at my bed, tempted to crawl into it and tell Beau I'd talk to him later.

Seeing Travis had wobbled my shaky trajectory with... everything. I was questioning staying at Beau's again—which was meant to be temporary after all. Lately, it was as if we'd decided to live together...

"Hey," Beau said, rubbing the back of his neck in the doorway.

"Hi."

"Will you give me a hug?"

After a bare moment of hesitation, I capitulated and walked straight into his arms. They wrapped around me and pulled me in tight. I told him about the dead flowers and calling it in while we rested against each other.

"I'll check the video footage and see if we got his face this time."

I nodded, pulling away. "Right."

There wasn't a clear shot of his face. Rob had put the flowers on the porch with the same hoodie and ski mask covering his features.

"We'll get him," said Beau, closing his laptop.

Blinking, I stared at his haggard face. "Are you okay—did you sleep last night?"

He stood and pulled me up after him, off the couch. "Let's go lie down. I couldn't stop thinking last night."

I let him tug me down to his bedroom, too worn out to resist. And also maybe desperate to stop thinking. Heat coiled under my skin.

We collapsed next to each other on top of his covers. "Wow," I said. "It feels really good to lie down."

His big hand wrapped around mine. "I couldn't sleep last night. Kept worrying about us—that I'd screwed up."

I turned on my side and nestled against him, kind of wanting to distract him from that line of thinking. What was there to say? We'd rushed into our situation, but it didn't change who we were, fundamentally.

"We're still barely an us," I said. "I mean, we don't know what this is."

He pushed hair off his face, his arm muscles flexing. "I really like what we have. It's so easy—neither one of us is trying to be something we're not. I'm...happy. It's making me take a hard look at what I thought I wanted—what I said to my dad."

"Oh?" I rested my cheek on his shoulder.

"I want to give this a chance. I'm not taking anything for granted."

Did he mean it? Would he still feel that way after the first few times it got super tough…For me, there was something so bone-deep right about us while at the same time not being what I'd planned for myself.

Instead of answering, I climbed on top of him and put my mouth on his. My brain was half shut down. What I knew, for certain, was that I wanted to be touched by him.

Beau groaned, his big hands smoothing over my back and butt. We took our clothes off, and he pulled me over him, gripping my hips and arching up into me. It was somehow more intimate than anything I'd experienced—staring down at his blue eyes in the dim room while his hands seemed to worship me.

Afterward, he dozed off immediately with his arm cuddling me in tight. I crawled out of bed to shower and put on a nightgown.

Cheeto and Bubba followed me around the house as I turned off lights and checked the doors. We all settled in Beau's room together.

What was I going to do? Men, it often seemed to me, always wanted a game—a competition and a challenge. When you stopped running, they slipped past you. Maybe my heart was more like a man's than I'd realized.

CHAPTER TWENTY-THREE

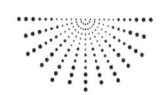

Monday started early with the furnace-like Beau wiggling against my side.

"Hmm?" I muttered, cracking an eye open.

"Did you have this on last night? God. I love this nightgown." His hand glided over my hip, hiking the satin material of my teal spaghetti-strap slip higher on my thighs. Beau shivered.

"What time is it?" I croaked, putting a leg over him.

"Seven." He rolled on top of me, very hard and ready.

I arched into him, completely on board with his mouth teasing my chest and a little giddy with Beau's total enthusiasm for what was happening. He made happy growly noises, kissing and stroking me, and then energetically bringing us both to a bright sweaty blast of Monday morning bliss.

After, we both had to rush to leave the house on time. I wasn't really thinking—except to notice that cohabitating with him wasn't what I'd thought it would be at all.

"I'll grill steelhead tonight," he said on his way out the

door, pausing to pull my back against his front and wrap his arms around me.

I leaned my head back to kiss him. "Yum."

He swatted my backside, grinning at me when I yelped, then hustled out the door.

I had to work hard to wipe the smirk off my face, standing there and watching his truck pull out of the driveway. "Wow." I patted my hot cheeks and stared up at the ceiling. Beau and I were moving way too fast...

The workday very soon completely distracted me from my love life—or should I call it sex life? Outdoors Adventures had a mountain of emails to respond to at the beginning of the week and that fall, it turned out, was a very busy time for them.

River Gorge, and Waterfall Canyon in general, had a booming tourist trade, with scenic outdoor ventures for every season. In October, the wineries and orchards were harvesting, and steelhead and salmon runs had people visiting from all over to fish in the rivers. Micro-breweries had a storied history in River Gorge, and the restaurant and bar scene downtown was packed nearly every night. So many of us came back, I think, not only because of the natural beauty but also the lively small city, made up of fine old buildings mixed with vibrant modern design.

At noon, I raced over to the hospice office to review the battle plan for the bachelor auction with Sasha. We were nine days out. Everything could fall apart so easily...

"The raffle permit," Sasha said to me with her hands shoved into her black curls. "Shit. I haven't heard back from them—I filed for it like fifty days ago."

I nodded, pulling out my phone and searching for a number to call. "The gambling exemption for nonprofits."

"Damn, damn, damn." Sasha stood up and paced back and forth. "We've already sold a bunch of tickets. I was hoping to convince you to go out to the retirement home with me today to sell some more."

"Wait." I held a finger up high. "How much money have we made on the raffle so far?"

"Maybe two hundred."

"Keep it below ten grand and I think we're golden. But I'll call until we get an answer."

Sasha sagged. "I'm never doing this again. What was I thinking?"

"Fun. Hold it together. We've got a list to tackle."

She took a big slug of her coffee. "Oh, yeah—how did I forget for so long? A massive flower arrangement was delivered. For you. They're by the front door."

I glanced up from our whiteboard. "That's odd..."

With my phone to my ear, I walked over to the lobby area and found a huge rose and lily arrangement. The card had a printed message on the inside. It read *I love you*.

My head jerked back. I texted Beau to see if he'd sent the flowers. The florist shop apologized when I called, but, no, they couldn't divulge their client's information—unless it was for a police investigation.

Sasha and I left for the retirement community to speak at their afternoon-tea function. The expensive bouquet stayed at the office, looking impressive on a small coffee table. Beau texted back that he had not sent the flowers—I tried to ignore my deflated heart. Then I called and emailed the police officer attached to my stalking case and my lawyer.

At the retirement home, I did my best to sell the bachelor auction in general and the raffle tickets in particular. Sasha and I put on our angel and devil costumes—she was the angel—and worked the crowd like a couple of Vegas performers at a casino.

"Are you excited?" I shouted.

I had whoops, clapping, and coughs.

"Do you like door prizes, giveaways, and raffles with prizes from the best businesses all over River Gorge?"

"Yes!" the crowd shouted.

"We'll have young bachelors, golden bachelors, and everything in between. We must put these men on the path to love. Are you with me?"

Three pretty ladies waved me over to their table while I was hustling around the room selling seats and raffle tickets. They were like the Golden Girls from that old sitcom my mother used to like. The tall one, with a helmet-like cap of gray curls, sat very straight and tall, examining me with her eyes narrowed.

She tapped a finger on the tabletop. "You don't have enough senior men in the auction."

"We want to nominate a couple," said the smiling lady sitting next to her. She had curly light brown hair. "Hazel and I have bought our tickets. Did you buy yours, Florence?"

The white-haired lady with bright red lipstick cocked her head and smiled. "Can't remember."

"Anyway," said Hazel. "Here's a list of the men we want."

She slid a piece of floral stationary across the table to me. On it was written two names in intricate cursive handwriting.

I nodded, winking at them. "I'll let Kurt and Tom know they've been nominated. They'll do the right thing."

"Good." Hazel tapped the table. "Now sign me up for four of those raffle tickets. I like to win."

∼

THE WEEK FLEW BY, every minute full. In the later afternoons, I took Bubba over to Lauren's backyard so that he could run outside while I visited. Lauren stumbled around, barely sleeping, worried about breastfeeding and Derek.

"I heard from him a little," she said on Thursday, pulling cherry tomatoes off a bush in her garden. "My husband. He likes the baby photos."

Baby Athena rested against my chest with her head on my shoulder while I rocked from side to side. She didn't like being set down. I was getting used to holding the tiny fragile bundle, even though my skin still prickled with nerves every time her life was put in my hands.

"Who wouldn't?" I patted Athena's back. "These bow headbands are so stinkin' cute."

Lauren pushed to her feet, grimacing and putting a hand on her back. "Something's up with him. I finally asked him last night, in an email."

I nodded. "Told him to spill it?"

"Just a 'is everything okay?' And that I've been a little worried because I haven't heard from him much." She pulled off her cloth garden gloves and shoved them in a pocket of her overalls. "I wish I understood him better. Some people don't communicate and it's basically normal—you know what I mean?"

"Sure." I did, but it still never seemed like a good thing. Lauren was an introvert who responded to messages—sometimes not until the next day, but she didn't ghost people.

"It will be better to know what's going on...I think." She stared down at her basket, her shoulders hunched.

"Yes, it will. Are you done? It's getting chilly out here."

Beau still wasn't willing to spend an evening in the same house as his father. Especially, he'd said, at the end of a long work week. He'd worked four ten-hour shifts in a row, and I knew he was run down.

I said goodnight to Lauren, Allison, and John. Bubba jumped into the back of my car, and I swung the door shut.

A man stepped out of the bushes just beyond their driveway. I halted. He gripped his crotch, rocking his hips. A chill shot into me. It was Rob.

Whipping out my phone, I turned on video recording and pointed the lens at him. He vanished.

I got in the car, locked the doors, and started the engine, breathing too fast. Gripping the steering wheel, I tried to rationalize what was happening in some way...He wanted my attention. Why was I getting more scared? It was just Rob. Had he been trying to catch me outside alone?

Pulling out onto that dark country road nearly made me throw up. I called Beau and put my phone on speaker. He wasn't done working yet. I kept the voicemail recording going as I drove too fast. Had Rob attached another tracker to my car?

When I parked at Beau's house, my heart was still thumping. I wanted to curl up in a ball in bed and pull the covers over my head. It seemed like it had been going on forever—I didn't know how much more I could take.

Chuck and AJ were out in the backyard with people over and a fire going. Reggae music was playing, and people were chatting and laughing. I exhaled, relieved to not be alone in a quiet house.

Beau came through the door about thirty minutes later. He dropped his duffel bag on the floor, greeting an ecstatically whining Bubba, then lifted me up in a bear hug against his chest.

"Finally," he said, swinging me around. "Ready to drink, babe?"

"I'm working tomorrow." But I had skipped my girls' night out to see him—and to visit Lauren.

He grunted, letting me slide down his front. "Smells good. You made your boxed rice stuff—and a salad. Nice. Can't decide if I want to eat the food or you first...Oh, spanking. Swat me again. I like."

"It's almost eight. I'm hungry—for food. Oh my God, you're such a horn dog."

Beau pulled his hands out of my shirt to crouch over and greet Cheeto. "Hey, buddy. Let's go cook some fish." Lately, Beau was taking Cheeto outside, with his harness on, the cat riding on his shoulder. Then he'd put Cheeto on a chair while he grilled.

The past few nights with Beau had flown by. He'd gotten home late and exhausted, so we'd had dinner, a drink, and gone to bed—or, rather, gone to pound town in his bedroom. I walked around with a tingly awareness of him from that morning, and the night before. A little flame of heat always burned in my belly, anticipating when it would finally be dark again.

Outside in the backyard, I stood by the firepit while Beau grilled, chatting with the familiar faces of the small crowd. Rob the creep slipped to the back of my mind—I refused to let him influence how I lived any more than I had to. In the morning, I'd fill out yet another police report.

Eventually, Beau and I sat down at the table next to the garage to eat, a little apart from the small party.

"Flaky bangin' fish tonight," I said, shoveling up another forkful.

Beau petted Cheeto up on his shoulder. "The grill was working with me."

"We should go cook for Lauren and your parents this weekend. They're all exhausted over there."

Beau put his fork down and picked up his beer. "Lauren could come here."

I took a sip of my wine, staring at his set face. "Is it... partially about us? You don't want your parents to know?"

He pushed a hand through his hair. "I think they've guessed."

"Right."

"But I don't want to talk to them about it. My father... pressurizes everything. I don't react well...I'm afraid of screwing up. With us."

I took a deep breath. "All right."

We cleaned up dinner, Beau teasing and kissing me until we were making out against the counters. The worry didn't leave me, though. It lingered. Another mess I had to deal with. The bachelor auction was less than a week away and I wasn't sure what I wanted Beau to do. I didn't understand why he wasn't ready to talk to his dad about me. Probably, I wasn't a person that mattered enough to him to compromise for.

CHAPTER TWENTY-FOUR

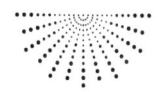

Friday afternoon, I walked out of the KIRG local country-music radio station sweaty and wondering if my on-air interview about the bachelor auction had completely tanked my reputation as a reputable spokesperson. How had we started talking about chest hair?

I turned my phone back on as I jogged through the freezing wind to my car. There were a pile of missed messages from Lauren.

> LAUREN
> Any chance you can come out?
>
> Sorry, you're working. And I'm always taking you from Beau. Sorry. I'm a shitty friend.
>
> Actually, I'm a little desperate...
>
> Call me?

My head drooped forward—I had a feeling she'd heard from Derek. I dialed her number.

"Hi," she squeaked, sniffling, the baby crying in the background.

"I'm on my way. The radio station made me turn off my phone. Just saw your messages. Should I pick anything up?"

"Mom's sick. She's staying in her room trying not to pass it to us. I don't know—couldn't sleep last night."

"Okay." I drummed my fingers against the steering wheel, staring out at the trees in front of the parking lot. "I'm going to stop at home first and change out of my work clothes. Check on the animals—not sure if Beau has Bubba..."

Lauren cried, blowing her nose and gasping. "All right..."

"You heard from Derek, didn't you?" Might as well get it out, so it didn't start her crying again later once she'd calmed down.

"He..." She gulped. "Met someone. Wants a divorce."

I blew out the breath I'd been holding. "Damnit. I'm sorry, Laur. That freaking asswipe—does he have any idea what you're going through?"

"Said he waited until after the baby came to tell me...how did he meet someone already?"

"No idea. Probably by being a liar. Damn him."

"What—I can't think—this changes everything. What am I going to do?"

I started my car. "Live your best life, that's what. Screw that asshole—he doesn't deserve you. Or Athena. Hang on, I'll be there in forty."

~

"What's going on?" Beau asked, leaning on the doorframe with his arms crossed, watching me pack a bag in my bedroom.

"Hey, I'm glad you got back before I left—"

"Left?"

"For Lauren's. Your mom's sick and Lauren's...really struggling. Derek wants a divorce."

"Oh, shit." He scooped up Cheeto and put him on his shoulder. "But they're only ten minutes away—why sleep there?"

"Okay," I said, standing up and putting my hands on my hips. "Your sister has hardly slept since the baby came home. Athena's fussy and needs to be fed like every three hours."

He put his hands up and took a step back. "That's rough—"

"It's hideous. Your mom is the one that knows what's up but she's quarantining in her bedroom. And working a full-time job the rest of the time. They're all in shock over there. Your dad hides in his office and flinches every time the baby cries. Nobody's sleeping well."

"Oh." Cheeto rubbed his face against Beau's stubbly cheek.

I stumbled forward and wrapped my arms around him, burying my face against his chest. "Wish me luck?"

He rubbed my back, exhaling a big breath. "I'll come too. And cook."

"Thank you." I kissed his chest.

"Do me a favor?"

"What?"

"Don't let us get pregnant. I need more time."

I smiled up at him, my heart leaping ridiculously. "Yeah. Me too. But she is pretty cute. When she isn't crying."

"You're cute." He leaned down and kissed me while Cheeto's tail twitched by my ear. Pulling back, he frowned at me. "Stop teasing me and go. Bubba and I will meet you there."

I had a hard time letting him go. Stepping away, I straightened out my shirt. I picked up my bag and forced myself to march out the door.

When I arrived at the Martins', Lauren was pacing in the driveway in her pajamas, a rainbow knit cap on her head, and pink bunny slippers on her feet. Athena had her eyes wide open, little face peeking out of the many layers of her bundle.

"I'll get an apartment," was the first thing Lauren said to me. "Start over and start fresh."

Carefully, I took Athena and put her against my shoulder. "No decisions today," I said. "Or for a while. Ready to go inside?"

Lauren inhaled shakily. "My life is garbage. I'm not cute anymore. My parents hate me. And I'm screwing up you and Beau—it's wrong. Everything I do is wrong."

"Hey, no. Not true. Is anyone cute after not sleeping for a week? We're going inside now. Beau is coming over. You're going to shower and put on fresh pajamas. Then eat and go to bed. That's it. Let's go. It's cold out here."

Wiping her face, she trudged inside next to me. "I had to give up on breastfeeding. Too stressed for my milk to come in." She sniffed, her face crumpling again.

"Well," I said. "It has its upsides, right?"

"Yeah." She grabbed a tissue from a hallway table and wiped her face. "Bottles are in the fridge. There's a warmer on the counter. Takes about five minutes."

We stripped the layers off Athena inside the very warm house, and Lauren showed me her feeding and sleep schedule taped to the fridge. To me, bottle feeding was an improvement over Lauren spending all her time breastfeeding, but I knew she was upset about losing the health benefits and closeness with her baby. She was still agonizing about it. I kept my mouth shut and learned her bottle system.

"Go." I pointed at the stairs. "Beau and I have everything covered. Your dad is home soon too."

She picked up the cup of tea she'd made for her mother. "Thanks. I hate being such a leech—I'll make it up to you somehow..."

"Don't worry about it. Just go to bed if you're too tired to come down."

Yawning, she stumbled on the stairs, caught herself with the handrail, then wiped up the tea she'd spilled with the bottom of her sock. I exhaled.

Beau arrived at the same time as his father. They came through the door, stiff and hard-faced. It was such a mystery to me how two individually charming men could have such a difficult time with each other.

"I brought steak to grill for everyone," Beau said tensely. "If I can use your kitchen."

"Fine," John answered, frowning and sharp. "Plenty of gas for the grill." He veered off into his office and shut the door.

Beau's face relaxed as he walked over to me. I was sitting in the big recliner chair and giving Athena her bottle.

"Hey. I made it."

"Yay." I smiled at him.

He leaned over and kissed me softly on the mouth. His father cleared his throat in the hallway. Beau pulled away and raked back his hair.

"I'll do baked potatoes and veg from the garden," Beau muttered.

"Great."

Athena dozed off and didn't finish her bottle. I followed Lauren's detailed instructions until I could lay the baby down in her travel bassinet set up in a dim corner of the dining room. I tiptoed out, chest prickling with accomplishment. The baby was sleeping and I was whooping with joy—on the inside.

"Raven," John said, startling me. "Come into my office for a minute. I'd like to talk to you."

"Sure."

I closed the door behind us and switched on the baby monitor connected to a camera trained on Athena's face. She turned her head, and I held my breath. Her eyes stayed closed. I collapsed in the chair facing John's desk.

John cleared his throat. "I hadn't realized you and Beau were...together until today. There's been a lot going on. You've moved into his house as well?"

"Yes. He's been incredibly generous."

He harrumphed softly. "You're like a daughter to me—"

"Thank you."

"Beau has always been wild. We've had more than one upset young woman show up here at the house."

I wanted to speak up for Beau—Harper's behavior had been wrong. It didn't matter to me that he hadn't done everything perfectly right as a teenager. In a way, he'd taken care of her. I remembered him constantly talking her out of her rages, hugging her, and making her laugh. It was too much to explain to his father in that moment. I knew what was coming and I didn't want to argue with him.

"Saying this isn't easy," John said, rubbing his face. "Beau runs away as soon as he's unhappy. He doesn't accept adult responsibility."

I stared up at the ceiling, trying to sort through my roiling emotions. "Beau and I," I said slowly, "are doing really well. It's surprising—to both of us."

He sighed. "He's impulsive."

That was true. I twisted my bracelet around. "I do want a settled life. It was impulsive of me to start something too. But he's a good person."

John nodded. "You're wasting your time. I know I sound harsh, but Beau was born with some privilege and will take care of himself. I'm sorry."

I stood up. "I'm going to go check on Lauren."

He drummed his fingers on his desk. "Did she hear from Derek?"

Stopping with my hand on the doorknob, I chewed on

my lip. John was harsh sometimes with his children, but he really cared. Lauren would have an easier time, I thought, if John had a chance to think through the situation before she talked to him about it.

"Yes," I said, turning to look at him. "He said he's met someone and wants a divorce."

John thunked his elbows down on his desk. He put his head in his hands. "Unbelievable."

"She's...shattered. But hopefully finally getting some sleep."

"Right."

I slipped out the door, my shoulders dropping as soon as I was out of the office.

Upstairs, Lauren had passed out on her bed with her bathrobe on and a towel wrapped around her head, turban-style. I turned out her light and shut the door.

After checking on Allison, I found Beau outside by the grill flipping his steaks while a cold breeze bent trees over in the backyard. Bubba woofed and trotted over to me.

"Hey," I said, putting my hands out over the grill.

"Baby sleeping?"

"Yes." I held out the monitor so he could see. "And so is Lauren."

Beau's eyebrows were drawn together. His messy hair was particularly spiky, like he hadn't been able to keep his hands out of it. "That's good."

"You okay?" I bumped his side with my shoulder.

"Saw you go in Dad's office."

"Oh." I put my hands in my pockets, shivering as the wind hit my back. "I've always listened to what he has to say. He's a sensible man—really different from my father."

"Was it about me?"

I hesitated, wishing he hadn't asked. He knew how his father felt, so why did he need me to confirm it?

"He's concerned," I said carefully, after pausing for too long.

Beau gave me a sharp look.

"With what Lauren's going through, I think he's feeling protective. I'm his part-time foster kid. I told him how amazing you've been."

He rubbed his face. "When we were teenagers, he told me I'd be out of the house if I touched you."

"Wow." I smiled a little, my eyes big.

"Your brother promised to break every bone in my left hand."

"Ha—the left hand?"

"Said that's where he'd start."

"That's my brother. Normal until he starts talking. You and I were mortal enemies—all I did was snark at you and plot my petty revenges. Remember when I put toothpaste and peanut butter on your phone? God, I was awful. Not sure why they were worried."

The sides of his mouth twitched. "Because I liked you. Everyone seemed to know but you."

I chuckled, my hair whipping around in the wind. "Guess so."

"Dad still doesn't trust me to treat you right. Unreal."

"That isn't it." I swallowed, surprised he kept digging us back into that hole. But maybe we did need to talk about it. "Your dad likes to talk about goals—five-year-plans and where I see myself. I think I was the only one really paying attention to him—it felt like a gift, to me."

"Yeah?" He watched me, his arms folded across his chest.

The bracelet my mother had given me was cold against my skin. "My parents...weren't settled. My mom was so strong—risking everything to perform and do theater. But every time we moved, or lived on someone's couch for a while, I hated it. My dream is to have what your parents do.

But you grew up with that and you want freedom. I heard Chuck talking about your clubs and contests in the house—the no-marry club and loudest-sex contest."

He flinched. "Drunken bullshit."

I shrugged. "We're really good together—but your dad's right. Our ideas about the future don't line up."

"Jesus, Raven." He picked up the steaks with prongs and flung them onto a plate. "You sound like him. Arguing a court case. I can't think with all of this pressure." He turned his back to me.

I picked up the plate of steaks. "Should I make you a plate?"

He shook his head. "No. I'm leaving. He always does this to me—I just need a little time to calm down."

"All right." My heart curled up into a ball inside my chest. John had been right. Beau ran away when he was unhappy.

He glanced at me and away. Then stalked out of the yard toward his truck, Bubba at his heels.

CHAPTER TWENTY-FIVE

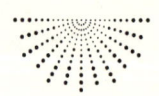

The baby woke up as I was taking my first bite of dinner, crying so pitifully I jumped up and ran to her. That's pretty much how the night went—I did the best I could but probably made a dozen mistakes.

Beau storming out sat on my chest like a sore. I tried watching television but kept going over what he'd said again and again. Giving up, I paced around the house with Athena on my shoulder, patting her back while she slowly digested her tiny portions of formula.

I set up an air mattress in the dining room close to Athena's travel crib, determined to let Lauren sleep. John focused on dishes and checking on Allison. He seemed unwilling to risk staining his nice dress shirt, or something, with the baby.

When I checked my email, there was a message waiting for me from Travis.

Hi Raven,

It was really good running into you at the coffee shop last weekend. I've missed you. Did I tell you that? I meant to. Also wanted to ask if you'd meet up with me. For a walk or a coffee.

I get caught up in my routines—of being a dad and working. Change, even a new schedule, throws me off. It's a rut and I've been stuck. You're so bright and quick, always moving and adapting. I've felt like a snail in comparison.

So perhaps asking in an email is how I can catch up to you long enough to finally say I'd really like to spend more time together. Will you meet up with me?

Travis

Reeling, I sank into the couch cushions, staring up at the family-room ceiling and holding a sleepy Athena against my chest.

"Doing all right?" John asked, briefly glancing away from his sports show to look at me.

"Yeah," I lied.

He yawned. "I'm headed up. See you in the morning. I'll make waffles at eight-thirty."

"Great. Goodnight."

He shuffled off to the kitchen to rinse out his wine glass. I watched a football player cartwheel in the end zone after a touchdown on the replay highlights. Was Travis serious?

I read the email again. He wanted to meet up for coffee—was he deliberately not saying a date? Friends did coffee. He'd been friend-zoning me for the last six months and I'd thought I was stuck there.

Did I miss Travis? He was intelligent, insightful, and a great listener. There used to be chemistry there for me, but Beau had subsumed all of my physical needs lately. I closed my eyes, my skin flushing, trying to block out the last week in Beau's bed.

Athena went back in her bassinet, hopefully for a slightly longer nighttime stretch. I crept off to the downstairs bathroom to change for bed.

My phone vibrated. I answered the call, taking a deep breath. "Hi."

"Hey," said Beau. "How's it going over there?"

I rolled my eyes—was he going to pretend like nothing had happened? "Athena's fed, sleeping, and has a dry diaper last time I checked. Sounds like such a minor thing but it's like I passed an exam. Scared I'll sleep through her next feed up. Am setting an alarm on my phone."

"Lauren's still passed out?"

"Yeah. And your mom's really coughing up there. Says she's okay."

"Thank you. For doing this for them."

"Yep." I pulled my pajama pants on one-handed.

"You're mad at me, aren't you?"

"No. I'm disappointed," I said in a shrill voice. "Come on, that was a joke."

"Uh-huh."

Well, he'd caught me on that one—it was only half a joke.

"Did you calm down?" I asked.

I could practically hear him shoving his hand through his hair. "Not really. I miss you. It makes me kind of lose it, thinking about him turning you against me."

Scoffing, I dug my toothpaste out of my bag. "He didn't do that. I already knew who you were. And we didn't talk about you anymore."

He breathed into the phone, and I heard Cheeto purring. "What's happening tomorrow?"

"We're distracting Lauren. I'll take her to your house. And

for a walk, if it isn't too cold. I think I can kit her out to travel for a few hours."

"Yep. I'll fish in the morning and cook in the afternoon."

"Win the fins," I said.

He sniffed, then swallowed—probably a beer. "Your bachelor auction is coming up. You're pulling me out, right?"

I stared down at my jar of cold cream—the same brand my mom had used. She'd always had a soft spot for Beau.

"No. Your picture has been advertising this thing for weeks."

"Raven. I don't want to go on a date with someone else. It's dishonest."

"No, it's fundraising."

"Babe, come on."

"It's too late. Think of yourself as a devil. Or as the bachelor, like that show on television."

"What?"

"I'll talk you into it more later. Sweet dreams."

"You're so mean sometimes. Why does it turn me on?"

∽

Lauren rushed down the stairs at four in the morning. Athena had just woken up for a bottle and I was blearily testing the warmed milk against my wrist.

"Raven," Lauren gasped. "Sorry—how did it go? I didn't mean to fall asleep."

I yawned. "On schedule. Is okay. I'm…go sleep now."

Lauren hugged me. "Thank you. I feel like I live in my body again. That didn't make sense—never mind. Go sleep."

At ten that morning, I forced myself out of bed and went downstairs for coffee and hopefully a leftover waffle. I found a plate with my name on it in the fridge.

In the family room, John had his arm around Lauren. She

leaned against his side, wiping her face, with Athena resting against her shoulder. I sagged against the kitchen counter.

"Let's get out of the house today," I called to Lauren.

She nodded, her mouth turned down. "I'm taking you out to lunch. And let's go to a craft store. I'm trying knitting—or maybe crochet. Not sure."

"Very ambitious."

It took a couple of hours to have all the gear packed, the car seat ready, and everyone dressed for a chilly and sunny October day. Athena fussed a bit in her car seat, then fell asleep, sucking on a pacifier.

"Dad said I should stay with him and Mom," Lauren said in a wobbly voice, staring out the passenger window. "Save money to buy a house."

"He's so great."

She sniffed. "I hate asking so much of them."

"Well, you'll just have to take good care of them when they're a couple of golden raisins, watching the news all day and shaking their heads at the gadgets."

"What?"

"I'm a little tired."

She rubbed her face. "Yeah. It hit me today—I'm going to do all the things by myself. Dad said try to buy a house and I thought, right, when I'm married. Now I'll be divorced. With a baby. My dating life is over. Single dads are hot. Single moms are sad."

"Whoa. Are you serious? Get your head out of that misogynistic sinkhole."

"How can I trust a man around my daughter?"

"Carefully."

Lauren yanked tissues out of her purse. "Why did I assume everything would work out? I thought I was a little bit smart. Now I know I'm a naive idiot."

"You are smart. And hot. With a good job. But most of all you're you and that's enough."

She had her face covered, hunched over in the passenger seat. I zipped into an open parking spot in front of the yarn store, then put an arm over her shoulders.

Obviously, being a parent changed everything. Yet, at the same time, it was so Lauren. She'd rather be at home, digging in her garden or baking a pie, than out socializing. There wasn't a doubt in my mind that she'd be a great mom. I hopped out of the car to set up the stroller.

By the time we went to lunch, Lauren had bought soft wool yarn for a knitted hat and a cross-stitch kit that created a picture of a chicken. It all passed by me with zero temptation—sewing clothes had crossed my mind a time or two, but I didn't have the patience.

I ordered a loaded bacon burger at the brewery restaurant and an iced coffee. "We should do a sip and see," I said. "Show off your beautiful girl."

Lauren put the bottle she'd warmed up under the bathroom faucet in front of Athena—whose face was scrunched up like she was considering crying. The nipple made it there in time. "Maybe—"

"Before Christmas. Your mom decorates everything so cute—yes. A holiday sip and see. I'll talk to Allison, once she's feeling better. Cookies and spiked coffee? Mulled wine and fruit platters..."

"Celebrate my divorce?" She frowned down at the table.

"Loud and proud."

Huffing, she glared up at me for a moment then her face relaxed. "There's no stopping you once you go into party mode. I'll think about it. Probably is best to rip off the Band-Aid."

"Nobody's going to be on his side—that's for damn sure."

"Yeah, I suppose so." She took a sip of her iced tea. "Tell me about you. How are things with Beau?"

My heart squeezed. "I don't know. It's Beau. Everything's great until suddenly it isn't. And…Travis has noticed I'm not there anymore. He wrote me an email last night saying he misses me and wants to spend more time together."

"Whoa." Lauren shifted Athena in her arms. "Do you still…I mean, it used to be like you couldn't see anyone but Travis."

"I—don't know. His mother is a cactus. I sat with them for minute in a coffee shop last weekend. She lives in his house… Or maybe he's in hers? I'm not sure."

"But have you told Beau?"

"No. There's barely anything to tell."

She gave me a look.

"I told Beau he's doing the bachelor auction. And, yeah, I'll tell him I'm thinking about meeting Travis for coffee. Beau will stop talking to me and storm off."

"He really likes you." Lauren put Athena over her shoulder and patted her back. "I made him swear to leave you alone in high school. It would have screwed everything up."

"Huh." I twisted the napkin around in front of me. "Surprised I didn't know how much he wanted in my pants."

"You liked him too."

"It's all kind of blurry for me. Mom…" I turned to stare out the window at the bright blue river curving below us. My mom had died and I'd shut down. Then been recreated as a girl without a mom.

The cancer had come for my mom during Beau's senior year, and she'd died shortly before he'd left for college. I'd clung to Lauren and Allison and survived from one moment to the next. Even a decade later, I crumbled every time I tried to remember that time.

"Yeah," said Lauren. "That was really rough."

I nodded, my throat tight. My mom had been fierce and hilarious, and I'd always been a little upset with her for not being more sensible. She'd seemed to love me unconditionally.

"But you and Beau—you're like a match. Energy wise. I don't know. Not sure I trust my gut anymore…"

"I want to get through the bachelor auction. Spend this week with you and take a breather."

Our food came and Athena needed a new diaper. Then a couple people came over to our table to say hello and have a look at Lauren's baby. By the time Lauren had eaten most of her fish tacos, she was droopy eyed.

"I've gotten used to an afternoon nap," she said, trying to sit up straight.

"Want to go home?"

"No. Beau's. I'll lie down in your room for an hour and be back in business."

I texted Beau and then we loaded up, after the stroller and I came to an understanding, and drove over. Beau was there, hosing off his raft in the backyard while Chuck and AJ kicked around a Hacky Sack.

Beau met us in the driveway and lifted Athena's car seat out while Lauren and I grabbed her bags. His T-shirt was tight on his big shoulders. He smelled a bit like the river, and soap, and popcorn. I liked it way too much.

Cheeto meowed from his tower. I paused to scratch his head, then rushed ahead of Lauren to tidy up the cat mess in my room. I stripped the hair-covered comforter off the bed, scooped the litter box, cracked the window, and swept the floor before I'd let her go in.

Beau sat on the couch cradling Athena, giving her a bottle while Cheeto perched on his shoulder and sniffed. He glanced up and caught me smiling, staring at him with my heart in a puddle at my feet.

"Okay," Lauren huffed, "stroller's set up like a bassinet. I have diapers. Bottles are in the fridge…"

"There you go, girlie," said Beau. "Fell asleep swallowing."

"Put her stomach on your chest and her head near your shoulder," said Lauren. "Keep her upright."

"For how long?" asked Beau.

"About twenty minutes." Lauren yawned.

I picked up my comforter and headed for the laundry room. Bubba followed me. It was like Beau and I had switched pets.

"Sorry about the dipshit," Beau said to Lauren. "He's lost my respect. You'll be better off without him."

"I keep telling myself it's better to do it now instead of later."

"Yeah. Hang in there. You'll get through this."

"Thanks. Dad wants me to stay with him and Mom. Can you believe it? I thought he'd be tough-loving me right through the door."

"That's good."

I tidied up the kitchen, catching glimpses of Beau with the baby whenever I could. He was so at ease, supporting her weight like he'd burped babies a hundred times, careful and gentle with his hands. I didn't want to take my eyes off him.

A little while later, Lauren took the baby into my bedroom. Beau found me in his office, sorting through my clothes in the closet.

"How are you?" he asked, propped against the doorframe with his arms crossed.

"Tired. And wired. I've had a lot of coffee."

He stared down at the ground, his eyebrows pinched together. I knew what was coming—he was sorting out the words to say the hard things.

I dropped the hanger in my hand and crossed the room to press my body against his. He inhaled, his hand on the small of my back pinning me closer.

Our mouths met, and need jolted through me. We sidestepped further into the room, our mouths moving ferociously, and he snapped the office door closed.

I slid my hands over his back and chest, shivering when he went straight for the zipper of my jeans. He pulled his mouth away, then stripped off my shirt. My pants and underwear were yanked down my legs while I kicked off my shoes. I hopped on one foot so he could free me from my tight jeans.

"Want you so much," Beau murmured, walking me back against a wall. "Babe." His fingers pushed between my legs, pumping in and sliding out to rub between my folds.

"Yes," I moaned. "I'm ready."

He pulled a condom out of his back pocket. How long had that thing been in there?

"It's new," he said, as if he'd read my mind. "Just for you."

Then he kissed me again and lifted me off my feet, erasing the five inches of height difference. I wrapped my legs around his hips, and he gripped my thighs and braced my back against the wall. We both gasped when he thrust inside in one hot glide so that our bodies were pressed all the way together.

"Yes," he hissed, resting his forehead against mine.

I closed my eyes, lost in the ride, arching into him when he ground against me. He pumped hard and we both panted. Something hanging on the wall fell down and clattered on the floor. I didn't care. It was fast and his hands were rough on my thighs.

"Ah," I gasped, loud, finding my release in a bursting twist of shockwaves and blasts of tingling heat.

Beau finished too and I cracked open my eyes to see him

—the slope of his shoulder and the muscles in his neck. His cheek pressed against my temple, the bristles almost soft after a few days of not shaving.

He put me on my feet. "You're so pretty," he said, leaning in for a kiss.

"You're so strong." I watched his arms, wondering if he'd hurt himself.

He grinned at me. "Not as tough as it looks. When you're motivated."

Somehow, I wasn't surprised he was experienced at banging against a wall. We dashed across the hall to clean up in the bathroom, our post-sex ritual.

"Come rest with me a minute," Beau said as I tucked the front of my shirt into my pants.

I followed him down the hall, holding his hand, totally dreading what was coming next.

CHAPTER TWENTY-SIX

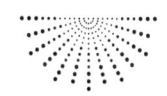

Both of us collapsed on his messy bed. It was so amazing to lie down that it almost made up for the awfulness coming my way.

Beau sighed. "We need to talk about the bachelor auction."

"Okay."

"You really want me going on a date with another woman?"

Staring up at the ceiling, the resounding answer coming from my gut was no. *Hell no.* I shook my head.

"No," I said. "But there's a but."

He put a hand over his eyes. "What?"

"Wait, I have a question first."

"Fine." That was a very grudging fine.

We were side by side and he wasn't touching me. It seemed all wrong. The bed was our happy place—we should be doing this somewhere unconnected to our daily lives, like a desert of parched land. I rubbed my face.

"Why didn't you say hello when I moved back to River

Gorge?" I asked. Looking back on it, he might have been actively avoiding me for us not to run into each other. River Gorge wasn't that big.

"I saw you a couple times from the patrol car. Dressed up outside a bar."

"Yeah?"

"My last serious relationship ended badly. Typical stuff—she's a little dishonest but we weren't right together. I thought about you a lot after you moved back. Wanted to be ready. Work, the dog, this house, fishing to stay sane…time passed. I don't want to screw this up."

The air whooshed out of me. I teetered on my path, looking over my shoulder. Beau seemed so *there*—and I wanted to touch him so badly my fingers flexed.

"This has blown me away," I said, my voice scratchy. "But it's happened so fast…one day you were arresting me—"

"That wasn't me."

"And the next I was living in your spare bedroom, getting yelled at by your ex. You had that happening and I…had a thing going on too."

He stiffened next to me. I wanted to pin him down with my body, so he couldn't run away, until I could get all the words out. I restrained myself.

"A work thing," I said. "It never went beyond the office. We're friends."

"Are you sleeping with him?" he ground out.

"No. There's been none of that. You're the one I want like that. Okay?"

He didn't say anything, both hands in his hair.

I cleared my throat. "I'm trying to figure it out—for the last half a year I've thought he was it for me, even though he kept me at arm's-length. I ran into him a week ago and the chemistry wasn't there for me but…it feels like a dangling thread. He—might want more now. I need a little time."

"What," Beau spat, "to try him out?"

"No. I'm not going to sleep with him. Or anyone."

He huffed, pressing his fists against his eyes.

"Lauren needs help while your mom's sick. The auction is in four days. A breather might do both of us good."

"A breather." He sat up with his back to me. "And you think I'll put up with this bullshit?"

"I'm not sure you're thinking past sleeping together for a few months. Which is fine. I get not knowing until you're in it."

"Then what the hell do you want from me?" He stood up and glared down at my face.

Love. A life together—plans for the future. At least the willingness to have those things manifest. "I want to figure out if being with you means I'm not going to get what I want."

"What—a bigger house? You're cold-blooded. But, hey, don't worry about me. I'm leaving." He stalked out of the room.

~

Let me know if you want Cheeto out,

I WROTE in a note for Beau on the kitchen counter.

If he can stay for a week or two, I'll stop in once a day and clean up after him. And walk Bubba if he's here. I'll have a paycheck soon— I owe you rent. I'm with Lauren helping while your mom's sick. Thinking about you. <3 R.

I slumped on Beau's kitchen counter with my head in

hands, staring down at my totally inadequate note. Please don't be mad, I wanted to write. And trust me. Ultimately, though, he wasn't wrong—I was definitely screwing up with him.

The comforter I'd washed came out of the dryer at the same time that Lauren shuffled out of my bedroom, yawning, Athena in her arms.

"We've got to go," I said. "Beau's upset with me. He left."

"Oh—no…"

"Will you call your parents? Ask them if they'd mind if I moved in for a week?"

She waved a hand. "They don't mind. But, yes, I'll call right now."

I packed a few bags and moved to Allison and John's, with their permission, saying I was staying for a week to help Lauren.

That night I babysat until ten, when I took a drowsy Athena up to Lauren's room and put her in her crib. Lauren roused from napping and took over the night shift, flashing me a thumbs-up.

And so my evenings became Athena-time and missing Beau. There was too much quiet and stillness and sitting—my mind spun in circles. On Sunday, I texted a photo of Athena staring at her fingers to Beau. A while later he messaged me back.

BEAU

Cheeto's staying. I don't want rent from you. Walking Bubba would be good. I'm 9-7 again.

ME

Thank you. We'll talk about rent later.

He didn't respond. I put my head back against the couch and stared at the ceiling. Saturday nights were casually lively over at Beau's—a fire in the backyard, the grill going, friends over. I suspected Beau had slept with one of the women that regularly came by, and I pressed my lips flat, a burning in my chest. What if he drank too much and did something rash?

Before I went to bed, I emailed Travis. It took a long time. I stared at the screen, not sure what I wanted to happen. Finally, I wrote, *Lunch time coffee Monday or Tuesday? I can meet around noon.*

He wanted to meet on Monday. I walked over from Outdoor Adventures, my jacket zipped up against the biting wind blowing through the gorge.

The steamy inside of the coffee shop was a familiar haven, my favorite barista glancing up and smiling at me. Travis waved from a table close to the door.

"Medium roast, right?" he asked, that crooked half smile dimpling one side of his face. There were two cups in front of him, a plate on top of mine to keep it warm.

"Yes, thank you." I unwound my scarf and took off my jacket.

"How are you?"

There was a chair close to him. I hesitated then sat in the other chair, stretching out my legs in front of me.

"A little tired, honestly. I'm helping Lauren with her baby, and it's been a wake-up call. I never did babysitting." I pointed at myself. "Youngest."

He nodded, still smiling. "I remember. A wake-up call how?"

"How hard it is. The sitting and waiting. She's precious. But messy."

"Piper was such a sweet baby," he said wistfully. "It's easier when they're yours."

"How is Piper?" I asked, changing the subject. The baby thing was a little raw for me—it threw me off. My settled life future plan had included children. I wasn't giving up on that, exactly, but a new wariness accompanied the thoughts.

Travis updated me on the Piper doings, our ritual conversation topic. And why wouldn't it be? He was a devoted father. It was my failing for finding it a bit tedious.

My stomach growled and I wondered why Travis hadn't wanted to have lunch. Perhaps I was reading too much into his actions? I forced my foot to stop tapping and tried to refocus on the conversation.

"I have a question for you," he said, hunching over his coffee a little.

"Oh?"

"Will you be bidding at the bachelor auction?"

I put a smile onto my face. "No. I'll be the auctioneer, most of the time, and one of the MCs. If someone doesn't get a bid, I'll step in for the organization and smooth it over—not totally sure how yet."

He frowned down at the table. Apparently, he didn't know how financially strapped I was. That was fine with me. I stared at his beautiful cashmere sweater and wondered if he could even imagine it.

"I see. I've been hoping it would lead to you and I going on a date."

My belly flipped over, and I sat up straight. That was actual concrete proof that he did want to date me. Why hadn't he asked me out before?

"Wow—I didn't know that's how you felt."

He raised his eyebrows at me. "I...tend to overthink things. And we were working together."

I nodded, sucking in a breath. "Things have changed for me since leaving the hospital. I...reconnected with an old friend. He helped me through a rough couple of weeks."

Travis sat back in his chair. "I'm sorry I didn't reach out. I assumed you'd want privacy."

"I understand."

"So...are you dating now?"

I twisted Mom's bracelet around on my wrist. "I asked for some space this week. Everything was happening too fast. Then I heard from you. I need to figure it out. I guess I'm trying to say that I'm not in the same place. But I really value our friendship."

Geez—*I really value our friendship?* What a cliché. At this rate I'd lose both Beau and Travis.

He covered his mouth with his hand, staring down at our mugs. "I wish I'd...well, I'm realizing I'll be going on a date with a stranger. Instead of you. Can I withdraw—"

"No. Please consider how much this event is helping all kinds of people. It's just a bit of fun. You might be snapped up by one of the seniors attending who wants an outing. Nope—don't make that face. You're going to be fine. And have a story to tell Piper."

"Maybe in ten years."

"There you go. Making teenagers laugh can smooth out all kinds of thorns. You'll be saying, 'Can you believe it, Piper, the whole town wanted a date with me?'"

He groaned. "I can't believe you talked me into this."

I grinned. "I'm that kind of devil. Should we call you an angel? Good and respectable?"

"Yes." His fingers slid over mine. "An angel who would really like a devil in his life."

My skin flushed, all of my awareness on our touching hands. "They might kick you out of heaven..."

The crooked grin I liked so much was back. "Too boring there anyway."

It was so...Travis, I realized, to talk out what could happen and turn hand-holding into a major event. There was a confidence to him in that moment that drew me—as if he could finally enjoy himself after taking the major leap of deciding. Could being together be easy?

I turned my hand under his and squeezed his fingers then slid away. "Speaking of the auction, I have to run and check up on a dozen details. The clock is really ticking this week."

CHAPTER TWENTY-SEVEN

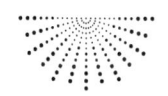

Travis had finally declared himself interested—he wanted to go on a date. I tried to be excited. Instead, it was like a sack of rocks had been dropped on my shoulders.

The rest of Monday flew by. I stopped to check in with every vendor helping with the bachelor auction and fired off emails and social media posts about the event.

My heart skipped a beat when I thought I saw Rob that afternoon, watching me as I hustled to my car. A big truck blasted by on the road, breaking my line of sight. By the time I could see again, no one was there.

I decided to ignore it—I had too much to do. At Beau's house, Cheeto scolded me with a litany of meowing. I gave him a can of cat pate stuff. He scarfed it down like no one had thought to feed him in days. Patently not true since his bag of kibble was nearly gone.

Bubba ran circles in the fenced backyard while I tidied up the house. Beau had left a note for me on the kitchen counter.

Hey. Bubba's been kicked out of his doggy

> *daycare. Again. Thank you for checking on him. I don't want to do the auction. You know you can't force me, right? If I show up, I'm giving the date a chance. Like you're doing with your 'friend' this week. Beau*

My forehead dropped down to the counter. I really hated fighting with Beau—the kind of fight where I'd probably lose everything.

> *I'll try to get Bubba out more tomorrow,*

I wrote on the back side of the paper.

> *That's fair, about the auction. Please come support the event. I'm gambling my career on this working. Raven*

The next day I jogged out of the Adventure Tours office at noon, stumbling over my feet a little. Athena had had a bad night, for some mysterious reason, and no one had slept well. Lauren had gone into the doctor that morning to try and get answers.

My plan was to get Bubba before taking a load of supplies out to the bachelor auction location. He could tag along with me, on his leash, during most of my errands and burn off some of his extremely high energy.

My hand groped for my phone—I had to call the caterer with the newest head counts. My car keys crashed down to the sidewalk.

"Crap," I muttered, squatting down to snatch them up.

A man stepped in front of me from the road. "Oh, hello, Raven."

I yelped and fell back on my butt. It was Rob, smirking down at me with one hand jiggling his pant pocket. I scrambled to my feet.

"Oops, did I scare you?" He put a hand over his mouth and made his eyes big.

Fumbling with my phone, I tried to start it recording in my pocket without him knowing. "Shouldn't you be at work?" I blurted out, taking a step away.

He shrugged. "Got canned—for no good reason. Fuckers. Said I'm 'erratic.'" He did air quotes with his fingers. "Your fault, I think. For messing up my head."

My chest was so tight it was hard to breathe. My eyes scanned everything around me—we were basically alone on that stretch of sidewalk, parked cars blocking us from the traffic whizzing by in the road.

"Listen," Rob said, holding his hand palm-up. "I need for us to happen. You know? It's like this whole thing for me. I'll drop the assault charge. We can start over."

My fingers were freezing. I squeezed my hands into fists and didn't say anything—which had been drilled into my head many times by my lawyer and the police officers. Including Beau. My eyes darted sideways, hoping his patrol car would materialize.

Rob took a step closer, and my stomach clenched.

"I think about you." His upper lip curled back in a weird smile that showed dark coffee stains on his teeth. "A lot. Too much."

His mouth slashed down. He smelled sour and his face was shiny like he hadn't showered in a while. The general grubbiness was new—there were what looked like food stains and crumbs on his jacket.

"Don't be a bitch. You whore. Why the fuck are you doing this? Answer me."

His hand reached for me and my nerve broke. Dizzy and holding my stomach, I veered out into the road, glancing behind me to see if he'd followed. He stayed where he was, kicking at the chain-link fence next to him. I bolted up the hill to my car, trying not to whimper, and flung myself inside. My hand jammed down on the automatic lock button.

"Dang it." I pressed my head against the steering wheel, while I fumbled to put the key in the ignition. Black fuzz crept around my vision.

A shoe scraped on the sidewalk outside and I jumped. I twisted my body to search all around my car. It was a man I didn't know in a delivery uniform. I pulled out my phone—the video recording was still going and had been for a few minutes. Exhaling, I started my car and pulled out onto the road.

Rob had seemed…even more not well than usual. This new version gave me cold chills. I hated being afraid. Hated it.

At Beau's house, I hugged Cheeto and Bubba until my heart stopped racing. I called the police station and left a voicemail for the officer on my case, asking again for them to come inspect my car for a tracking device—so that it would be solid evidence. I filled out yet another police report and emailed my lawyer.

The video recording wasn't much. With the microphone covered by my pocket, all that I could make out was cloth rustling. I emailed it to Mr. Mesh, hoping the crafty old lawyer would have an idea.

My court date was approaching fast—only seven days away. I collapsed on the couch, taking deep breaths, and covered my face with my hands.

CHAPTER TWENTY-EIGHT

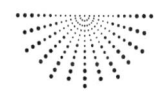

The next day, I picked up Bubba in the morning and took him with me to the Outdoor Adventures office. It was Wednesday and there probably wouldn't be many tourists walking in.

I scolded Bubba—for a lot of things—but particularly for growling at anyone that approached the door. In response, he stared at me with his tongue hanging out. His big amber eyes were watery and kind of vacant seeming.

"Sorry," I apologized to the guide Bubba snarled at, making him leap away from the fishing poles. "I'll take him outside while you load up."

Bubba and I walked out front to a patch of grass next to the parking lot. I scanned everywhere for Rob, my neck twitching with tension, but didn't see anything.

Later, Bubba did better at the hospice office, seeming to appreciate being surrounded by women and adopting his visiting manners. There was a lot of petting and someone actually produced a dog biscuit.

"So. Tomorrow," said Sasha, chewing viciously on a pen cap. "Oh my God. Tomorrow."

I nodded, putting one hand on my hip and raising a fist to the ceiling. "We shall conquer," I bellowed, in what I imagined was a superwoman voice.

"Um. The board keeps calling me—my internship is on the line. They're worried about the tone..."

I flung an imaginary cape over my shoulder and flicked my styled ponytail. "Already signed off. We're locked in—decorations, balloons, banners, prizes, branding...Okay, deep breath. We've taken your idea and run with it. It's different. All the seniors are excited. Cross your fingers that everyone else shows."

Bubba put his head in Sasha's lap. She frowned down at the drool dripping on her cute yellow dress. "Yep," she said, holding up her hands twisted together in a finger knot.

"Now let's head out there with the last of the gear and cheer on the decorating. Did you print out the charitable gambling license?"

"Got it. And the raffle wheel put together. Glad there's going to be wine tomorrow. Might have to sneak in something stronger..."

Actually, I was more jittery than a squirrel and as nervous as a long-tailed cat in a room full of rocking chairs, as my nanna used to say. So, in typical manic over-compensation, I put on cheerful and excited relentlessly, moving too fast, living for when I could cross another thing off my list.

That night at Lauren's house, I poured myself a glass of wine and flicked around the internet to distract myself. An email appeared from Dominic. I chewed on my lip—I'd totally forgotten about him, somehow. How had that happened?

Raven,

Is there still time to volunteer for your bachelor auction? I'm willing. Can donate an evening at my restaurant and club, at the least. I'd be another devil, if you'll have me.

Dominic

My answer was an immediate and resounding *hell yes*. I got to work on adding Dominic to the auction right away, around seeing to a fairly tuckered out Athena—who'd had a bit of a gas problem, apparently, but was doing better.

Then, too quickly to believe, it was the day of the auction. John, Lauren, and I were all in the kitchen at the same time that morning. I sucked down my coffee, scanning emails and the hospice social media accounts, bouncing a little as I stood by the kitchen counter staring at my phone.

"Can I have some of your energy? Please?" Lauren poured herself a glass of orange juice.

I reached over with my finger and touched her arm. "Zap. There you go."

Lauren rubbed her face. "That did nothing."

John glanced up from his newspaper. "Go to the event tonight, Lauren. Your mom and I can manage."

"But—"

"She's feeling better. Get out of the house for a few hours."

"Yes," I said, slapping the counter. "Lauren, I need you there."

Mostly, I needed her to perk up a little and not be so depressed. Dressing up and getting pretty was medicine in my book. Not to mention seeing our brothers on stage could be either hilarious or tragic—and not to be missed.

"But—"

"You have time," I said, pointing at her, "to take a nap and find something to wear. Curl your hair and put on lipstick. No—no excuses. It's happening. You'll sit at a table with

Autumn, Maria, and Kelsey. Hopefully watch them spend a ton of money for a date with a man. And take pictures. I'm off—be ready by six."

~

THE DAY ABSOLUTELY FLEW BY. I spent it at the retirement center, overseeing the ballroom setup with Sasha and a couple of board members that dropped in. River Gorge businesses had shown up to deck out the space with balloon arches and flowers, fruit bouquets and draped tulle, signs for the parking lot, and a hundred other things that—placed all together—were like an adventure park for dressy grown-ups.

"Wow," said Sasha, a hand on her chest. "Gold, plum, and crimson, stacks of pumpkins—and white feathers. Like a wedding and cute Halloween had a baby."

"Like it?" I bumped shoulders with her.

"Yeah." She sniffed, taking off her red-rimmed glasses to wipe her eyes. "I love it so much."

I glanced at a clock on the wall for the thousandth time—two p.m. "Time to dress. I'll check on the caterers one last time. And the building manager. Be back as quick as I can."

At Beau's house, Bubba practically tackled me with kisses then ran in laps around the backyard with his jowls flapping. I made some calls, then had to bring him in while I showered and dressed. Otherwise, he'd bark nonstop at the squirrel in the neighbor's yard.

In the kitchen, there was a new note from Beau, pinned to the counter with an empty beer bottle.

Doing it. I'll try dating someone else and see how I feel.

The paper crinkled in my hand. I sank into a chair by the table, my stomach queasy. Cheeto jumped up into my lap.

"We'll be even," I said, scratching Cheeto's head. Except Beau hated me for having a second thought—was taking it as a rejection.

My heart seemed suspended. There was so much going on in addition to Beau and all of it hammered at me. It reminded me a bit of the time after my mom had died. I'd organized her funeral—as best I could as a shattered teenager. I'd moved several times and had lost my life as I'd known it.

I forced myself to my feet and into the shower. There was too much to do for moping—and if I was going to face Beau and Travis that night, I'd at least look good doing it. I had a glistening black sequin gown with a low-dipping strappy back. Sleeveless, the drop cowl neckline, column silhouette, and floor-length skirt would glam me up enough to match our sumptuously decorated ballroom. The dark shimmering dress tied in nicely with my devil's horns hair attachment.

Hair and makeup nearly done, I jumped when Bubba started barking like the house was on fire. Heart racing, I sprinted out into the living room in my bathrobe.

I got there in time to see Bubba throw himself against the window. One of his paws snagged on the curtain rod and tore it down.

"Whoa," I yelled, running over.

Bubba kept barking, pointing his body toward the driveway like he was about to bust through the wall. I pushed him over enough to see out the window.

A hooded figure ran up the driveway, something metal flashing in his hand. I fumbled for my phone to take a picture, but the bathrobe pockets were empty. He disappeared out of my sight down the sidewalk.

Panting, a hand on my chest, I stared at my car. It tilted

oddly. There was a note stuck under the back windshield wiper with black marker on it. I couldn't make out the words.

I called my brother and begged him to head over. "With floor jacks. I think the two driver's side tires were slashed."

"Shit. Yeah, okay. Poor little car's in pain. I'll be there in a bit. Better shower for your damn auction."

"Don't work on the car in your dress clothes. You can change at the event."

"Pshh."

I filed a police report—taking time I didn't have. Texted Sasha to let her know but she didn't respond. I called the police and the officer wanted me to wait around to answer questions. I told him about the event, talking fast, and shamelessly begged to do it after. He didn't promise anything, grunted, and hung up.

"Dang it." I squeezed my eyes shut and massaged my temples. My momentum had hit a wall—I was off-kilter and had to be pumping up a crowd in two hours.

"Screw it." I stood up and ran for my dress, deciding to pay for a ride. I had to get out of there immediately.

On my way to the taxi, I paused to bend over the note left on my car. *Your pussy is trash. STOP FUCKING HIM.*

CHAPTER TWENTY-NINE

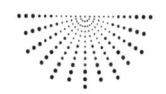

"Raven." Sasha rushed over to me and grabbed my shoulders. "Are you all right? I finally looked at my phone—oh my God. Slashed tires?"

I forced a big smile on my face and waved at one of the Golden Girls, Ms. Hazel, arriving over an hour early. My heart drummed in my chest. The night was here, and I was wound up so tight my neck twanged when I turned my head.

"Yes. To both questions. I'll deal with it later. Let's test the PA system volume again and see if it's loud enough for Ms. Hazel over there."

Sasha nodded at me, her eyes big.

Even with dread sitting in my stomach like bad shellfish, I had to put aside what the stalker had done. My poor car...I squeezed my eyes shut for a moment. There would be time to fret and agonize over the cost later—I'd force myself to forget it if it killed me.

We put on the cultivated play list Sasha had been working on for weeks...romantic upbeat pop music mostly. The bachelors began arriving—everyone except Beau, Travis, and

Dominic. Mason walked in, covered in grease stains. He took one look at my face and veered toward the men's restroom.

The musicians warmed up. Our wine and beer bar opened. Sasha and I brought pitchers of beer to the bachelors' table, welcoming them all. We passed out their gift bags which had luxury shaving kits, chocolate, and nips of whiskey. They'd picked either devil horns or angel halos, which waited for them at their place settings.

"Angel, really?" I asked Mason as he poured his whiskey sample down his throat.

He grimaced, showing his teeth. "Totally," he croaked, obviously not as prepared for hard liquor burn as he'd thought.

I gave all of the bachelors name tags and asked them to mingle with the crowd, and especially potential bidders, during our meet and greet before the auction began.

Travis rushed into the room, pulling at the collar of his fitted tux. He veered to Ms. Hazel and bent over to speak to her.

The room filled up. People were holding drinks, grazing at the snack tables, and taking pictures in the photo booth. Bachelors greeted people at the door and helped them find their assigned seating.

"You look amazing, as usual," I said to Travis, interrupting his conversation with Ms. Hazel because, really, we were about to start.

"No, that's you." He kissed my cheek.

A warm flush spread out from where his lips touched my face. He smelled like expensive cologne and dry cleaning. His hands slid down my arms, his hooded brown eyes warm as half of his mouth turned up in his lopsided smile.

"Thank you for doing this," I said. "Will you come mingle with the other bachelors? I'm about to go up and start gushing about our sponsors. River Gorge has been spectacular."

He nodded, stepping away. "Do I have time for a glass of wine?"

"Of course. There's a server waiting to help you at the bachelors' table. Are you nervous you'll cause fist fighting among the women?"

He raised his eyebrows at me.

"What's that?" Ms. Hazel called. "Someone's fighting?"

"No. Everything's fine," I half shouted down at her.

She gave me a gimlet-eyed stare as Travis headed off. "Keep it civilized, girl. They're men. Not exotic dancers."

I saluted her. There wasn't any more time to wait so I headed up to the front and tapped on the microphone. My heart thumped loud in my chest while I smiled out at all of the faces—staring hard at me.

"Welcome, everyone. While we're all mingling, I want to say a few words about our absolutely wonderful sponsors. This is, without a doubt, one of the best places to live on the planet. I'm so proud to call River Gorge my home. River Front Reality Group has generously provided…"

There was sporadic applause for the many different businesses named. I forced individuals and groups in the crowd to stand up and take a bow for contributing, referencing notes on my phone to make sure I didn't forget anyone.

Public speaking made my pulse beat fast and my skin tingle—I didn't hate it but found myself counting the seconds until it was over. Even so, I gave it everything I had, pulling out all the tricks I could remember to be an entertaining speaker.

Dominic walked in and ambled over to the bar. Heads turned to stare at him. There was just something exotic about the man. His fitted black suit was stunning. The open collar of his white shirt brought to mind James Bond.

I'd put all of my friends at the same table and most of them were sitting down in front of their name cards, grinning, in formal dresses or midi cocktail sparklers. Lauren waved at me from her seat beside Autumn. Still no Beau.

"Have I said yet that you all look remarkably fine?" I asked the crowd. "Go on and let us know, angel or devil. You'll find what you need on your table. We're starting this unforgettable night with an introduction to the incredible organization we're here to support, Riverside Hospice. These are true angels. We honor their work tonight and the many people they help. I'd like to introduce Sasha Barry, the smart and dedicated intern that has made this event happen. Originally from Chicago, we're truly blessed to have this PhD candidate working in our community."

I spoke for a while about all of Sasha's many accomplishments. The crowd clapped politely as she took the stage. She was a bit breathless, but her bubbly energy carried her through. She in turn introduced tall Gail Fraser, the nonprofits acting executive, and Indra Nooyi, leader of the board.

The crowd drooped a bit under the onslaught of speechifying that followed but were too well-behaved to do more than stare blankly. I made sure the appetizers flowed out to the tables.

"Raven," Dominic said, stepping up to me after I'd encouraged another server to get out there and keep the drinks orders going.

"Thank you for coming—really." I gave him a side-hug.

"It's good to see you. Nice event. I'm impressed."

I grinned. "That means a lot coming from a restaurateur. Will you come sit with the other bachelors?"

He followed me over to the men's table, prominently placed so everyone could see them, and I introduced him around. The men were bright-eyed and drinking fast. I asked their server to bring out another round of appetizers.

At last, Indra finished her college-dissertation-style presentation. I'd learned a lot, but my job was to get people in the mood to spend money. After the applause wound down, I went back to the microphone.

"Let's take a short break. Then are you ready for a prize? I think that's a yes. And we have a few hunks to talk about. We'll be back in five, after a song from Sonic Pulse."

The band burst into a rollicking tune. Smiling and waving at people I knew, I made my way over to my friends' table. Kelsey was there without her controlling boyfriend, I was happy to see.

"Raven," said Autumn, leaning toward me. "Who is that tall dark hunk that came in late? Dressed like he has a million bucks."

I waggled my eyebrows at all of them. "Restaurant and club owner. With an obviously wounded heart. Brooding. Only interested in no strings…encounters…"

"Oh," said Phoebe, shimmying her shoulders. She'd been traveling to visit family in Korea and was recently back in town.

Phoebe was a fun kind of person, an artist who liked neon hair colors and wearing faux leather. She was in a tight black-and-red dress and had what appeared to be a short riding whip in one hand.

Lauren swatted me with her cloth napkin. "What's his name?"

I bent toward them, and they all leaned forward. "Dominic. Lockwood."

Kelsey fanned her face with her name card.

"All the bachelors showed?" asked Maria.

"But one." I glanced at the doors and there was Beau,

walking in with a hand pushing through his hair. He looked over and our eyes met across the room. "Here he is now."

CHAPTER THIRTY

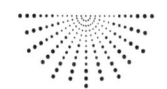

Beau stalked over to the bar, where he was immediately surrounded by attendees wanting to talk to him.

"Excuse me," I said, squeezing through the people so I could take Beau's arm. "We're about to start the auction."

One of his hands slid down my back. Electric jolts shot through me. I dragged him toward the bachelors' table, disengaging my hand from him when we'd stepped out of the crowd.

"I've got to get on stage," I said, scanning him. He still had on his patrol officer pants and boots but had thrown on a black polo—hardly formal attire but it would have to do.

"We need to talk," he said, stepping closer. "I found out some things about your case."

I startled—all of the horrors I was trying so hard to forget about rushed into my mind. My eyelid twitched. Taking a deep breath, I pushed my shoulders back.

"Later," I said. "Drinks and food are waiting for you at that table." I pointed at it and saw Travis staring at us.

Beau nodded, his eyes raking over me and his mouth set

in a firm line. We both walked away at the same time. My heart moaned and held a tissue up to its face.

People were clapping for the band. I rushed up on stage where Sasha waited for me with the brass raffle drum. "Okay?" I asked her.

"Yes." She grinned, sucking in a breath.

"Are you ready to meet our first bachelor?" I boomed into the microphone, standing behind the wooden lectern we'd placed on the stage.

Women shouted and cheered. I glanced over at the bachelor table and saw them wide-eyed and tipping drinks down their throats.

"I have a little surprise for you," I said, conspiratorially. "I'll be projecting a slideshow of these men's social media accounts so we can get to know them. What do you think?"

Laughter and cheering greeted that announcement. I hadn't found dirt on any of the men—they would have been excluded—but I did have almost all of them in their swimming trunks.

"Your brochures have a photo and short description of all of our bachelors tonight. Scan the QR code to see more photos, their bios, and the date packages they've picked for your magical evening. As the bidders are well aware, this has been online for the last couple weeks. However, there's one surprise addition. He's definitely worth giving a second glance."

Sasha took the microphone. "First, let's do a raffle drawing!"

The band did a drumroll. An older lady squealed in the crowd when Sasha drew her number, and then tottered up to the stage. Sasha gushed about the prize provided by one of our sponsors. It was a fruit basket from a local orchard. I flicked on the projector and adjusted the focus.

"Folks," I said, taking back the microphone. "We're going

to start with a man very dear to me. My brother, Mason Brown."

Women screamed in the audience—that surprised me. Mason waved and made his way on stage, grinning at the cheers. I'd found a picture of him, shirtless in front of his truck, darkly tanned skin glistening over all of his bulging muscles.

"Mason is a firefighter and a homeowner. Loyal and bighearted. He can fix nearly anything—saving my bacon more than once. The man has energy to spare. He uses it to renovate houses, work on and ride dirt bikes, and hunt in our great outdoors. His coworkers call on him for his strength, fearlessness, and can-get-it-done attitude."

Mason smiled a little sheepishly while women in the audience hooted.

"Now, everyone," I said, "the critical question. Is Mason an angel or a devil? Place your flags according to how your table votes."

Every table had two flags and a stand, one for angels and one for devils. Individuals voted with smaller flags put at each place setting.

Sasha listed the date package and thanked our sponsors. Mason had gone for go-karts and mini golf at a local family-fun place.

"Mason, is there anything you'd like to say?"

He took the microphone. "Ladies. I might have been dragged into this by my sister here, but you're making me feel pretty damn good. I'm a simple dude with rusty manners. But I know what to do with fire."

More screaming. Mason did a little dance, turning to shake his booty at the crowd. I gaped.

Everyone cheered and it was generally agreed that he was a devil.

"Mason, put on your halo. This man is an angel. And

now," I said, "it's time for our first silent auction. Bidding starts at fifty dollars. Raise your paddles high, ladies and gentlemen. Sixty. Seventy. A lot of interest, I see. How about one hundred?"

Some of my friends were voting—Phoebe, primarily, who kept her arm straight up.

"One hundred fifty. Two hundred."

There were still a lot of hands.

"Two hundred fifty—"

"Five hundred," shouted Phoebe, slamming her bidding paddle down on the table. Lauren, sitting next to her, covered her grinning mouth with her hand.

"Five hundred dollars," I called. "Going once...going twice...gone!"

My gavel banged on the lectern. Everyone clapped. The board members had big smiles on their faces.

Phoebe beckoned Mason. He jumped off the stage, flicked his hair back, and sauntered over to her. She swatted his butt with her whip. He jumped as the crowd twittered.

We had small tables set up on the far side of the ballroom for each bachelor to take his bidder to. Phoebe herded Mason over there, brandishing her whip at him. She sat down at the first table and pulled him onto her lap.

The next two bachelors were lovely older men, who made heartfelt speeches about wanting love and companionship in their lives again. It made my chest ache—I wanted it so much for them. For myself too, and Lauren, and all of my single friends.

"Next," I announced, "is a man many of you will recognize as an active member of our community. Mr. Travis Dashiell. Please come up on stage, Travis."

He stiffly climbed on stage as women cheered and whistled in the audience. My social media photo of him was in a lounge chair, on some tropical beach, holding a pina colada. He glanced at it, his eyes a little sad.

"Travis is a medical and health services manager at our local hospital, where he is respected and valued by all for his kindness, generosity, and support of others. He's a man that believes in integrity and holds himself to a high standard. A widower, Travis is dedicated to his young daughter. They're members of River Gorge Methodist and he's involved with several charities there. He's a deep-thinker with an agile mind. And, last but not least, is a gorgeous dresser."

Catcalls and general hoots of approval. Travis was smiling at me, his eyes warm.

"I can see there are already angel flags appearing on most of the tables. Travis, would you like to say anything to your admirers?"

He cleared his throat, taking the microphone. "This is stunning. Thank you for supporting this amazing organization. I'm an introvert, who probably spends too much time reading, but I'm truly looking forward to what the night has in store for me."

Sasha listed the sponsors for Travis's date. He'd chosen an evening at the local live music venue that also hosted open mics and had a small bar—the same place where he'd rejected me at the hospital's fall employee party.

"Here we go folks. Fifty?" There were a lot of bidders. "Seventy-five...One hundred, one hundred fifty, two hundred?"

I could see Peggy at a front row table, and Marla too, both of them smiling rigidly up at Travis. Maria had her paddle up over at my friend's table.

"Three hundred, three fifty, four hundred?"

Marla dropped out of the bidding and so did most of the other women in the room. Maria flicked her long dark brown hair and smiled cheekily in Peggy's direction. Peggy's eyes were squinted, glaring up at the stage.

"Five hundred dollars." I paused to fan my face. There was a scattering of applause from the crowd. Maria and Peggy both had their paddles up. "Five hundred fifty—"

"One thousand smackers," shouted Ms. Hazel, wobbling to her feet and slamming her paddle down on her table.

"One thousand," I repeated to the startled faces in the ballroom.

Maria's paddle dropped to her table, and she picked up her wine glass, smiling and shrugging her shoulders. Peggy glared behind her at Ms. Hazel, her paddle slowly sinking down.

"Going once…going twice…and congratulations, Ms. Hazel."

Ms. Hazel made a fist and pumped in her elbow. The crowd clapped, everyone leaning over to chatter to their neighbors.

I stepped over to Travis, smiling with my eyes big. "Well," I said to him. "That was unexpected."

He huffed out a breath, pulling his jacket straight. "Not to me. Set that up. I'll be paying the thousand myself."

"My gosh—well, thank you for your generous donation."

His dimple peeked out. "I'm not going on a date, unless it's with you."

I shook my head at him. His words gave tingles of warmth—who knew he was capable of so much romance? "I'm shocked. You're something else, Travis Dashiell."

He grinned. "So are you, Raven Brown."

Our gazes were sinking into each other. Peggy coughed at the table below the stage and Sasha was wrapping up another raffle drawing. Travis made his way off stage.

"Our next bachelor," I said into the microphone, touching

his name on my list with the tip of my finger, "is Beau Martin."

CHAPTER THIRTY-ONE

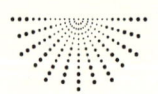

The picture of Beau on the wall, enlarged by the projector, showed him holding up a giant fish, grinning, with a backward baseball cap on his head and his shirt off.

My eyes burned as he stepped up onto the stage and I had to swallow hard. There was a lot of cheering. Beau smiled and pushed his hair back off his face.

"Beau Martin is a patrol officer for the River Gorge police station. He takes pride in never having pulled his firearm. He genuinely cares about our community and finds a sense of achievement in peaceful resolutions to conflicts."

There was a big spontaneous applause from the audience. Beau stood very straight with his fist against his chest.

"He's an outdoorsman who loves to fish, river raft, and snowboard. He's quick to laugh and doesn't hold a grudge. Charming and playful have been used to describe Beau. He juggles projects easily and is well liked and positive at work. To everyone that knows him, he's incredibly generous—a man that would rather give than receive. Beau Martin, ladies and gentleman, is an absolute winner."

Women in the crowd hollered as everyone cheered. Beau's face was a bit flushed as he turned and met my eyes. I inhaled a shaky breath.

Flags were going up on tables across the ballroom. The majority of them voted angel.

"Beau, is there anything you'd like to say?"

He stepped close to take the microphone. His fingers covered mine for a moment.

"Hey," he said. People whistled. "I didn't know what to expect tonight. River Gorge is a special place. Thank you for coming out. And for thinking about your neighbors. As a famous man said, 'All we're ever asked to do in this life is to treat our neighbor, especially our neighbor who is in need, exactly as we would hope to be treated ourselves.' Do you know who said that?"

Beau leaned forward, cupping a hand against his ear.

"Mr. Rogers," a few people shouted.

He nodded. "Mr. Rogers also said, 'There are three ways to ultimate success: The first way is to be kind. The second way is to be kind. The third way is to be kind.'"

People stood up from their tables, clapping. I blinked hard, a hand on my heart. It was a moment I hadn't expected. There was an arresting presence to Beau on stage—a man who knew who he was, completely comfortable in his own skin.

"Thank you, River Gorge. I'm honored to be here."

"Wow," said Sasha into the microphone. "Thank you, Beau. He's chosen for his date a romantic dinner at our local winery, Mountain Vista. With over fifty acres of planted grapes, nestled between two volcanoes, with unparalleled views from the main tasting room, Mountain Vista Winery is a River Gorge top ten destination."

Beau stood very still, not smiling, his eyes on the boards of the stage. I'd picked that date for him weeks ago—before anything had happened between us—because I'd thought it was the best one. I pressed my lips flat, a burning in my chest.

I cleared my throat. "Folks, Beau couldn't decide if he was an angel or a devil. I think he should trust the judgment of this audience. His actions speak for him."

They had, overwhelmingly, voted him an angel. I wished his father could have seen it.

"Do I have a fifty-dollar bid?"

Paddles went up all over the ballroom. Beau rocked back on his heels.

"Do I see a hundred? Yes. One twenty-five? One fifty? One seventy-five?"

The crowd was engaged as I talked fast. At the friend table, I saw Lauren had her paddle up.

"Three hundred. Do I have three twenty-five? Three fifty. Three seventy-five. Four hundred."

Most of the paddles had gone down, including Lauren's. My heart twisted as I saw my friend Autumn, the gorgeous blonde, with her bid unwavering. A couple of other women were battling it out with her, but I knew that look on Autumn's face. She wouldn't give up.

"Four hundred seventy-five. Going once, going twice, gone."

Without a glance back at me, Beau stepped off the stage and went to Autumn. She stood up and they walked off together toward their private table.

I'd been quiet for too long. People cleared their throats in the audience. Sasha took the microphone and did another raffle giveaway. I trembled, my jaw clenched tight, as I walked to the far back of the stage for a sip from my glass of water.

We still had four more bachelors to auction. One of them

was a local celebrity, a morning news anchor for a big city television channel. He brought in a very high bid.

"And now," I announced, "is Harry Watson."

Elderly Mr. Watson had nominated himself. The only recent picture I could find had him scowling at the camera with a birthday cake full of candles below him. He frowned out at the audience, one of his eyes twitching.

There wasn't a single bid. I stared at Sasha, my eyes big. *Why hadn't we planned for this?*

"Hold on a minute," I said, whipping up my phone from its cubby in the lectern and glancing at the screen. "I'm seeing that we're missing a few women—the ones I think would have been bidding now."

I stared hard at the Golden Girls in the audience, raising my eyebrows at them. They smirked back at me, clearly having none of it.

Swallowing, I said, "I will be placing a bid on Mr. Watson. Thank you to River Gorge Coffee for sponsoring my favorite way to spend part of an afternoon. Going, going, gone."

My gavel banged on the lectern. I plastered on my biggest smile and escorted Mr. Watson off the stage, gripping his arm tight when he tottered on the step down.

"Thank you, dear." He sniffed. "I expect to see you soon."

We were down to our last bachelor. The crowd was merry, the servers rushing to fill drink orders. People were buying raffle tickets and adding on donations with their credit card transactions. The board members smiled warmly at me. All I could do was not stare at Beau, stones in my belly, as he laughed with Autumn.

"Last, but by no means least, is Dominic Lockwood," I announced, back at the microphone.

There hadn't been any shirtless pictures of Dominic—disappointing, since he had a long lean figure that would be easy on the eye. The projector displayed a grinning Dominic, skiing, with a beautiful snowy mountain range behind him.

"Dominic is new to our Northwest community. He came here from New York City, where he decided to retire from investment banking. With a master's in finance from Notre Dame University, he's a highly educated and sophisticated bachelor. Currently, he owns an eclectic and fascinating Portland restaurant called Sidus and the hip Club Invocation. He's a board member of two environmental justice charities. Dominic is a thoughtful, generous man—that obviously needs a River Gorge woman in his life."

The crowd cheered. He was last and it seemed to me that many of the faces out there were hoping for a chance.

"Dominic, would you like to say anything?"

"Thank you. It's only fair to say that I'm pessimistic about love and not likely to settle down. You might call me a devil. However, this has been a surprising night. Thank you for including me. I promise to provide an exciting and special date. And I will double the donation of my bid."

Everyone shouted their approval. Women were hooting and catcalling. Dominic put a hand in one pocket, posed like a runway model, smirking out at them.

"Well," I said. "He's a challenge worth taking on—don't you think, ladies?"

Hollering agreement.

"Here we go—no brawling. Fifty? One hundred? I think we're still way too low. Do I have one fifty? Two hundred, yes, two hundred fifty...three hundred?"

Maybe it was the alcohol or maybe it was the man, but there were still a lot of paddles held high in the air. I hit five hundred. Then six. The field narrowed.

"Six twenty-five, yes, six fifty? I see six fifty—"

"One thousand," shouted Kelsey, standing up at her table.

I closed my mouth. "One thousand. Last chance. One thousand, going, going, gone!"

CHAPTER THIRTY-TWO

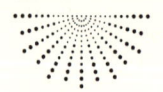

The board members took over the microphone for thank-you speeches. Our band headed on stage and checked their instruments. Sasha and I hustled the lectern and raffle drum out of the way. We stashed them behind the payment table we'd set up by the main doors.

"Everyone," I said into the microphone when the board members were done. "Has this been a great night?"

The crowd let me know it had with clapping and whistles.

"We're going to end the night with dancing and music. Bachelors, I encourage you to take to the floor here, in front of the stage, for the first song."

Some cheering from the bidders' tables rallied the couples up onto their feet. We'd left a small dance-floor clearing in front of the stage and Sasha clicked on the disco ball lighting as the couples sheepishly walked in front of the crowd.

"I didn't rest until I'd secured for you, tonight, the best band in River Gorge. They're in demand all over the Northwest and beyond. Be sure to visit their swag table by the door."

When I glanced behind my shoulder, the lead singer gave me a thumbs-up.

"It's my very great pleasure to have back on the stage, Sonic Pulse!"

I hurried off the stage, picturing the hundred and one things I needed to do, and almost ran into an old man blocking my way.

"Oh." I screeched to a halt.

Mr. Watson glared at me. "It's time, Ms. Brown, for our dance."

"Ah." I gave him a big smile. "Right. Give me one minute. Be right back."

He opened his mouth, appearing ready to argue with me, but I rushed off. I had to check on the payment table and make sure Sasha was ready to take credit cards.

Sasha and I frantically organized ourselves on the banquet table. We pulled out a charitable contribution receipt for each bidder and set them out on the table.

"Harry Watson's staring at us," Sasha mumbled at me. "Are we supposed to do something?"

"Oh crud." I waved at Mr. Watson. "He wants a dance with me. I'll be back."

Mr. Watson and I made our way onto the dance floor. He held his arms up in a classic ballroom hold, standing very erect. I stepped forward and pressed my palm against his, hoping I'd remember how to waltz. Luckily for me, Mr. Watson was a confident dancer, transforming into someone that seemed about twenty years younger.

He smelled a bit like rubbing alcohol and those chewable stomach pills. We shuffled in closer to the other older couples. I noticed Travis close by, dancing with Ms. Hazel.

"How soon can you pick me up for coffee?" Mr. Watson asked. He sniffed in what seemed like a disapproving way.

"Not sure. My car…needs repairs. I won't forget. That's my favorite coffee shop."

"Oh?" He squinted at me. "Must be good."

"The best."

He nodded, seeming satisfied.

"Excuse me," said Travis, who had maneuvered closer to us. "Can we switch? I have an idea for Raven."

Mr. Watson frowned. "Well—"

"Of course," I said, stepping back.

Both of the older people glared at us. I grinned at Travis and stepped up to him, putting my hands on his shoulders. We did a sideways shuffle away.

"How are you?" Travis asked.

I forced my smile to brighten. "There's a lot going on—but the auction has been a success. I wish I could make myself enjoy it a little more. I keep jumping to what's next."

He smiled down at me. "You seem like you could take on anything. It surprises me when you're stressed out like a normal person."

"Ha. I'm a very normal person."

We gazed at each other. I tried to keep my thoughts present—to enjoy what should be a triumphant moment. My inner pirate queen should have been holding up her cutlass and shouting victory.

"I have an idea," Travis said. "Why don't we do a double date? Perhaps Saturday afternoon?"

"Oh—yes. I'd really like that."

"In that case," he said, his eyes twinkling down at me, "can we finally exchange phone numbers?"

"Of course." My mind turned over possibilities—all revolving around my car. Could I borrow Lauren's? She might have a doctor's appointment…I decided to text with Travis about it later.

The music wound down and we stepped apart. I did my

best not to glance openly at the other dancers—even though I'd known where Beau was the entire time. Harry and Hazel were still locked together and appeared to be in a heated argument.

"Work tomorrow," said Travis. "And Piper is probably waiting up. This has been…more fun than I thought it would be."

I grinned. "I'm glad."

Peggy waved at him from one of the tables. "Oh," said Travis. "I should say hi, shouldn't I?"

"Yes. You definitely should."

He sighed. "Right. Good night. I'll see you on Saturday."

"Good night."

I slipped away before Harry Watson could grab me. At the donation table, two board members and the head executive had joined Sasha. I veered off to find Lauren.

She waved at me from the friend table. I collapsed into the empty seat next to her.

"Phew," I said. "That's done."

"Look at Kelsey," Lauren hissed close to my ear. "They're totally pressed together."

Kelsey and Dominic were having a moment—staring into each other's eyes, his hands low on her back and her arms looped around his neck. He bent over and whispered something in her ear.

"Wow. Score for Kelsey—I didn't know she had it in her."

"Right?" Lauren cleared her throat. "Beau wanted me to tell you an officer did the report on your slashed tires. After Mason jacked up your car, they took the two damaged wheels off and dropped them at the tire store."

"Oh. That's amazing."

My eyes slid over to Beau. He stood very close to Autumn, bending over to listen to her with a smile on his face. They looked like a matched set.

"Where's Mason?" I asked, trying to distract myself.

Lauren shrugged, pulling on her earlobe. "Phoebe was, um, very flirty."

"Where's Maria?"

"She left. I should get going too. Can you leave yet?"

"No. I think Sasha will drop me off later. Better see this through."

"Back to my baby—I miss her. Can you believe it?" Lauren pushed to her feet. "This has been great. I never want to leave the house, then I'm usually glad when I do."

I began the epic process of clearing out the ballroom, loading up Sasha's little car until it was stuffed to the roof. There were volunteers to thank and present with the gift bags Sasha and I had put together.

The band was nearly done with their set when I noticed Autumn giving Beau a long hug by their little table, off in the dim part of the ballroom. Swallowing, I forced myself to march out of the ballroom, the raffle drum tucked under my arm.

Down the hallway, something clattered then banged. I halted, worried someone had taken a fall.

The door of a supply closet opened, and my brother stumbled out followed by Phoebe. She smacked him on the butt with her little whip. He grinned and said something to her over his shoulder. I hurried away. That had been far more than I'd wanted to know.

I was waylaid by my high school literature teacher, Ms. Jacobs, and congratulated on the event. She'd helped me get through my awful senior year—and prevented me from failing out of school. I hugged her, my eyes burning, and attempted to tell her how much I appreciated her.

We both smiled, embarrassed by my gushing, and said goodnight. The band was done by the time I beeped Sasha's car unlocked.

Grunting, I squeezed the raffle drum into the backseat of her little hatchback. Footsteps approached nearby. I looked up and Beau was staring at me, his arms crossed.

"Hey," I said. "How was your night?"

He shrugged. "Good, I guess."

I closed the car door and locked it. "That was beautiful, what you said on stage."

He pushed a hand through his hair. "Lauren tell you about your car?"

"She did. Thank you—so much."

"Found out about those flowers sent to you at the hospice office." He glanced over his shoulder at a group of people walking to their cars. "Come over here."

I followed him down the sidewalk, away from the crowd of people. He turned into a dim little garden with a path.

"Not my case but I snuck a look for you. Those flowers were sent from a dead man."

"What?"

"Man named P.L. Barnes. He died, recently, somewhere in the area. Of old age, it appears."

I rubbed my forehead. "Another thing that doesn't lead back to Rob. Damnit."

"You saw him, today, in my driveway?"

"He had the ski mask on and the dark hoodie pulled up. But it was him. He surprised me in the street this week. Said we should be together. He looked bad—dirty. Lost his job."

"Jesus."

He pulled me against his chest, and I wrapped my arms around his waist. I panted, my face in his neck. Beau's reaction to what Rob had done brought it all back and my chest squeezed down tight.

At the same time, it was Beau, his hands sliding low on my back and then his mouth pressed firmly on mine. We both made hungry noises. I wanted him to push me against a wall.

He pulled away and we gasped in breaths. "Come home with me, Raven. I'm done with this bullshit."

Oh, I wanted to. I closed my eyes, trying to think. "Bullshit?"

He took a step away. I opened my eyes and stared at his back.

I cleared my throat. "When's your date?"

He shrugged. "Maybe next week."

"I'm—I hated seeing you with her. But…I'm going to Lauren's tonight. And on a date Saturday."

He whipped around and glared at me. "Travis Dashiell. Makes sense it would be him. All you can see are dollar signs."

I crossed my arms. "Not true."

"Forget it. I'm done. We're through."

He walked away.

CHAPTER THIRTY-THREE

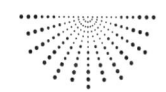

"Are you all right, Raven?" John asked me Friday morning.

I'd caught a ride with him into town. Hopefully, I'd have my car back that afternoon.

"Didn't sleep well last night. A lot's been happening."

He nodded. "Have you updated your lawyer about everything?"

"Yes, by email. The arraignment is next week."

My stomach clenched. I needed more proof against Rob, badly. There still wasn't concrete evidence that he was the one stalking me.

"Mm. Have you talked to the neighbors around Beau's house?"

I sat up. "No. I'll do that."

Fridays were always busy at Outdoor Adventures. I slouched in my chair, drinking black sludge out of the terrifying old coffee maker I'd found on the back counter. The hairs on the back of my neck were on end, sure Rob was watching my workplace. I stayed put in the office.

Grimly, I tried not to think about Beau—he'd already kept

me up all night. I called the tire store about my wheels and they said it had already been taken care of. My chest seemed like it was full of thorny brambles. Had he fixed my car for me?

At noon, I dashed out the back door, with the hood of my jacket up over my head, and ran down to a bus station next to the busy road. A bus came a few minutes later and I hopped on, not caring that it wasn't the right one as long as it carried me away.

Out of the window, I saw Rob, scratching his face next to the fence up the hill. I collapsed into a bench seat, wrapping my arms around my chest. Clearly, I needed to buy another stun gun.

At the hospice office, I was wrapped in hugs and congratulated on a successful night. I tried to take it in—it was supposed to be a win. It was all I could do to control my antsy twitches.

We wrapped up loose ends and plastered socials with thank-you messages. I said my goodbyes to everyone, promising to stay in touch, but sensing it was time for me to move on. Sasha offered to drop me off at Beau's house.

"I can't believe it's over," she said as she drove. She'd dressed up in a cat costume for Halloween.

"Right? October has flown by."

She smiled at me. "I'm going to miss seeing you in the office."

"Me too. But there's a group of us that meet up on Thursdays downtown for drinks. It started as a networking event for women—still is. Mostly, we buy cocktails."

"I'd love that. Text me?"

"Will do. Yay."

We said our goodbyes in Beau's driveway—where my car sat as if nothing had happened, all four tires fully inflated and the jacks gone. Beau's truck wasn't there and the house was missing Bubba's racket inside. They were off fishing somewhere, most likely.

Cheeto and I spent a while cuddling. I cleaned up his cat room and left him eating his favorite chicken liver pate. There were so many things I needed to do—find a place to live chief among them. My shoulders seemed weighed down by slabs of ice.

I knocked on Beau's neighbor's doors, keeping notes on my phone as I went. Only an older woman, that didn't hear well, answered. She hadn't seen anything.

That night I asked Allison and John if I could stay longer.

"I'm sorry," I said, "I know it's a lot—"

"Of course you can stay," said Allison. "We want you here as much as you're willing to be. You've been a huge help with the baby. We should be paying you."

"Yes." John refilled my wine glass.

I smiled, slumping against the counter. "No payment. Thank you."

Travis and I texted a little that night. He asked if I'd like to meet him at his house and pick up our elderly dates together in his Lexus TX. I agreed to come at three in the afternoon.

In the upscale neighborhood close to downtown, Travis's house sat on a big corner lot, perched up high on the hill with a view of the river and mountain. It was one of those landmark homes that stood out with big, beautiful trees and lovely shaded garden beds. The house had been built at the beginning of the twentieth century, a sprawling two-story with arched gables and bay windows, surrounded by porches, sunrooms, patios, and trellises.

I knocked on the front door, then bent over to pick up a tiny shoe that had fallen onto the front porch, next to a carved jack-o-lantern. Travis opened the door, wearing slacks and a knit sweater.

"Hi," he said, his eyes crinkling with his smile. "You look gorgeous."

"Thank you." A little flushed from his compliment, I hesitated, thinking he'd kiss my cheek again.

He only held a hand out to enter.

"It's finally sweater-and-boot weather," I said. "My favorite. Did you have a fun Halloween last night?"

"Piper was a Thing Number 2. Lots of candy. You?"

"Oh, I stayed in. Was a diehard trick-or-treater as a kid, usually dressed as a pirate."

I followed him inside. Warm oak floors and creamy walls set off a collection of gray and beige furniture. The old thick woodwork trim everywhere had been painted white and the house was obviously thoroughly updated for modern living.

"Your home is lovely." I smiled as he glanced around as if seeing it again for the first time. "No wonder you like to spend so much time here."

"In my office, mostly. Still writing."

He'd told me a little about his book projects. There was a memoir about his wife, and some fiction he worked on.

"Would you like something before we go—a glass of wine?"

"Harry and Hazel will give us a scolding if we're late. Don't they sound like they belong together? I wonder what Hazel's holding against him…"

"Oh, right." He rubbed his cheek. "I'll grab my keys."

I followed him into the kitchen, unashamedly glancing around at everything I could see. "I found a tiny Mary Jane doll shoe on the porch. Is there a good place to leave it for Piper—like speared to the top of this mandarin as if it's been hiking?"

"Sure. Or on the counter. She's with her cousins today."

Apparently, we had his house to ourselves. Unless his

mother was lurking somewhere. If she was, I hadn't heard a peep.

We talked about his daughter and the hospital. I didn't bring up Rob, my slashed tires, the court case—any of it. I didn't want to burden him or our fledgling date.

Picking up Hazel and Harry was almost a relief. I could make small talk all day long, but I kept holding back from teasing or joking with him. I didn't know why. *I'm tired.*

"You two, huh?" Hazel asked us as we drove to the coffee shop. "This why you had me shut out all those bidders?"

"That's right," said Travis.

"Could've had your pick." Harry sniffed.

I grinned at Travis. "I guess he did."

He gave me that crooked smile.

"Are there bathrooms at this place?" Hazel called out. "What is it—an open mic?"

"Can't you relax?" Harry snapped.

"There are bathrooms," I said.

Hazel glared at Harry. "Why am I sitting next to this troll? I'm supposed to be on a date with Travis."

"Here we are." Travis swung into a parking spot. "Raven's favorite coffee shop."

"Can't drink coffee. They'll have tea, I suppose."

We escorted our two dates inside and got everyone settled at a table with drinks. Travis had an urgent call from his mother about Piper. He excused himself and rushed outside.

"What's the matter?" Hazel asked me. Did she do anything but fire out questions? "Don't you like him?"

I startled. "Of course. He's great—there isn't anything that I don't like."

Hazel shook her head at me. "Got somebody else?"

"Are you a retired attorney?"

She blinked. "No."

Harry flapped his hand at her. "Let the girl figure it out herself. Travis is a catch, isn't he?"

"Definitely." I sipped my latte. "The real question is, why aren't you two together? All those fiery arguments…"

They both gave me dour glares. I winked at them and pushed the plate of pastries closer to their side of the table.

"I've asked her," Harry said, darting a look at Hazel over his held up cup. "She told me no."

Hazel pursed her lips. "I'm not anybody's second choice. You'd just asked Natalie."

Harry huffed but didn't answer.

Actually, after a little adjusting, I found them both endearing. They wanted to know all about my family and patted me consolingly for losing my mother young, and my grandparents. They'd both had spouses die. Hazel had children, and grandchildren, that visited. Harry had none.

Travis rushed back in. "Sorry—Piper had a fight with her cousin. Then fell down and was hurt. I think it's okay now."

"Bathroom, Raven." Hazel held out her hand to me. "Bladders only get smaller as you age."

Eventually, we shuffled everyone to the Old Cannery Concert Hall. It was a bit surreal being back there—like it had been a different lifetime.

Travis pulled out his phone and checked it often. Even though he was distracted, he was such a pleasant man to sit next to—very nicely dressed, his posture upright, and well-mannered. Why did it still seem like we were at work together?

"Are you worried about Piper?" I asked him quietly as we sat in chairs outside waiting for the first performer.

He nodded. "My mother wanted me to leave. She's…well, she's very protective of Piper."

It seemed like there was a lot going on there. "She wanted you to cancel our date?"

He frowned, as if realizing he'd said too much. "No. It was the accident. Anyway, I know I need to get out more."

"Are you..." I swallowed. Then I forced myself to go on. "Are you ready, do you think? To have a woman in your life."

"Oh." His mouth twitched up a little. He reached out and took my hand, holding it in his. "Yes. It's been five years."

"Right." I squeezed his fingers. That was a long time.

"I...well, I hate dating. When it doesn't work out, I mean. There was someone, a few years ago. We lasted three or four months."

People edged past us to open seats. Harry and Hazel were in the front row and we were in the back—a feat I'd barely managed to pull off. I took a sip of my wine, picturing dating Travis and realizing he would probably be very slow to get into the bedroom.

"What happened?" I asked.

"Nothing bad." He took a sip of his water. "We had a lot of differences, and I began to feel like her project. She was ready to push things along and I...wasn't."

"You take things slowly."

He stared into my eyes. "Does that worry you?"

"A little." I twisted my bracelet around my wrist. "Life is happening pretty fast for me, right now. My next job search will have to be broader than River Gorge. I'm not sure I can afford to stay."

"Ah." He put his hand on his chin.

An a cappella group began singing "Mr. Sandman" on stage. I didn't want to leave the Waterfall Canyon area, move for a job to some new city with no friends or family. And then there was creepy Rob. Taking a deep breath, I shook out my hunched shoulders a little.

Travis and I didn't have another chance for an in-depth conversation. We cheered on new performers. It was a nice afternoon, sitting outside in bright sunlight with fall color in the plants on the forested slope above us.

Even so, it was like I had a chunk of ice in my belly. I had to force myself not to fidget. A decision was barreling at me and I couldn't dodge it any longer.

CHAPTER THIRTY-FOUR

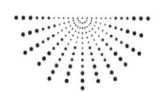

"Dinner's at six," Harry reminded Travis and me between performers. "Best get us back to the home so we don't miss it."

Hazel had already made her way inside to the bathrooms. When she was done, we loaded everyone up and made the short drive to their residence. Travis and I separated, with our dates, to walk them inside.

"I'd like to see you again, Ms. Raven," Harry informed me, scowling. "You let me know."

I dipped my chin, suppressing a smile. "Would you like to come to my father's birthday party? It'll be at the bar he manages. Probably rowdy."

A rare smile lifted up Harry's craggy face. "Yes. I'd like that. Call me with the time and date."

Nodding, I waved goodbye and made my way to Travis's SUV. The last week of not enough sleep was crashing in on me all at once. I swayed a little and had to lean against the side of the car. Mostly, I really wanted to put off what was coming next.

Travis rushed out. "I forgot about dinner. Let me call my

mother and check in on her and Piper. Then we can make plans?"

"Sure," I said. "Let's drive to your house first."

We got inside his Lexus, and he put in earbuds for his call. I stared out my passenger window as he drove and talked, trying to give him the illusion of privacy.

There wasn't much to glean from his jilted half sentences, except that his mother was not happy about the change to everyone's schedule. Travis calmly agreed to call her again and hung up.

"Here we are," Travis said, parking in his driveway. "What's next?"

I closed my eyes for a moment. My stomach constricted. The world sort of tilted sideways like I was inside a hamster wheel being tossed around.

"Can we sit on the porch?" I asked, my voice hoarse. "We need to talk."

"Oh…right." He nodded, his face serious.

Pressing on my belly, I got out of the big car and made my way up onto the porch. I'd always wanted to sit on it. Wide enough for an outdoor furniture set, the painted covered porch stretched grandly along one side of the house. There was even a porch swing.

We each sat on a wicker chair. A lovely view down the hill toward downtown stretched out before us. My nose stung, horribly. I gasped in a breath through my tight, burning throat.

"Raven, is this…" Travis cleared his throat. "Are you ending us already?"

I reached out and took his hand, hating the expression on his face. "I'm sorry. What we've had has been wonderful. I really care about you. But things have changed for me in the last month. I'm not in the same place that I was while I worked at the hospital."

His hand gripped mine back hard. He looked away from my face, staring down at the gray deck boards. "Because of Beau."

I startled, surprised that he knew that. "Yes."

Beau was not the person I'd imagined a life with—and it probably wouldn't work out. I'd always wanted to control my own destiny. Redirect the sails even if I couldn't control the wind.

My parents had been reckless risk-takers, impulsive, and always chasing their desires. It turned out I was more like them than I'd realized.

"Okay." Travis was a little shaky. He gasped in a soft breath, putting his free hand over his eyes.

"I'm sorry." I scooted closer to him so that I could bring our hands against my chest. "We could have had a wonderful relationship. You're everything I wanted."

He pressed his sleeve to his face. "I waited too long. Neglected you when you needed help. Life is passing me by."

Patting his clasped hand, my mouth trembled. "I recklessly jumped into an intimate relationship. It turned into something more. And now…it's not right to walk away. For me or him."

He nodded. "I see."

I let go of his hand to wipe the wet off my face. Steering clear of emotions was so much easier than completely cracking open. I was seconds from losing it—jogging off to my car so I could sob until it was all out.

"Is it because I'm a father?"

"No." I took a breath. "Piper is a charming eight-year-old—not a baby. An infant would be tough. I already have one in my life…that's been a shock. Your mother, on the other hand, does seem like a bit of a…dragon."

He huffed.

"It wouldn't have mattered though," I said. "If the timing

had been right. You're a special man. As the bachelor auction showed last week."

Shaking his head, he rubbed his face. "I don't know what those women think they know about me."

"That night, what you did, was the most romantic thing anyone's ever done for me. Thank you. It was...I'll never forget it."

He stood up and so did I. When he held open his arms, I walked into them gladly. We hugged for a long time.

"Goodnight, Travis." I pulled away, wiping my face.

"Goodnight." He reached out and cupped his hand around my shoulder. "I'll miss you."

"Me too."

I forced my feet to move away, stumbling a little on the porch steps. Even as I kept myself from glancing over my shoulder, I couldn't believe I was walking away from him. For the chance to maybe be let into Beau's bed again.

With questionable driving, I got myself back to Lauren's and parked in the gravel side yard. Then I laid my seat back and stared up at the moon, which had risen early.

My tears dried up. The air grew chilly and I began to think about a mug of hot tea, inside, watching a late college football game with the Martins in their family room. It was dim in there—maybe I'd get away without explaining my red puffy eyes.

I'd followed my heart. The pirate queen inside me was calm, staring out at the horizon, waiting for what came next. I took out my phone to text Beau.

ME

> Hi. I'm home at Lauren's. Done with my date. Talked with Travis and we're going our separate ways. Just wanted to let you know.

I didn't hear back from him at all.

CHAPTER THIRTY-FIVE

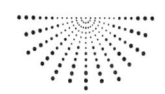

By Sunday morning, I was convinced that Beau was already sleeping with Autumn. I gritted my teeth as I imagined him meeting her at a bar—angry with me and determined to feed me my own medicine. They'd drink. One thing would lead to another...

It was like a dagger sinking into my side every time I went over it in my head. I woke up early, still half dreaming about him grilling fish with Bubba following Autumn around.

Massaging my face because I'd been clenching in my sleep, I tried to let go of the idea of anything working out in my life at that time. I put my feet on the floor and shuffled into the bathroom then downstairs. The house was still dim and quiet. Coffee and television was what I needed to do with myself.

Lauren startled me when I turned on the light. She was pacing with Athena over her shoulder.

"Morning," she muttered, barely getting out the word before her mouth opened, overcome with a giant yawn.

"Good morning. What happened? Did you sleep last night?"

She stared at me blankly for a moment. "Um—yeah, I think we did. Earlier. Heartburn. Maybe. Cries when I lay her down."

"Oh, dear. I'll watch her. Go and get some sleep."

"Really?" Her eyes were closed.

"Yes."

"Thank you. Bottle...thirty minutes ago."

We put Athena down in the bassinet in the dining room and she dropped off into a deep sleep right away. Lauren shuffled out, shaking her head and muttering. I set up the baby monitor and crossed my fingers for an easy morning.

Allison and John came down a couple of hours later, on their way to an early church service and a Sunday brunch with friends. They always dressed up and held hands on their way out the door.

I smiled and waved. Then had to hunch over another mug of coffee. It had been how I'd imagined Travis and I together.

Athena slept for a solid four hours and woke up ravenous. She waved her little mittened hands around as I fed her, staring up at my face, and patted my chin. Something burst in my heart—I got it, the baby love, I really did. I smiled down at her and cooed.

"Well, hello there, angel. Auntie Ray Ray loves you. Yes, I do..."

We went for a little walk around the backyard together with her in the chest-mounted carrier. I picked apples and produce from the garden. Actually, having a baby cuddled up against me was pretty wonderful.

Beau hadn't responded to me, and I wondered what to do next. While Athena napped, I did a job search—the pickings locally were slim and didn't pay well. I texted Beau again.

> ME
>
> Hey. Going to get more of my stuff today around 2. Let me know if that doesn't work. Wondering what you're thinking about Cheeto? Also am talking to your neighbors to see if anyone saw Rob.

After Lauren emerged, I showered and made an extra effort with my appearance—perhaps there was still a part of me ready to fight. The pirate part. It was just a cropped sweater top and jeans, with spotless white sneakers, but I needed a little something to be able to walk away with my head held high. If I got to see him at all.

At Beau's house, the driveway was empty. I parked, then had to put my head down against the steering wheel and take deep breaths. How could it keep hitting me that he'd broken us up? *Dang it. Screw him.*

Pinching the bridge of my nose, I reviewed my notes about the neighbors. If anyone could confirm they'd seen Rob lurking around the street, it would be a start.

I grabbed my shoulder bag and opened the door. As I stood up, I noticed someone approaching on my side and swung around.

"Get back into the car. Now."

I froze. *Scream, damnit.*

There was a big-ass knife pointed at my chest. My throat was pinched closed. My heart rammed my chest. The person rasped in breaths through a ski mask. A hooded jacket was pulled low over their face.

"Rob?" I croaked, pressing my back against the car.

He twitched, crouched over. The knife had a long black blade, the top side serrated like a saw.

I gulped, shaking my head. Pain flared in my chest, and I struggled not to curl over. I pressed a hand hard against my heart.

"Shut up. In the car, bitch."

He lunged at me and I screamed. The knife ripped open a cut on my chest.

"Fuck," he whispered, yanking the knife back. It pulled threads away from my sweater on the curved tip of the blade.

The scratch stung, then became a sharp mind-altering ache, blood flowing out quickly. *More than a scratch.* I pressed a hand on it, my vision blurry.

"Wait," I gasped, edging sideways. He flicked the knife at me again. My heart beat so hard my ears hurt. "What—where is it you want to go?"

"East," he barked. "Fucking away, okay? I can't think."

"Don't do this." A sob burst out of me. "Damnit, Rob. You're better than this."

"Shut up. Whore—"

Beau appeared, sprinting from the backyard toward us. Rob swung to face him, the knife held out.

There was nowhere for me to go but back in the car. Rob's knife was inches from my face. I dove down onto the driver's seat.

I screamed because Beau didn't slow down—he kept running straight at the knife. At the last moment, he dodged to the side and Rob lunged into empty air. Where was Beau's weapon?

Rob whipped around. The blade landed against Beau's arm and slashed open a bloody gash. Beau's other arm flashed up and punched Rob hard in the belly.

Hunched over, Rob spat at Beau's face. Rob dove forward, the blade pointed at Beau's belly. I jolted up and rammed my elbow on the steering wheel.

Beau jumped away fast, angling his body sideways, and the knife cut down the side of his leg. He stumbled back.

I lurched out of the driver's seat so that I stood right

behind Rob. He was bent over with a hand on his gut. I kicked him as hard as I could right between the legs.

CHAPTER THIRTY-SIX

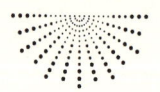

Rob collapsed forward onto his knees. His knife clattered to the ground.

I rushed around him and kicked the knife further away from Rob's hand. He lashed out with a fist and hit me hard on my thigh. I stumbled, gasping, that leg buckling under me.

Beau tackled Rob. He smashed Rob's face down onto the ground. Rob flopped and struggled like a caught fish, trying to kick his foot back. Beau kept him pinned, blood smearing everywhere, until he had Rob's arms held behind his back.

"Grab the cuffs in my jacket pocket," Beau shouted at me while Rob yelled and cried.

I darted forward, leaning over both of their shoulders, and found the cuffs. Beau slapped them onto Rob's wrists.

"Beau," I gasped, "are you okay? God, you're really bleeding." I wiped my wet face on the sleeve of my sweater as I tried to think what to do next.

"I'll live."

He looked pale—I trembled, not believing him.

"Call nine-one-one," Beau said over Rob's hollering. "And look for rope or a zip tie—something to tie his legs."

"Garage?" I yelled, already pushing buttons on my phone. "Tool chest."

I ran to the side door, fumbling with my keys.

"Nine-one-one. What's your emergency?"

"Stabbing." I grabbed a dog leash off the wall.

"Where's your emergency?"

I rattled off the address while I darted out to toss the leash at Beau. The calm dispatcher asked question after question as I ran back inside for the first aid kit.

It was hard to believe that no one else had heard or seen the fight, but the street was empty. I put the phone on speaker as I crashed down beside Beau, pressing a clean kitchen cloth against his leg. His blood was everywhere.

Rob's legs were bound together with the dog leash. He had his face down on the asphalt driveway, sobbing.

"Beau," I yelled, ignoring the dispatcher. "Stay with me—please don't close your eyes. There, sirens! Hold on."

He put a hand on my arm. "You okay?"

"Me? No. No—don't you dare die on me. Why the hell did you run at him without a weapon? Damnit, Beau."

"No time," he croaked. "Tell you later."

"Oh, God. Hold on, babe. They're here." I replaced the bloody kitchen towel with a big sterile gauze pad I'd managed to unwrap one-handed. "What's your blood type?"

"O negative. Get my keys. Bubba in truck—two blocks down…"

"Beau!"

His eyes closed. Police officers ran up the driveway and a minute later paramedics too.

I couldn't track what anyone said to me. My pulse drummed in my ears as I called Beau's name over and over. The paramedics pushed me aside, and then an officer took my arm and walked me away from the action. I whimpered, my ears ringing.

Beau was put on a stretcher and loaded into an ambulance. Sirens wailed as they sped away to the hospital. A paramedic approached me and guided me to the front porch.

"Let's take a look," she said. "Get you cleaned up and bandaged. That slash on your chest needs a doctor."

She cleaned and covered the cut while I cried with a hand over my face. A different person put a paper towel in my hand and suggested I clean some of the blood off. I crinkled it up into a ball in my fist and pressed it against my throbbing forehead.

It was about then that the fog began to clear. I had to pant for a minute with my head down between my knees. I started answering questions.

The interrogation seemed endless when all I wanted was to fly to the hospital. Rob was led to a police car, the leash off his legs and the mask taken from his face. He stared at the ground and didn't fight them.

I found my phone and called Allison. She was frantic and I heard her and John running to their car while she shouted questions. When I choked up, gasping too hard to speak, she promised to update me and we hung up.

"I need to get Beau's dog," I started saying to everyone.

More questions and double-checking that I wasn't going anywhere but the hospital. I refused an ambulance, worried about Bubba. At last, I was released.

Beau's truck keys had gone with him. My car was locked in the crime scene, blocked in by the yellow plastic tape that surrounded the driveway. I rushed inside the house.

Cheeto meowed nervously and jumped out of his cat room to follow me as I ransacked the house searching for another set of truck keys. I had to pause with a fist against my forehead, taking deep breaths, while I tried to think like Beau—not his desk or the key rack…

I ran to the kitchen and pulled open the junk drawer. They were there. I turned and ran to the front door. My phone pinged with a text message.

ALLISON
He's stable. Wants you to feed Bubba.

CHAPTER THIRTY-SEVEN

When I got to the hospital and found Beau's room, Autumn was already there. It had been a really long day of explaining what had happened to me, over and over. I ducked into an empty room.

"Thank you, dear," I heard Allison say, sounding frayed. "I'll tell him you stopped by. But he's resting right now. They had us all leave the room."

"Let me know if I can do anything," Autumn said. "I know people that can get blood stains out of anything."

"Will do. Thank you."

Autumn's high heels clicked down the hallway. I peeked past the doorway and saw her push a button for the elevator.

I sagged with my forehead pressed against a clean whiteboard in the dark room. *He's alive. It doesn't matter.* I wanted to curl into a ball on the floor.

Someone gasped in the doorway and switched on the light.

I pushed off from the wall. "Sorry. I'll get out of your way."

"What..."

"Didn't touch anything but the whiteboard."

I slid past a giant mop bucket and out into the hall. The slash on my chest ached. I stopped in the middle of the hallway, not sure where I was going.

"Raven?"

My shoulders sagged. I turned and Lauren was quickstepping to me, Athena in a carrier on her chest.

"Hi," I said.

We side-hugged, leaning our heads together. Lauren wiped tears off her face. Athena slept, with a binky half in her mouth.

"Are you okay? Is that a bloody bandage on your chest? What the hell is happening today—no, don't start crying. It's okay. Do you need a doctor?"

"Stitches."

"Right. Let's go get you checked in and on the waiting list in the emergency room. Come on. Can't see Beau right now. Better sneak out of here—I'll find coffee. And send Dad for burgers or something. Go. I'll meet you there."

I did what I was told. Lauren knew me well—the last thing I wanted was to devolve into a puddle of weeping so violent I couldn't speak. Had happened before.

She found me ten minutes later hunched over in a plastic waiting-room chair with a clipboard on my lap.

"Oh my gosh," she said quietly, sitting down next to me. She pressed a cup of coffee into my hands. "I haven't seen you like this since...your mom. I'm so sorry. Here, I have some tissue somewhere—hang on."

The coffee was very sweet and creamy. Lauren always insisted on doctoring my straight black whenever she thought I needed it. I wiped my face then turned in my clipboard.

"Any news about Beau?" I asked, sitting back down next to Lauren.

"Not really. He lost a lot of blood—nicked an arterial vein. I saw him for a couple minutes. Was groggy. Asked about you. Had to answer a lot of questions with the police."

I nodded, blinking hard. "I saw Autumn here."

"Oh." Lauren sat up straighter. "She drove by the crime scene tape. Bullied her way in—well, she called me. I told her the room number and she came up."

Exactly what I would have done if the person I was dating landed in the hospital. I glanced away from Lauren's probing blue eyes and dabbed at my face.

She leaned in closer. "Are you worried they're together?"

I nodded a tiny bit.

"No way. He's upset about the Travis thing but that doesn't mean he jumped into something—I mean, besides promising to go on a date." She waved a hand around. "Wait. Talk to him."

The hot coffee down my tight throat shot a little life into my veins. I told Lauren what had happened in Beau's driveway. She gasped and cried a little too. Then Allison and John found us, with paper bags full of delicious greasy food, and I repeated the story again—with the whole waiting room leaning in to listen.

Allison hugged me the entire time, telling me how brave I'd been and thanking me for taking care of Beau. The words, the love, the food, and more of Lauren's disgusting sugary coffee slowly brought me back to myself.

"What about Bubba?" Allison asked. "Beau asked."

"With AJ. In the house. After your text, I found Bubba. And Beau's housemate came home." I'd also slowed down enough to clean the blood off my face and hands and change into different clothes. Once the animals were set, I'd driven Beau's truck to the hospital.

"Beau should be released in a few hours. He's been stitched up."

"Raven Brown?" called out a clipboard-holding medical assistant.

"Here." I stood up.

"Come to the waiting room upstairs when you're done," Allison said.

I nodded, trying for a smile. My leg ached where Rob had hit me. I limped into the labyrinth of emergency room treatment areas.

~

AT MIDNIGHT, Beau was released. I'd been in the waiting room on his floor for about thirty minutes—still trembly and yet struggling not to nod off.

"I'll text Lauren," I said, pulling out my phone. She'd had to leave a few hours earlier with the baby—too much exhaustion and not enough prepared bottle formula.

A nurse pushed Beau out in a wheelchair. He had a sticker on his shirt and a lollipop in his mouth. Our eyes met. I wanted to throw myself against his chest. *Why hadn't I put lipstick on?*

"Be good," Nurse Linda said to him—she'd known him since he was a kid.

"I always try," Beau said.

Allison and Nurse Linda hugged then walked off toward the checkout counter down the hall, speaking about a potluck coming up.

John put a hand on Beau's shoulder. "Well, son, where to now? Your mother and I would like to have you with us."

Beau rubbed his face. "Nah. Dog needs me. I'll go home."

"Okay. Don't scare us like that again. You hear?"

Beau reached up and patted his dad's hand. "Yeah."

John blinked, his eyes shining. "Proud of you. Always."

A tired smile curved up Beau's mouth. "Well, we'll see how you feel in a week or two."

"No," John said, lifting his chin. "We're done fighting. I'm done."

Beau glanced up at him and held open an arm. They hugged, the muscles on Beau's uninjured arm flexing as he gripped his father in tight.

Turning away, I gathered up the lingering trash around the room. There was a lifting in my chest. John had been quiet all night, his face in his hands for long stretches of time. Maybe some lasting good had come out of the disaster.

"Raven," Beau said.

I whipped around and went to him, crouching down beside his wheelchair. John walked toward Allison. I took Beau's hand without thinking. He gripped mine back and didn't let go.

"You really scared me with that stunt." I tried to glare at him.

"Worth it. We caught that asshole." He reached out and tucked hair behind my ear. "Will you take me home? Could use a hand with Bubba and Cheeto."

"Of course."

Allison and John walked us to Beau's truck. They wanted to follow us to Beau's house, but Beau refused, holding up his crutches, and telling them to go home and get some sleep.

"You saw a doctor?" Beau asked as I pulled out of the parking spot.

"All stitched up. Nothing serious." I fought back a yawn.

"Good."

"So, why did you run at him without a weapon? And you came from the backyard, right?"

He nodded, then winced as he shifted his leg. "Figured out what he drove. He traded in that orange Kia Rio for a gray Nissan Versa."

"Aha." I had been on the watch for the orange car.

"Yep. Kept him out of sight for a while. I changed the porch camera to watch the road. Spotted it. He drove by a lot. Bastard parked down the road and watched with binoculars."

I blew out a breath, my stomach flopping.

"He stayed away when I was home—watched from a corner of the park two streets up I'm guessing."

"Wow. That's all he did? Quit his job to be a full-time stalker…"

Beau nodded. "He lost it. I cleared out on Sunday—meant to drop Bubba off at the trainer's place, park far away, then hide in the backyard until you arrived." He huffed, rubbing his face.

"What happened?"

"Bubba attacked another dog. Derailed me bad—other dog's okay. Anyway, I was late and worried. Rushed into the backyard from the property downslope and heard you scream. Saw him holding that knife. Wasn't going to give him another chance to cut you."

I shook my head, my eyes burning again. "Damnit, Beau."

He leaned back in the seat and closed his eyes. "Worth it."

"I don't think anyone saw the attack. Rob's going to try and lie his way out of it."

"Nope. I set up a camera on top of the garage. Can see the whole driveway. It's over for Rob Campbell."

CHAPTER THIRTY-EIGHT

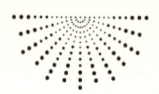

I held the door for Beau as he maneuvered himself inside the house on his crutches, his face pinched with pain. Bubba howled and barked from the basement.

"Let me get to bed so he doesn't knock me down," Beau said.

Cheeto meowed and darted around our feet. "Are you hungry? Thirsty?"

"Thirsty. They fed me at the hospital."

When he opened his bedroom door, I went through the mudroom and opened the door down to the basement—where there was another door, with Bubba scratching and whining behind it.

I knocked on the door then opened it. Bubba paused to try and jump on me, then barreled up the stairs fast.

"Hey," Chuck called. "How's Beau?"

"You both all right?" asked AJ.

I propped myself on the doorway. Chuck and AJ were in their recliners, cords connecting them to their complicated video games. They'd pulled headphones down from over their ears.

"He's on crutches and lost a lot of blood. We made it—really tired. Anything else happen here?"

"Crime lab guys came," said AJ. "I think they're done processing. Nobody's out there guarding, right?"

"No."

He sniffed and nodded. "They're done."

The yellow crime scene tape was still up, blocking off my car and the driveway. I waved goodnight, too tired to ask questions. I stumbled upstairs.

I'd emailed my lawyer while I was at the hospital, so he'd see everything first thing Monday morning—in about six hours' time. There was only one more day before my arraignment in front of a judge. Rob had attacked me, but I wasn't sure it was enough. There still might need to be evidence of him threatening me before I was arrested.

I brought a glass of water back to Beau's room. He'd collapsed on top of his covers, still wearing thin hospital pants over his boxers and with his jacket on. I rested my head against the door, watching him sleep.

Faster than I would have thought possible for myself, I'd totally fallen for Beau Martin, my old nemesis. I pulled covers over him, turned on his bedside lamp, and switched off the overhead light.

He was still mad at me. I didn't think it would be enough that I finally understood my own heart.

∽

Monday morning, my phone woke me up too early with nonstop incoming messages and calls. I dragged my eyes open, afraid someone would bang on the door.

Lauren's messages concerned me the most. Call me NOW. Followed by CALL ASAP. I managed to press the phone icon, my eyes drifting closed again, and held the phone up to my ear.

"Raven—Mrs. Garcia called me last night."

I sat up. "Really?"

"Yes. I thought it was a scam number. She called again this morning—she wants to make a statement about Rob."

"Today?"

"Only if I can catch her before she has to start work in two hours. I'll drop Athena off with you. Be there in twenty."

She hung up. Cheeto rolled onto his back, staring up at me. We'd slept in my little bedroom next to the front door. Very cozy in there, when Rob was in jail.

I limped into the kitchen and started coffee. The bruise on my leg was bigger and more tender than it had been the day before. Bubba trotted out of Beau's bedroom, and I put him in the backyard for his morning run around.

The house had missed me, and I did what I could to get ready to host Lauren and Athena. I texted my boss to remind him that I had taken a couple days off. Lights flashed in the driveway, and after checking it was her, I rushed out in a bathrobe to hush Bubba and help Lauren with the gear.

"Fell asleep in the car," Lauren whispered at me. "I'll bring her in."

I grabbed the portable napper out of the trunk, the slash in my chest aching. Lauren set everything up in my bedroom and loaded the fridge with bottles.

"Remember those awesome breakfast burritos over by your old apartment complex? I'll grab a bunch—Beau loves them."

Lauren didn't appear to have slept much either. I tried to give her coffee, but she only ran out the door, bumping into the doorjamb, worried Mrs. Garcia would turn her away. I was too—and I didn't know if there'd be enough time to get her statement to the judge.

While Athena slept in my room, I paced and returned an urgent phone call from the police department about the flower bouquet delivered to me. It seemed like they wanted another charge to stick to Rob Campbell. Apparently, he'd been stealing money from an elderly great-uncle and then impersonated him after he died. Rob had been connected to the flowers.

Mr. Mesh called me when he got into the office at eight. He wanted a video file from the driveway camera emailed to him right away. And the signed witness statement from Mrs. Garcia delivered to his office.

"As absolutely soon as possible," he said. "He's a hard judge but frugal—we have a chance. Another call coming in. Talk soon."

I drank too much coffee and paced some more. My friend Shep, the apartment manager, had provided a statement and so had his wife. Along with my photos, video, and audio recordings of Rob, and what had happened since, it might be enough for the judge to throw out my case entirely.

Lauren did a video recording of Mrs. Garcia telling her what she had seen. She typed it all out on her laptop and did a translation. Both of them went to a copy store so Mrs. Garcia could sign and date the printed documents. Lauren drove to Mr. Mesh's office and delivered everything.

She arrived back, four hours after she'd left, holding a take-out bag of burritos. "Got it," she said, plopping the bag down on the table. "Food and another strike against Rob."

I leaned in sideways to hug her while Athena rested on my chest. "Thank you. That was beyond heroic. And I think you just saved me from thousands of dollars of legal fees."

Lauren shrugged. "Best friend. That's what we do."

I grinned at her, wiping my leaky eyes—damn, would the crying ever stop? "That's what you do."

"Better sleep now. I ate on the way here."

"Do it. My bed even has the cat hair washed off."

"Awesome. Babe's up for a while?"

"Seems like it. I put her sleeper in the living room. Go. Rest."

After kissing her baby, she staggered into the bedroom.

Athena and I checked on Beau. He'd been up a couple times to use the bathroom but had gone straight back to bed. I'd kept his water glass full and fresh.

He blinked at me when I peeked through the door, and so did Bubba. "Do I smell breakfast burritos?" he asked.

"Yes. Would you like to eat back here?"

"Sure."

I'd never seen Beau so weakened. He struggled to sit up, flinching when he shifted. I tucked pillows behind his back and resisted cupping his face with my hand.

More of the day passed. I had to stop myself from contacting my lawyer and demanding an update. Not hearing anything was destroying my stomach lining.

When Athena slept, I cleaned the house, desperate for some way to burn off my nerves. A new idea started forming in my brain—something I could do for Beau. It would mean risking everything and laying myself bare. A messy gamble.

The doorbell rang. I moved my mop bucket and drying towel into the kitchen then hustled over to the door. Autumn stood on the other side.

"Oh," she said when I opened the door. Her mouth transformed from brilliant smile to shocked frown. "Raven? What are you doing here?"

"Hi. Here comes the dog—Bubba, hush!" I looked up at Autumn. "Can you chat on the front porch for a minute? People are sleeping in here."

"Okay. Here, take this sushi platter. For Beau. Is he in there?"

"In his room resting. Be right back."

I had to shut the door on her so Cheeto didn't dart outside. After checking on the still sleeping Athena, I put the food in the fridge and then went out front.

Autumn had her arms crossed and was staring at the driveway. "That's your car over there, isn't it?"

"Yes. I've been living here. Rented the front bedroom from Beau about a month ago." I collapsed against the side of the house. There weren't any chairs.

"What? Why didn't you tell me?" She stared at me, hurt and shock on her face.

I took a deep breath. "A lot happened to me. It's been awful. When I saw you, I wanted a break."

"What happened?"

"My neighbor started stalking me. He hurt my cat—then I got him with a stun gun. Had to move because he was getting violent. He tried to kidnap me yesterday and Beau stopped him. That's how he got hurt."

She paced back and forth in a tight circle, watching me with narrowed eyes. "There's more going on here. I can smell it."

"There had been. We ended it before the bachelor auction."

She snorted. "Oh, really?"

I held open my hands. "Messy life happening. Nothing about my month has been what I expected. Was arrested. Lost my job. Had a stalker trailing me around and leaving creepy crap everywhere I turned. Beau helped me."

With her hands on her hips, she stopped in front of me. "What about Travis Dashiell?"

"We're only friends."

"Damnit, Raven. What the hell?"

"I did pressure Beau into doing the bachelor auction. But he decided to really give it a chance. I was planning to move my things out of the house yesterday when the stalker attacked. Good intentions, Autumn, from both of us." I swallowed, my ears burning. "But I do…care."

She put her chin up. "I'm leaving. Going to think about this."

I rubbed my forehead. "I'll tell Beau you stopped by. He's really out of it."

She marched away without another word.

CHAPTER THIRTY-NINE

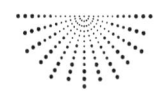

Lauren woke up not long after my confrontation with Autumn on the front porch. I was out in the backyard with Athena and Bubba, taking a hard look at myself.

"You know what? My sleep schedule is totally bonkers. I feel like a vampire." Lauren took Athena, snuggling and kissing her. Athena wiggled and waved her arms.

"Gotta get your sleep." I scratched Bubba's head and caught sight of Cheeto. He stared at us from a window, tapping on the glass with his paw.

"Have you heard from your lawyer?"

"No." My head dropped back and I stared up at the blue sky and fluffy white clouds. "Seems like I'm going to have to go in tomorrow and plead not guilty."

"And sue the River Gorge Police Department." Lauren huffed. "Talk to my dad about it."

"He's helped me a lot." I stood up. "I'll be right back."

I looked in on Beau, Cheeto at my heels as I stood in the doorway. He seemed like he was sleeping. His good arm was over his eyes and the bandaged one was propped up on pillows. My heart twisted every time I saw him like that. I tiptoed away and shut his door.

Cheeto was more than ready to go outside. He hopped up on my shoulders and then slipped, unused to such a narrow platform compared to Beau's. Inspiration hit and I tried putting on a backpack, stuffed with a towel, and found a system that worked for us. Cheeto's claws still dug into the back of my neck—were Beau's shoulders covered in scratches?

"How's Beau?" Lauren asked.

"Not sure—I'm worried. But I keep reading his discharge papers and this is what's supposed to happen. He has a follow-up appointment tomorrow." I helped Cheeto get over to the patio table. "Autumn stopped by today."

"You answered the door?" Lauren covered her mouth with a hand. "What happened?"

"She wanted to punch me, I think. I told her we had a fling that ended right before the bachelor auction. A weird thing happened."

"What?"

"The more she strutted around laying claim to him, the less sorry I was. I mean, I'm ready to fight. Not sure I'm a good person…"

"Yes—to fighting for him." Lauren raised a fist in the air, then started patting Athena's back again. "Wait—I never asked you about Travis. Didn't you go on a date with him a couple days ago?"

"Technically, I was on a date with Harry Watson from the retirement home."

"Uh-huh."

"But Travis and I talked. I told him that I have feelings for Beau."

"Oh my."

"I—haven't handled any of it right. Beau is upset. So is

Autumn. Travis finally takes a chance on me and I shut him down."

Lauren elbowed me. "Travis will be fine. And so will Autumn. Her and Beau would be a disaster. She's a…perfectionist. He's a slob."

I snorted. "That's true."

"What are you going to do?"

"I have an idea. And could really use your help."

∽

Tuesday morning, I put on my best pantsuit, with the hair and makeup I'd wear to a dream job interview. If only the day had that in store. My belly was too tight for anything but dry toast and black coffee. In a few hours, I'd face a judge.

AJ wasn't working his pizza delivery job until the evening and so had been willing to drive Beau to the doctor early that afternoon. I left Beau with his side table stocked with drinks and snacks and his pill bottles in easy reach.

I arrived at the courthouse early. It was all I could do not to gnaw on my hands like a cornered animal. The security guards put me through the weapons screening station, checked my ID, and searched my bag. My hands were sweating by the time I put my shoes back on.

My stomach gurgled as time crept by at the pace of a slug on a leash. I stood up and tried to take a deep breath. It was almost time to go in. My phone rang.

"Morning, dear," Mr. Mesh said. "The motion to dismiss was granted and the pretrial hearing canceled."

I collapsed into a chair. "We're done?"

"Yes, we are. Heard some news. Judge Smith was out of court yesterday. I'm guessing he didn't see anything until this morning."

"Oh my God." I put my head between my knees.

"I'm glad you're all right. Tell Beau Martin good job from me."

"Thank you, Mr. Mesh. Thank you so much."

"Pleasure to help."

We hung up. The big courtroom doors opened to start the day's proceedings. I wandered over, in a daze, to get a glimpse inside at the red carpet and antique wood benches. There was wood paneling on the walls. The air whooshed out of me.

I stepped aside as a number of tense-looking people filed in and sat down on the hard benches to wait for the judge. The clerk at the entrance assured me that yes, I could leave. I walked out of the old downtown building into bright morning sunlight.

Hand a little shaky, I called Lauren. She picked up after one ring.

"What happened?"

"Dismissed—thanks to you. And Rob trying to kidnap me."

"Good. Are you okay? You sound like you aren't breathing right."

"I'm not." I stumbled over to a bench and sat down. My nose stung—I really didn't want to mess up my makeup.

"Breathe."

I fanned my face with a hand. "It's over. Finally."

"Yes."

"Well, except I have to file a petition to expunge the arrest from my record. Dang it."

"Wow. You sounded like a lawyer for a second."

I took a deep breath. "Time to do something really scary."

"Oh?"

"The Beau prank. It's go time. Are you with me?"

"Yes. Everything's almost ready."

A few of the figurative sandbags I'd been carrying around slipped away. I stood up and straightened my jacket. It was time to hazard all. My inner pirate queen held up her cutlass and roared.

CHAPTER FORTY

Lauren hired a babysitter, for the first time, to help me carry through my mad plan. We flew across town, both of our cars stuffed to the ceiling, with only about two hours to set everything up.

"Good grief," Lauren said as we stood in front of Beau's house. "This yard is a mess. You're really going to waste all these flowers on this jumble?"

"Hand me the spray paint. It's all happening."

"At least you cleaned the inside," she mumbled, heading through the door with a big cardboard box.

I ran like piranhas were nipping at my heels. When the outside of the house was done, I put on Bruno Mars singing "Uptown Funk" and pulled Lauren into an impromptu dance party with me—but only for a minute.

AJ and Chuck had been cajoled into helping the day before and I found the bags of balloons they'd inflated for me next to their video-game recliners. It all took longer to put together than I'd hoped. I ran out of the office still buttoning my favorite green dress and holding heels in one hand.

Lauren gave me a quick hug. "I better go so he doesn't blame this all on me."

"Yes. Run along, little lady—it's showdown time."

She shook her head. "Only you would prank the guy you're trying to win back."

I hopped on one foot to pull on a heel. "Find a forgotten bottle of liquor in your parents' cabinet for me. For when this doesn't work out."

She nodded, solemnly. "Peach schnapps and reality television will be waiting."

After she left, I taped up the finishing touches and lit the candles. Beau's truck pulled into the driveway. I peeked out of the curtains and saw AJ emerge from the driver's seat. Bubba jumped out too. Beau leveraged himself out of the passenger side more slowly, staring around the house with his mouth hanging open.

I rushed over to the dining room table and positioned myself in a chair where I could see the mudroom door open. I reclined back and crossed my legs, a wine glass dangling from one hand. My heart thumped in my chest.

The mudroom door cracked open. I bit my lip, watching the newspaper sheet pull taut—one side was taped to the top of the doorframe and the other to the wall above the door. Beau's low voice mumbled words to AJ and they both laughed. What was probably Beau's crutches scraped as he positioned them closer to the door.

Beau kicked open the door and swung through in one quick movement. Pink packing peanuts and confetti fell on his head. He flinched then stared around the house, an expression of horror on his face.

"Oh," I said, inconsequentially. "You're home."

Bubba charged past Beau and leaped into the piles of balloons—pink, red, and white balloons covered all of the main floor. Eighty heart garlands hung from the ceiling.

Thirty bouquets of roses—that I'd bought in bulk and Lauren had put in glass jars—decorated the surfaces of the house.

Balloons burst under Bubba's claws. He barked and yipped. I pretended to take a sip of wine. My glass was actually empty.

"You did all this?" Beau asked, bewilderment on his face.

I put my glass down with a clunk. "This is payback."

"What?"

"Would you like to sit down?"

He nodded and used his crutches to swing his way through what appeared to be a little girl's dream ball pit—in his house. Balloons swirled up around him and Bubba made happy growly noises as he popped them with his teeth.

I helped Beau to lean back onto a pile of cushions and prop his injured leg up, standing on my knees next to the couch. He seemed to notice my dress for the first time, his eyes sliding down me like a caress.

"So," he said, a smile tugging at the edges of his mouth. "Hearts and flowers?"

"That's right. You're lucky I decided against the glitter bombs."

He tucked a strand of hair behind my ear. "I like the flowerpots around the doors. The big spray-painted heart on the lawn won't last long."

I'd written hero in fluorescent pink spray paint on the grass in front of his house, then sprayed a big heart around the words. Lauren and I had found some old plant pots in a shed at her parents, and she'd help me plant them with every kind of pink flower I could find.

"This is part prank—because you've always hated everything pink except Pink Floyd—and part…declaration."

"Oh?"

I took a deep breath, closing my eyes for a moment. Beau

reached out and held one of my hands. Putting both of my hands around his, I pressed his fingers against my chest.

"For the last ten years, I thought I knew what I wanted. To be normal. Find a settled life—the opposite of what my parents had. I forced myself not to take risks. But I…I can't force my heart into a square box. I don't want to. I've fallen for you. And you're everything I want."

He inhaled, and then so did I while I tried to smile.

"I had to find myself—I had to realize that I was lost. People have called me pigheaded in the past and there might be a crumb of truth there."

"Not pigheaded. Hotheaded, maybe. I like it."

Huffing, I shook my head. "That job at the hospital was a dream come true. But…not what fills my heart. I'd thought my parents did everything wrong. Now, I know I'm more like them than I've wanted to admit."

Smiling, he pushed hair off his forehead with his free hand. "Your mom was amazing."

I gasped, letting go of his hand to pinch the bridge of my nose. "She was."

He cupped my cheek. "You're you. One of a kind."

Blinking, I leaned into his touch. "I've never had chemistry like this. Or been with someone that would throw themselves on a knife for me. I can't wait to see you, every day. I love everything about you. I pranked you to make sure you know—I want to be with you. Will you, please, give us another chance?"

My heart stopped for the instant that I waited for him to say or do something. His face was flushed, and his eyes were bright. I tried to prepare myself to hear a no—

"Yes."

We both bent forward at the same time and our lips met. I moved closer to him, pushing him back against the pillows. His hand slid down my back.

Balloons flew up in the air next to us and floated down onto our heads. Bubba barked, sounding very proud of himself, and jumped away.

I pulled back, afraid of jostling one of his injuries. He smiled up at me.

"Autumn called today," he said.

Swallowing, I sat on my heels. "Yeah?"

"I told her I wanted to buy back the date from her. She sent me an invoice about three minutes later."

My grin almost hurt my face. "Well, that was probably the right thing to do…"

"Raven."

"Yeah?"

"I love you."

I stopped breathing and my eyes opened wide.

He squinted at me. "You're acting like you didn't know."

Blinking at him, I shook my head.

"I was a little mad, about your date. I might not handle rejection well. When it comes from you."

I kissed his hand. "Treat me right, and it won't happen again. I love you too."

"Hey. I'm going to—treat you right. I'm ready. Excited. We fit together. I think I got so mad because I've never been so happy. Stay with me, babe. Live here, I mean. Don't take a job in another city…please. I'm pretty damn selfish sometimes but I need you. With me. You, me, Bubba and Cheeto. And the guys downstairs for now. And Lauren whenever she wants. I'll even put up with your brother."

"I adopted a grandfather too. He's going to Dad's birthday."

"Okay. So, will you stay?"

I put my hands on either side of his face. "Yes."

CHAPTER FORTY-ONE

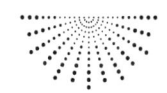

Four months later, I cuddled on Beau's chest, recovering from our Saturday morning spelunking—a euphemism that Beau wasn't giving up on. I was still catching my breath with sparkly starbursts glimmering in my head.

"Stop trying to distract me," I said. "We're going on this hike."

He hummed. "I'm not the one draped over my chest."

"That doesn't even make sense."

"We should take a hot shower together and then decide. It's cold out there."

I slapped his chest gently. "No. Clear skies today. Perfect for the photos."

"Okay."

I took a deep breath and tried to muster the will to put my feet on the cold floor. Beau rolled me over and kissed me. By the time he was done, we were both sweating.

With slippers and a thick bathrobe on, I did at last venture out into the still dark house for coffee. It was late February and we'd had a cold winter. The old oak floor creaked under my feet as I turned on lights.

In the living room, Bubba and Cheeto were curled up together in their nest of fleece blankets. I grabbed my phone and snapped a picture. The two of them had become best buddies lately—who still squabbled and stole each other's food.

We drove south out of town toward our nearest mountain, breakfast burritos in hand, as the sun rose.

"I haven't been to Tamanawas Falls since I was a teenager," Beau said.

"Me either. And only in the summer."

Mount Hood's snow-covered top appeared to be just over the next rise as we ascended to its base on Highway 35, the sides of the road flanked by fir trees. We trekked outside nearly every weekend, and I was documenting it all for my website.

Beau and I had healed from Rob Campbell's attack. Rob was in prison, probably for the next ten years. Chills still crept along the back of my neck when I thought about him—and shock that I'd somehow functioned with him stalking my life. It wasn't right for anyone to live with that kind of fear.

After the attack, I'd kept working for Adventure Tours in downtown River Gorge—and started my own freelance PR company. I wasn't making as much money as I had at my hospital job, but I was on my way up.

Dreams were sneaking into my plans. I'd started to create my own tour company, centered around women—to empower and educate them in technical outdoor adventures like rock climbing and wilderness hiking. The problem was, I didn't want to presume that my partnership with Beau would last.

We turned toward the start of the trailhead, the chains on Beau's tires cutting through the snow in the parking lot.

"Snow's packed down on the trail," I said. "Spikes should be enough."

"Sounds good to me."

With micro-spikes strapped on over our snow boots, and trekking poles in our hands, we moved confidently over the slick, icy surfaces of the parking lot. The trail was a quiet surreal place, winding through white-capped old-growth firs, hemlocks, and cedars.

I grinned at Beau when he turned around at a log bridge to wait for me. His face softened and he bent down for a kiss, his lips like chilled fruit against mine.

"You're about the best hiking buddy," I said. "Ever."

"Buddy?" He put a fist against his chest. "Is that all I am?"

I rolled my eyes. "Fishing for compliments?"

His arms snapped around me and he lifted me off the ground. "Always."

"Fine." I kissed him. "You're the best partner—so good I couldn't even have imagined it. I love you. It's like an icicle in my heart sometimes."

The truth was, I was so happy it scared me. Beau and I had it—that elusive something between two people that made every day full to bursting. Soulmates. One true pairing. Whatever it was, it filled me and kept me on the edge of my seat. I couldn't stand the thought of losing him. The scars on Beau's leg and arm were a daily reminder that I almost had, only four months before.

Sighing, he rubbed the tip of his freezing nose against mine. "That'll keep me going for a little while."

He put me down and straightened out my hat. "I want to get a picture of us in front of the frozen waterfall."

"You bet we will." Maybe I'd even frame it and hang it on the wall—if I was feeling brave.

I wasn't sure where Beau was at, with us. We'd settled

into partnered life almost too easily. Beau had wanted to stay free and untethered—that had been his goal for a long time. He seemed to have altered his position on all that. Wouldn't the urge to be independent come back?

We hiked along Cold Spring Creek, its clear water iced over as it twisted around snow-covered boulders. The bent trees and blue-tinged snow created a fairy-tale landscape from a frozen land, stark and haunting.

"There it is," said Beau, staring ahead at the waterfall coming into view. "Look at the size of those icicles."

"Beautiful."

The frozen waterfall was like a giant chandelier, perched on the edge of the hundred-foot cliff. Massive boulders of the same andesite rock as the cliff face protruded from the snow-covered slope, like the craggy shoulders of slumbering giants.

"Hey," Beau said as I took photos. "Left-field question—what do you think about big weddings?"

"Like organizing them?" I asked, fiddling with the camera on my phone. "Hell yes. I'd rock it. Have been thinking about throwing my hat in. Two mill visitors a year to Waterfall Canyon. Lots of marriages. The wedding business is booming."

Beau pulled the tripod out of his bag. "So you like them?" He sounded disappointed or something.

"They're amazing. I've been to a few big dollar ones and—wow. Stunning."

"Huh." He took a deep breath, frowning.

We climbed closer to the frozen falls. Beau didn't have many materialistic tendencies, unlike me. He splurged on his hobbies. Apparently, a boat was happening very soon. On other fronts, he preferred to cook at home and didn't care much about his clothes or furniture. I didn't mind. Beau could make a burlap bag look good. He was incredibly generous to me. Someday I'd buy the furniture—if I knew I was staying.

Beau held out a hand. "Raven, come here."

After one more shot, I shoved my phone in a pocket. I wrapped my arms around his waist and stretched up to kiss his cheek. "Hey, you."

He cleared his throat, stepping away a little with my hands gripped hard in his. I cocked my head at him—a bit like a confused chicken.

"When I was in the hospital," he said, "the whole time, you're were the person I wanted by my side. That day woke me all the way up. I'd already realized that you were it for me, without really thinking through what I wanted that to look like. That taking responsibility for our future together would give me peace and purpose."

My heart beat too fast. Breath burst out of each of us in white clouds. I blinked hard and pressed my lips together.

He smiled, his eyes shining. "You're my number one, babe. I want to be settled, with you. Make sure everyone understands they don't have a chance. We're taken."

I gasped as he sank down on his left knee. "Oh my God."

"Hey. I love you. If you'll have me, whatever's mine is yours. I want to always be there for you. Raven, will you marry me?"

"Yes." I crouched down and wrapped my arms around him. "Beau. I love you so much—are you sure though? We don't have to rush if you're not ready…"

It seemed a little fast—not for me, for him, the guy that had refused to ever marry.

He pulled a box out of his pocket. "One hundred percent sure. Are you ready to see the ring?"

I put a hand over my mouth and nodded.

He held the box up high, close to my face. The lid popped open.

A giant spider crawled forward and jumped at my face. I screamed and stumbled back.

Beau dropped the box and grabbed me, pulling me against his chest. We were both laughing, tumbling sideways in the snow with our arms around each other. He'd put a remote-controlled plastic spider in the ring box.

"I can't believe you just did that." I covered my face.

"See? I have to marry you. Who else is going to put up with me?"

He took another box out of his pocket. "So, Lauren helped me. I wanted you to pick it out, but she said I had to have something. We'll pick our bands together along with a big engagement ring that matches."

This box he opened carefully. The interior lit up and revealed a vintage ring—a rose gold band with five rectangular diamonds set in an art deco 1920s style.

"Oh, I love this so much. It's gorgeous, Beau."

He slid it onto my finger. "Good fit." He brought my hand to his mouth and kissed it.

I cupped his cheek. "We're going to have the biggest wedding the gorge has ever seen. I'll use it to promote my business."

He swallowed, hunching in a little, like a turtle. "Okay. Whatever you want."

"I'm thinking champagne wall, ice sculptures, live peacocks, fireworks—oh, we'll do a flash mob. Ride in on horseback to the ceremony. Llamas with saddlebags full of beer…"

His eyes narrowed.

I rolled on top of him. "Just kidding."

"Well, squeeze in an ax-throwing contest and I'd be on board."

"Nah. We'll go to Vegas."

"Really?" He grinned. His legs wrapped around mine.

"Yes." I poked him in the chest. "And you're going to wear a tux. Fitted."

"Anything, babe. All you have to do is ask."

The End.

SIGN UP FOR MY AUTHOR NEWSLETTER

Please help other readers find this book by leaving a review. Also, receive a free sign-up bonus and learn about new releases through my author newsletter. You'll hardly hear from me. Hugs, Anna.

www.annaalkire.com

ACKNOWLEDGMENTS

Biggest thanks to the two best guys in my life, my husband and my son, whose timely hugs and shoulder squeezes have powered my writing life. Love you.

Special heartfelt thanks to my editors and beta reader. Thank you Manda Waller (copyedit), A.M. Vivian (beta), and Gennifer Ulmen (proof).

And thank you to the fabulous illustrator, Ashley Santoro, who designed the cover.

FOR A SAMPLE OF ANNA ALKIRE'S
LIGHTHEADED HEART, TURN TO
THE NEXT PAGE...

Lightheaded Heart: Waterfall Canyon Book 2

Lightheaded Heart

Waterfall Canyon BOOK 2

Anna Alkire

WATER'S EDGE PUBLISHING

CHAPTER ONE

The thing was, my partner was difficult—not some kind of monster. That's what I'd been telling myself for too long. *You're a bird-witted romantic.*

"Hon," Gerry called from the hall in his there's-a-problem voice. "You left your makeup tote in the bathroom—did you remember?"

"Oh, yeah." I cleared my throat. "Actually, can you come sit down with me?"

"Now? I'm a little busy." His door shut.

He'd watched porn in his office all morning. For the last month, he'd made it a part of our daily lives—at bedtime, before dinner, and right after kissing me. A woman moaned behind his door.

"'Courage is the price that life exacts for granting peace,'" I read aloud, staring at a black-and-white print of Amelia Earhart's twin-engine plane propped up on my dresser with the quote printed on the bottom. Those were her words, not something I'd ever think of.

I stepped out of our townhome's big bedroom with another packed bag bumping against the door jamb. My

CHAPTER ONE

shoulders tensed to granite—Gerry hated it when anything banged on the walls.

Leaning sideways into the bathroom, I managed to grab my tote with two fingers. I rushed down the stairs, the zippers on my bag rattling. On the main floor, I halted, staring at the living room set I bought three months ago.

It doesn't matter that you have cute couch cushions. Get the hell out. I'd built my own cage and trapped myself in a relationship like a penguin in a desert zoo enclosure.

Heavy footsteps came down the stairs behind me. I swung around too fast. My hairbrush flew out of the tote and crashed onto the floor.

"Kelsey," Gerry said, standing by my pile of bags, frowning at me like I'd left broken glass on the carpet. "What is this?"

He went into the kitchen, his slippers scuffing on the floor, and put his Coke can in the recycling bin. His short, auburn hair was combed and gelled into place, as usual. There was a bit of a flush on his pale, freckled skin. Stupid of me for still noticing how handsome he was.

I let my bag slip off my shoulders and thump on the ground. Taking a deep breath, I looked down for a moment, pulling my sweater straight. What I'd found out the day before changed everything.

Swallowing, I met the gaze of his dark gray eyes. "You have a week. Then I'm pressing charges."

He reeled back, his mouth gaping open. "What are you talking about?"

Heat burned in my cheeks. *God, he was such a good liar.* "I'm an accountant, Gerry. I have proof."

"What—that I paid our bills?"

I stared at him. He'd drained our mutual account—after hacking into my personal accounts and transferring my savings into it.

CHAPTER ONE

He held his hands out to me, palms up. "Okay. I had a high-interest loan to pay off. We talked about it at dinner last week. Don't you remember?"

We hadn't. "My credit cards are maxed out."

"Not me." He leaned forward, his eyes open wide.

I was already disputing the charges with my credit card companies, but the process would take weeks. "We need to sell the townhome right away. If you'll leave, I'll handle it."

"Jesus." He stormed over to me.

I flinched when he reached out and grabbed my shoulders. "Let go."

He gripped them tighter, shaking me a little.

I stared at his chin, clenching my teeth.

"Stop." He crouched down so that we were eye level. "I love you. I'm going to make this right."

Everything in me wavered. His hands slid down my arms —I'd missed being touched. My chin snapped up, and I stepped back.

"No."

He crossed his arms. "I'm not going anywhere. You're blowing this all way out of proportion. I know I've...struggled lately. It's work—not getting the promotion. Don't do this—it's cruel. I need a little help, okay?"

I couldn't meet his eyes any longer. The truth was, I didn't know what to do or where to go. *You're sleeping in your car because you make stupid choices.*

"Hey." He put a finger under my chin. "I'm sorry. Give me another chance?"

"One week," I mumbled, stepping away from him. "And you're sleeping in your office."

He frowned, putting his hands in his pockets. "Alright."

Leaving my bags on the floor, I walked out the front door to sit in my car and try to breathe.

CHAPTER TWO

Heart still thumping, I drove to my refuge—the Indian Creek Trailhead, a lush greenbelt that ran across my town. I pulled on hiking boots and a ballcap from the bag stashed in my car and grabbed my binoculars and journal for birding.

When gravel crunched under my shoes on the path, my chest finally seemed to open all the way and I could take in a full breath. Big oaks stretched above me with crimson and gold leaves. A fluffy white Samoyed grinned at me as he trotted by with his human.

"Lady bug," a toddler shouted at her mother.

My stomach tightened. *Twenty-eight years old and starting over...*

I walked faster, part of me automatically scanning the trees for birds but mostly staring down, watching the terrain as my feet ate up miles. My walks were always solitary. Gerry hadn't hiked with me since we'd first started dating.

My youngest sister's ring tone went off on my phone— American Robin bird call. I stopped, sucking in air and wiping the sweat off my forehead.

"Tilly," I said.

CHAPTER TWO

"Kelsey? Are you jogging or something?"

"Speed walking. How are you?"

She blew out—cigarette smoke, probably. *Damn*. It seemed like smoking was going to stick. "In midterm hell. Housemate hell. And I'm probably fired from my job."

"Sorry to hear that."

"What are you doing for Christmas?"

I made it to the park bench that overlooked the river—miraculously empty—and slumped onto it. Then forced myself to sit up straight. "Not sure."

"Well, can I sleep on your couch or whatever?"

"Yeah, always." I ground dirt under the toe of my sneaker. "But things are...changing for me. Would you keep it private for now?"

"What's going on with you?"

I stared up at where an Osprey nest had been last year. "I'm...leaving Gerry."

"Shit—really?"

"He stole money from me." The admission came out of me, and it was like a bell tolling through my head. I'd said it. There was no taking it back now. Through all my years with Gerry, I'd never admitted my doubts about his character. He hadn't been physically abusive—it wasn't easy to explain. "On top of everything else..."

"What, you mean the fact that he's a shady asshole? Jesus, it's about freaking time."

Tilly had missed the parts of Gerry that I'd loved—or maybe depended on? He'd paid attention. Before the porn had taken over, our kinky sex had been a dirty secret between us that seemed to keep us close. *You were addicted to it.* I'd kept hoping he'd grow past the need to control the petty and small matters of our everyday lives.

"He won't leave the townhome. I'm not sure what's going to happen."

CHAPTER TWO

Actually, I had a bad feeling that I did. He wouldn't budge until I forced him to—and it would cost us both more than we could pay.

"Damn. I'm sorry, Sis. Can't you change the locks on him and throw his shit out a window?"

"No. I can't force him to leave—and I can't stand to be under the same roof as him."

"Why'd he steal money?"

I blew out a breath. "He spends too much." Called it networking, but it boiled down to chasing around the very wealthy and trying to be on the inside. "Started gambling, too."

"Did you, like, freeze your accounts or whatever?"

"Yeah." I'd had to take Friday afternoon off work to frantically call my credit card companies and go into my bank. I opened a private mailbox and changed all my account numbers. I emailed a lawyer.

"So now you're broke and basically homeless? Shit, we're in the same boat."

"Pretty much. Wait, you're not homeless, are you?"

More smoke blowing. "I'm behind on rent. They forced me into the basement."

"Is it a finished basement?"

"Not really. But it's dry. Don't worry about it—so, no, not really homeless."

I put a hand over my eyes. "I'm going to try and figure out Christmas. And Thanksgiving at Audrey's."

Audrey was our oldest sister, an engineer living in Portland with her wife. If the weather was good, they hosted big Thanksgiving gatherings in the yard of their tiny bungalow.

Tilly grumbled something about tofu that I didn't catch. "Yeah, keep me posted. Not sure I'm in the mood for an Audrey lecture...but it's probably better than staying here. Talk soon."

CHAPTER TWO

Stomach growling, I hiked back to my car and drove to the library. Why hadn't I put the bags I'd packed in my car? *Because you're a coward.* Gerry had been staring at me, and I'd fled.

Surrounded by a park, the library was a beautiful old brick building with a view of the Columbia River. I filled up my empty bottle and gulped down water, sloshing some onto my shirt.

"Kelsey? Oh, it is you." Deedee Fisher was one of the librarians—the one who knew my secret book hobby.

I wiped my mouth with the sleeve of my sweatshirt. "Hi. Sorry, I'm a sweaty mess."

Deedee squinted at me. "Working out?" she asked dubiously.

"Hiking." I pulled a leaf off my arm and glanced around for a place to toss it.

"Ah—great weather for it. Anyway, take a look in the section. You won't be sorry." Deedee adjusted her purple-framed glasses and blew out a low whistle. "Bunch of new ones."

I forced my mouth into a smile for her. "On it."

She grinned at me, then cocked her head, her smile fading. "Are you alright, dear?"

My eyes burned—*no, not now*. I gulped, shaking my head a little. "Just a breakup. I'll be fine."

Her eyes opened wider. "Oh—honey, I'm so sorry."

"Thanks."

She patted my arm, looking me over. "Go sit down. I'm going to bring over some cookies that I made last night. I always put them in the staff room, so I'm not the only one gobbling them down."

"That would be amazing."

Head spinning, I had to go to a picnic table outside and eat my cookies right away. I picked the crumbs out of the

CHAPTER TWO

plastic bag and mentally kicked myself for not eating anything before stranding myself outside my home. Going back was my only option—Gerry would be waiting, ready to concentrate on wrapping me back around his finger…

My phone vibrated in my pocket and made the Budgie bird call—Maria's ring tone.

"Kelsey," she sang out cheerfully. "What are we doing today? I woke up recently and can't let Saturday pass me by without day drinking."

Maria Adamos was my best friend—which would be news to her since she probably considered me little closer than an acquaintance.

About two years ago, we'd been introduced at a networking event for women professionals. A core group of us still met for drinks on Thursdays. People might consider Maria the party girl and me the designated driver. I'd always thought she had a deep well of compassion, along with her bright smile.

I cleared my throat. "Actually, can I come over? I, um, need a break from running around."

It sounded so awkward in my meek voice. I'd never been to where she lived. Was it too much? *Nice, push her away with your weirdness.*

"Oh—yeah," Maria said. "You don't care about messes or anything, do you? I mean, I'd get up and try to make this place presentable, but I wouldn't really get anywhere…"

"I really don't. Thanks. Text me your address?"

"Sure…my gut is telling me something is happening with you. You're going to talk to me when you get here, right?"

"I can talk," I said, trying to sound witty—and not pulling it off.

Lightheaded Heart: Waterfall Canyon Book 2

PRAISE FOR ANNA ALKIRE

Lightheaded Heart by Anna Alkire is an unforgettable romance that hooked me from the first page. As the second book in the Waterfall Canyon series, it stands out with its emotionally charged story and characters who truly make you feel.

— AMELIA, AMAZON

I absolutely loved the first book and was so excited to read this one! Kelsey was an incredibly awesome character and very relatable at times. The storyline flowed together so perfectly! This author did such a beautiful job on this story!

— DESTINY IMPERATI, AMAZON

This was so good. Great characters that you can't wait to read about In their own stories as well as the main characters and their intense roller coaster to get to their happiness. Both having gone through situations that they needed to overcome but knowing they wanted each other. I really really enjoyed this story.

— BUMPI, AMAZON

BOOKS BY ANNA ALKIRE

Buck Up, Buttercup: Montgomery Brothers Book 1
Signs of Trouble: Montgomery Brothers Book 2
Both Fingers Crossed: Montgomery Brothers Book 3

Sally Jones: A Trophy Wife Romance
Somewhere Beyond the Sea: A Trophy Wife Romance

A Gnome Inheritance: A Smitten in Seattle Romance

Hotheaded Heart: Waterfall Canyon Book 1
Lightheaded Heart: Waterfall Canyon Book 2
Bullheaded Heart: Waterfall Canyon Book 3

ABOUT THE AUTHOR

Anna lives in Washington state where she writes, reads, and sews every minute she can. Find out more about her (and grab a free story) at her website.

www.annaalkire.com

Made in the USA
Columbia, SC
29 May 2025